Whisper in My Ear

by

Teresa J. Reasor

Contact Information: teresareasor@msn.com

Cover Art by Tracy Stewart
Edited by Faith Freewoman

Teresa J. Reasor
PO Box 124
Corbin, KY 40702

Publishing History: First Edition 2015
ISBN 13: 978-1-940047-03-4
ISBN 10: 1-940047-03-X

Dedication

To Tracy Stewart, who is one of the best cover artists in the world.

To Faith Freewoman, who helps me make my writing so much clearer.

And to KaLyn Cooper, my fellow author and critique partner. Thanks for all you do.

All of you rock!

A special thanks to Beth Lechman for naming Drew's band. The name *Loud and Unbound* is perfect!

Table of Contents

Chapter 1

Drew waited for Sam to get to the point. Had he called him into the office to talk about extending their contract, or something else?

Sam Reeves rested his hands on his rounded belly and propped his feet on the edge of his scarred desk. "You sure drive those chicks crazy every night." He reached over, chose a cigar from the box on his desk, and rolled it between his fingers.

Though there had been a law on the books for almost forty years banning smoking in San Diego nightclubs, Sam ignored it in his office. The rich cherry smell of his cigar tobacco was embedded in the walls. The familiar, almost comforting rattle of the ceiling exhaust fan doggedly continued its wasted effort to extract the aroma.

Could Sirens die of secondhand smoke?

Drew palmed the sweating water bottle from Sam's desk, tilted his head back, and took a long drink to wash the scent from his throat.

"I can help you break your smoking habit, Sam," Drew said, nodding toward the cigar. As a Siren hybrid, he had the gift of healing, and could easily rid him of the addiction.

Sam stared at him for a moment, unmoving.

Did Sam know what he faced across his desk? Had he guessed what Drew was? Was it fear clouding his eyes, or was he debating whether or not to take Drew up on his offer?

Sam shook his head. "We all have our vices. Think I'll keep mine."

Drew shrugged. "Suit yourself."

Sam returned to what was on his mind. "You're going to be a superstar. You have record producers lining up at the bar to listen to you sing every week. And you being here has made me a small fortune." A frown flashed across his jowly face. "Why the hell haven't you signed on the dotted line?"

Drew smiled and tilted his chair back against the wall. Had his suggestion spooked the guy? "Eager to get rid of me, Sam?"

"Hell, no! You're keeping the place packed. But with all the interest, you have to admit it's strange you're dragging your feet about taking the next step."

Drew took another swig from the water bottle. He could control what he did to the women in person. To reproduce his *special magic* digitally might be dangerous.

He glanced over to find Sam studying him. Drew shrugged. "Signing a contract is a long-term commitment. I've got to be sure I'm—*we're*—ready for that."

"What more could you be waiting for?" Sam asked.

More than what they'd been offered thus far. But it was a balancing act. He could enflame women with his voice.

He could addict them to it if he wasn't careful. He'd learned that after being stalked by a couple of his fans. The experience was seriously fucked up.

Sam narrowed dirt-brown eyes. "Elvis had it. And Sinatra. But not the way you do."

Drew was pretty sure neither Elvis nor Sinatra were Sirens. They'd created an obsessive following without using any special powers. Could he reproduce the affect he had on women without projecting any of his subliminal tones? He'd never tried.

There was something ironic in being able to please hundreds of women without ever experiencing any satisfaction himself. Though he could give them physical pleasure, he couldn't seem to inspire any lasting emotional bond with any woman. Lately that had been driven home to him more than once. Why couldn't he stir more than short-term, temporary lust?

Sam stuck the cigar between his teeth, but thankfully didn't light it. "Let me give you some advice, Drew. Don't share this special something you have with anyone. Not even your band. It will make you a superstar and keep you there."

Drew remained silent a moment. Was that what he wanted? Fame? Fortune? It was certainly what his band expected. But wasn't there more? Drew rubbed at the dull ache between his brows. "Are you warning me about the power-play my drummer's trying to incite with the other members of the band?"

"None of my business." Sam waved the unlit cigar in a dismissive gesture. His chin jerked up, setting the flab beneath to jiggling. He tilted his head with a frown. "Hear that?"

A persistent beat, like a base drum came from down the hall. In the soundproofed office it was more a vibration against the walls and floor than a noise. "Yeah, I do."

Sam dropped his legs from the desk and shot to his feet. He rushed to the door and jerked it open.

"Drew. Drew. Drew."

The staccato chant brought Drew to his feet, and in two strides he reached the door, then stopped.

"Jesus," Sam muttered and stormed down the hall. He paused behind the curtain to one side of the stage. "You better get your guys together before these crazy women start taking the place apart."

Drew grimaced. He wasn't due to begin his set for another half hour. But the floor of the nightclub was already packed, and the exterior walls lined with standing patrons. A few men were scattered here and there, possibly having accompanied their ladies to the show, but for the most part his audience was composed of women. The second floor balcony was filled to the brim. His shoulders tensed as he studied the crowd pressed against the chrome railing.

"Did you reinforce the balcony, Sam?"

"Yeah." Sam pointed with his cigar at two girls whose bootys hung over the railings where they'd perched. "Crazy bitches." He jabbed his cigar into his shirt pocket.

Drew checked the stage. Rand's drums were set up. Tony's base stood upright on a stand waiting to be plugged into the amp. Drew's keyboard was positioned at an angle between the two. The only instrument missing was Simon's

Les Paul. He'd taken it with him to restring before the set this evening. "I can do a few numbers alone to calm them down until the band gets here."

"Thanks." Sam shook his head and took the stage. The chant lost a bit of its volume and finally died when Sam flipped on the sound system, then walked to one of the mikes. "Welcome to The Next Big Thing." His tone was upbeat, but Drew recognized nerves bordering on fear in the tension of his stance and the way he gripped the neck of the microphone stand. "We've been in business here in San Diego for ten years, and have had some groundbreaking acts in the past. One hundred and fifty-two acts have gone on to professional greatness from our stage. But we've never had anyone like the man you're going to hear tonight. The rest of Loud and Unbound will arrive in a short while, but Drew has agreed to come out and do a couple of numbers for you folks until they do."

Sam had formulated a brief introduction using the information Drew had given him, all half-truths. Every time he heard the intro, he experienced a twinge of bitterness. Humans responded to things they didn't understand in one of two ways. They either wanted to capture and study the creature, or they wanted to kill it, stuff it and mount it on a wall. The only way preternatural beings like him survived was to keep their true identity hidden. But he had to make a living, and he was good at singing. It came so naturally.

The audience clapped, stomped, and squealed their approval as he crossed the stage to stand next to Sam. The place vibrated. "Sure you can control this shit?" Sam asked, his pudgy features creased.

Drew nodded. The aggressive energy in the room hammered against him. With the house lights up, he scanned the audience. As his attention paused at one of the tables, several women lunged to their feet, their high-pitched squeals piercing. He forced a smile against the uneasiness that crept into the pit of his stomach. Had he underestimated his power? Had he allowed his magic to get out of control?

His attention lingered on the stunning blonde at the same table who'd remained seated even as he motioned the rest back down. Her expression mirrored his embarrassment and uneasiness. He fought the urge to rush and sauntered to the mike. "Thank you, ladies. Your appreciation is very flattering. Thank you for coming tonight."

Their tittering response, high and tinny, at one time would have triggered some satisfaction. But lately he'd gotten less pleasure from the audience's adoration. The milestones he achieved with his music seemed undermined by the sexual stuff.

The audience began to chant his name again, and he swore beneath his breath. Sam was right. He had to calm them. He strode to his Roland, flipped it on, dragged his bench forward and took a seat. He ran his fingers over the keys in an eight-measure intro to give them an opportunity to settle down.

When that didn't work, he took a deep breath and exhaled a low frequency hum meant to lull them into relaxing. He scanned the room as the tension eased. Those who had been so excited sat back in their seats, their air of expectancy emphasized by the languid pose of their limbs. One even caressed her breasts.

But now the blonde had slid forward and was studying him. Her dark eyes raked over him intent, searching. Her heart-shaped face settled into an expression of puzzled unease.

He recognized something different about her. Above the scent of expectancy in the air he smelled an unfamiliar fragrance that cut through the perfumes and human endorphins. His heart stuttered, then beat a frantic rhythm. The muscles of his neck tensed. He grew aroused. Tilting his head back, he savored her essence.

It had to be the blonde staring at him so intently.

He focused on her while he spoke into the mike punctuated by some slow breathing to still the heavy beat of his heart. "This is a song I wrote recently. You'll be the first audience to hear it. It's titled *Journey*."

His fingers managed to hit the keys for the intro again, though his mind seemed fuzzy as that scent looped through his nostrils and into his lungs before he exhaled.

He closed his eyes for a moment and eased into the song.

"The first step is the hardest
Like learning a dance you've never done
And the rhythm of the movements
Can be so overdone.
Let's ease into it slowly,
Practice the steps and learn them well.
I'll cradle the curve of your body
Against mine, and let it swell."

He hit the chorus with a little more emphasis, but contained the underlying power of his voice so it was just a whisper beneath the practiced human tone.

"And let me do my best for you.
I'll show you how it's done.
Then I'll let you be my teacher.
You can tell me how to please you.
With me by your side,
Holding you, loving you,
It's all a journey."

By the time he hit the second stanza, the audience was swaying to the music and settled into the calm place he wanted them to be. All but the cool blonde who was scanning the crowd, her features tense, her eyes restless. Was she as hyperaware of him as he was her? Was he making her anxious?

"Take my hand and walk with me
Through that open door.
I promise to try my best,
More than I've ever tried before.
Let's ease into it slowly,
Practice the beat and learn it well.
Cradle my body against yours,
And I'll show you how I feel."

He dropped into the alternative chorus and projected with his voice the low-level sensuality that gave the women such pleasure. He caught the scent of their arousal, felt the hum of their release building in the air.

> *"And I'll let you do the same for me.*
> *You can show me how it's done.*
> *If you'll let me be your teacher,*
> *I'll prove you please me.*
> *Take me into your heart,*
> *With you holding me, loving me*
> *It's all a journey."*

He repeated the first stanza, and during the chorus he noticed the blonde studying the other women at her table instead of focusing on him. He'd never had a female to lose interest in his performance before. How could she be looking at anyone but him when he couldn't take his eyes off her?

> *"And let me do my best for you.*
> *I'll show you how it's done.*
> *Then I'll let you be my teacher.*
> *You can tell me how to please you,*
> *With me by your side*
> *Holding you, loving you"*

A shimmering heat bloomed among the females in the audience, and their sexual energy peaked and fell over as he extended the end of the chorus.

"It's all a journey
It's all a journey."

Katrina Larson rolled the glass of rum and coke between her palms. What was she doing here? Since she was deaf, she felt as out of place as a cowboy at a fashion show. When her girlfriends leaped to their feet as soon as the singer's attention fell on them, she'd fought the urge to sink under the table.

Now she studied the man on stage. He was tall, at least six foot three, dark, muscular, and very masculine. He projected a raw sexuality every woman in the room responded to, including her. All her friends had talked about for weeks was Drew Saunders. They raved about his voice. But she would never understand what special quality they heard in it. Even with the cochlear implant she was considering, her hearing would be…different.

When he began to play, the vibration from his keyboard feathered against her skin and beat beneath her feet, but she couldn't hear the words he sang. Nor was she close enough to read his lips. When the other women lounged back into their seats, she took her cue from them and relaxed.

A low-level hum penetrated the silence she lived in, startling her and jerking her forward in her seat. She searched the room, eager, her heart pounding. It had been nearly six years since she'd heard any sound. She'd missed it, missed the ebb and flow of the pitch inside her head. Where was it coming from now?

Her eyes settled on the man on stage. She couldn't hear

a word of what he was singing, but beneath the surface tone there was a sensual vibration low enough to penetrate her deafness.

What was he? If he were a member of her Shoal, she'd recognize it. Though she wasn't of pure blood, she could still recognize her own. And being on land, he'd be as deaf as she.

Because of the pitch he was able to project, he had to be something aquatic, but not of her species. The resonance was too different.

Fascinated and hungry for sound of any kind, she strained to hear each note he projected. Sitting next to her, her best friend, Cheryl, grasped her wrist and leaned close enough for her to read her lips in the light of the candle on their table. "I just had an orgasm. I swear to God. All he has to do is sing and you just go. I wish you could hear this, Katrina."

Shock held her prisoner for several moments. He was seducing the audience with his voice. She spied a man two tables over from her, and he seemed more interested in checking out the breasts of the woman next to him than the man singing.

So only the women in the audience were affected. He had seduced her too, but the effect was blunted because of her hearing issues. Her stomach cramped. What he was doing was…*wrong*.

What could she do? She studied each of the women she'd come with, her coworkers. Cheryl, Jacqueline, and Hallee all seemed to be mesmerized. If she tried to explain, none of them would believe her. But she couldn't just sit here and watch him manipulate her friends. She had to leave and figure out what to do.

A movement from the side of the stage caught her attention. Drew Saunders stood and played the last few bars of the song. Then he motioned to someone offstage, and three men walked out.

Katrina rose and tapped Cheryl on the shoulder. Used to speaking instead of signing with her, she said, "I have to go."

"You haven't even finished your drink," Cheryl protested.

Katrina slid the rum and coke over to her. "I haven't touched it. You can have it. I'll see you tomorrow."

She collected her bag, and, glancing toward the stage one last time, wove her way through the crowd toward the door.

Drew motioned his band members on stage. "Ladies and gentlemen the rest of the band, Loud and Unbound. On drums is Rand Michaels."

As soon as he reached him, Rand said, "What the fuck's going on, Drew? You going solo now?"

The drummer's anger vibrated off him like static. It underscored his unshaven, tattooed, rocker look. His attempts to live up to his own hype were getting old, though. Drew gave him a long look. "The natives were restless. Sam was worried they might damage the club."

Rand scanned the audience. "They look okay now." A heavy undertone of accusation sharpened his voice.

Drew controlled his expression, and his anger, with an effort. There was a time and a place for everything. Who knows what an act of violence on stage could set off in this audience? "Take your bow, Rand, and get ready for the show." Drew threw out a hand toward the other two band members. "On base, Tony Cosimini. On guitar is Simon Fletcher."

While the men were getting settled, Drew glanced toward the table of women he'd been watching. The blonde was halfway across the room, winding her way toward the door. Her hair swung from side to side, brushing the small of her arrow-straight back, her gait purposeful. For a moment, he was distracted by the lush curve of her jeans-encased hips, and the graceful way they swayed with every step she took. Where was she going?

His stomach tightened. His heart hammered.

She was leaving!

Why wasn't she affected by his singing like the others? He had to find out. He had to stop her. He dodged the mike stand and leapt off the stage. Women surged to their feet and hands reached for him. Drew tugged free of one woman's grasp, then another.

A brunette with big hair and a sultry expression ran a hand down the front of his jeans and gave his gear a painful squeeze. Jesus! Grasping her wrist, he pushed her into her seat and shoved past the next two who stood in his path.

His hand closed around the blonde's shoulder and he swung her around. "Why are you leaving?"

Large blue-green eyes, the color of the sea, focused on his face, then widened in surprise. Her hair, a caramel color streaked with every shade of blonde from platinum to honey, tumbled forward to frame her high cheekbones. Her bow-shaped mouth parted in shock as she shrank from him.

He grasped her arm. "Don't go."

A high-pitched sound, piercing and sharp struck him like a blow. Pain lanced through the bones of his face, his teeth. He bent at the waist and covered his ears.

The frosted glass panes in the door shattered, throwing diamond-shaped pieces through the air and across the polished black and white tile floor. He threw up an arm to protect his face and twisted away.

Bedlam reigned as people sitting close by surged to their feet and ran toward the stage.

The sound ceased, cut off as suddenly as it had erupted. He straightened, panting. The aftereffects of the noise had left him dizzy. Even with his hearing blunted from the trauma, he heard the bottles of liquor behind the bar continue to tinkle like wind chimes, as though the glass retained a lingering resonance.

He turned to the door. What the hell was that? Was she okay?

An evening breeze wafted through the empty metal doorframe, carrying with it the smell of car exhaust.

The blonde was gone.

Chapter 2

D r. Graham Powell studied the X-ray, his eyes narrowed. What was that structure at the front of the skull? It looked like an extra sinus. He placed another film on the view box, examining the area from a different angle. The tissue looked healthy. It wasn't a tumor, and there was no evidence of infection. And it wasn't a sinus. It was a self-contained space. He could easily see the white edges of the bone. Perhaps a genetic anomaly. But it wouldn't interfere with Katrina Larson's hearing.

He moved to the computer, took a seat, and pulled up the CT scan images. The same abnormality was evident. Again, no sign of tumor or disease.

He clicked on more images and turned his attention to the structures of the inner ear. The cochlea appeared larger than normal. The ear canal opened wider, but the tympanic membrane stretched across the wider canal as though it was a natural fit. Yet she couldn't hear. Why?

If the inner ear mechanisms were somehow larger, could it retard their ability to react to sound? The nerve seemed to be intact, but if it was damaged, an implant would be unable to transfer sound to the brain. He traced the path of the structure and, aside from the nerve appearing thicker, saw nothing to indicate damage. But what could have made it thicken?

He had to figure this out. Why would all the structures of the inner ear and the nerve be larger than normal? Had there been some kind of glitch in the CT images or the viewer? He checked the magnification on the computer. No, nothing out of the ordinary.

Fifteen minutes later, he rubbed his eyes and rolled the chair away from the screen to take a break and mull over the puzzle.

He opened the file the audiologist had sent him and read through it carefully. All the readings of her hearing showed sound registered in all the higher and lower frequencies most people couldn't hear, but none of the octaves where the human voice usually fell. She could hear a dog whistle, but not the spoken word. What the hell?

Stranger and stranger. This was something totally new, something he had never seen in all the years he'd been practicing. His pulse revved with a sizzle of excitement.

The implant would adjust for those normal vocal frequencies, and as long as the nerve wasn't damaged, her brain would receive the signals. It would just be a matter of her brain learning to recognize those mid-range octaves between the frequencies she could already hear. Hearing could happen for her.

This patient could be the subject for a case study for a major article, if he could figure out what had caused the defect and why those octaves were out of her range. Would she agree to more testing? He needed to convince her.

Satisfied he had reviewed every test, he wrote a note to his secretary to schedule a pre-op appointment for the patient so he could explain the procedure. He picked up the phone and dialed Carl Turner's number from memory.

As soon as Carl answered, Graham said, "I've reviewed your patient's test results."

"And what did you think?"

"She'll be a good candidate for the procedure. What did you think about the area at the front of her skull?"

"I'd say it was a birth defect, but there's no reason why it should have any bearing on the surgery or her ability to hear. It appears to be self-contained," Carl said.

"Weren't you intrigued by the anomaly?"

"Of course, but from the standpoint of hearing, it doesn't have a bearing in your findings."

"Carl, your focus is admirable when it comes to your devotion to your practice as an otologist and a surgeon, but you need to look at the big picture now and then."

Graham clicked on Katrina Larson's file and brought up the CT images again. "Did you know dolphins and whales have a space in their forehead filled with fat that acts as an area of focus when they emit sound waves beneath the water?"

"Yes, actually I did. But they receive the reflected waves through their bottom jaw. It's called echolocation. Are you saying you think this extra space at the front of your patient's head is a fat-filled cavity?" Carl's tone sharpened to wariness.

"I thought I'd persuade her to sign some release forms

so I can do further tests in exchange for a donation toward her surgery."

"What kind of tests?" Carl asked.

"Nothing intrusive, just a more in-depth CT scan, showing a cross section so a forensic artist can reproduce the landmarks of the skull. I want a scale model so I can take photographs to include with the article I intend to write."

"And what if the patient doesn't want to undergo these tests?"

"I'll make it worth her while to do so."

Carl remained silent a moment. "I'd suggest you get a signed release for each test, not a blanket release. And I'd caution you to explain everything carefully. You don't want anyone saying you took advantage of a handicapped individual. It would reflect badly on our practice."

"I'll be careful," Graham said, an edge of irritation making the words terse. "Relax, Carl."

"We'll discuss it more after I've met with her. I assume you want to be there for the pre-op conference."

"Yes, I do." He wanted a look at the exterior of her skull to see if there was any noticeable difference.

Graham's gaze brushed over the picture of his parents on his desk. He glanced at his watch. If he didn't leave soon, he'd be late for his dinner engagement with them, although he knew they'd wait. Since he was their only child, they doted on him. He smiled to himself as he collected his briefcase.

In the parking lot outside his clinic, he tossed his case into the back seat and slid behind the wheel of his Mercedes-Benz coupe. The butter-soft leather driver's seat enfolded him, and he reveled in the new car smell. At the gentle push of a button, the engine sprang to life and purred with power, the sound thrumming along with the satisfaction that raced along his nerve endings. He shot out of the parking lot and turned east, heading downtown.

Swinging onto Broadway, he wove his way through traffic and pulled in front of the Art Deco entrance to the hotel he'd selected for his parents' anniversary dinner. A parking attendant took his keys and handed him a ticket.

He checked his watch again. Five minutes to spare.

The golden glow of the lobby reached out to embrace him as he entered the door. Beaded crystal chandeliers gleamed overhead, and inviting groupings of leather chairs and sofas beckoned guests to sit and enjoy the ambiance of the historic hotel. A grand piano sat beneath the overhang of a second floor balcony.

He wanted to treat his parents to an anniversary dinner they'd remember, and the Grant Hotel was the place to do it. He made his way to the grill to see if they had arrived. The hostess approached. "I'm looking for my parents, they should be waiting for me. Late fifties, Dad is about five nine, one forty-five with dark auburn hair sprinkled with gray. My mother has a touch of gray at the temples."

The hostess frowned. "We have—" She looked down at a chart on the desk. "Oh." Her expression cleared and she smiled. "They arrived just a few moments ago. Please follow me."

His parents sat side by side in one of the upholstered two-seat booths against the wall. Though both were in their late fifties, they looked younger. His mother's hair, pulled back in a simple bun at the base of her head, gleamed with honey tones beneath the golden glow of the lights. Was it more than good genetics holding the gray at bay and protecting her pale skin from the wrinkles normal for a woman her age?

Her dark gray eyes widened when she saw him, and she smiled. His father looked up from perusing the menu when she touched his arm, and he tracked Graham's progress across the room, a half-smile softening the firm line of his lips and crinkling the corners of his pale eyes. There was no lax sagging of his jawline, though a few wrinkles fanned from the corners of his green eyes, and his dark sable hair showed a smattering of silver sprinkled through here and there. In their dark evening clothes, they looked elegant and refined.

And he looked nothing like them. With his blond hair and large frame, he wondered for the millionth time where he might have gotten his looks. What ancestor had passed down his flat Nordic cheekbones and pale green eyes?

Their hands flew as they signed to him even before he reached the table. He laughed at their eagerness. "I can only read one at a time," he said as he pulled out a chair.

As a child, he'd felt locked out of their world until he was old enough to sign. Now they were locked out of his.

They had been deaf their entire lives, and had refused to allow him to examine them to see if implants would improve their hearing. Even though he'd helped hundreds of people hear again, his parents had refused, and he struggled to understand why. He had devoted his life to bringing the gift of hearing to those who were denied it. But he couldn't give it to his parents. Frustration tightened the muscles of his neck and shoulders. Why were they being so fucking stubborn?

He drew what comfort he could from knowing that because they'd been deaf their entire lives, the procedure probably wouldn't work for them anyway. But from a son's point of view, if there was a chance in a million he could give them the ability to hear…but after over fifty years in the non-hearing world, they were probably frightened of change.

Pushing away his frustration, he greeted them both, leaned forward to kiss his mother's cheek, then extended his hand to his father as he half rose from his seat.

"You've come alone?" his mother signed.

"Yes."

"Graham." She shook her head in disappointment while her fingers flew, the message adamant. "You work too hard. There is more to life than work."

He smiled. "I know. When I find someone to be serious about, you'll be the first to know. Tonight is about you and Dad. This is your anniversary."

His father rested a hand on his mother's arm, and they exchanged a quick look.

Since they were unable to hear, they had always shared a physical or mental connection that transcended their hearing loss. There had been times he'd watched them communicate without signing, as though they read each other's thoughts. What would it be like if a person could hear and also connect to another human being so complete-ly?

Was that why they weren't interested in the procedure? Were they afraid the results might damage their relationship if it worked for one and not the other?

Taking a seat across from them, he asked, "What do you think about the hotel?"

His mother looked around the room. "It's beautiful, but it must be very expensive."

"Expense doesn't matter. I want you two to enjoy being here."

"We already are, son," his father signed. "We appreciate you remembering our anniversary. It's an important day to us. But not nearly as important as spending time with you."

Graham smiled, though the small dig about his infrequent visits tweaked his patience. He was building a practice. What did they expect?

His mother signed. "We're glad you called. We have some news to share with you."

"What is it?"

"Your father and I have decided to visit Scotland for a few months. We haven't been back since you were a baby."

"It will be like a second honeymoon," his father signed.

They weren't harping at him. They were breaking the news they were leaving. He smiled through his feelings of chagrin. "I think it's an excellent idea. Neither of you has taken a break from your jobs at the institute in years. It's time you got away together."

"We will miss you, of course," his mother signed.

"As I will you, Mother. How long do you plan to be gone?" he asked.

"A couple of months at least. We hoped to connect

with some old friends while we're there." His father's hand gestures quickened with excitement. "We haven't seen some of them since we immigrated to the U.S."

A waiter appeared with water and they spent a few minutes studying the menus. They pointed out the items they wanted, and when the waiter reappeared Graham ordered for them all.

"So when will you be leaving?" he asked.

"In a month," his father answered. "There are a few cases I must see through before I leave."

"Any who could be a candidate for surgery?" Graham asked.

His father shook his head. "Not every deaf person should have surgery, Graham."

"They should if it will improve the quality of their life."

His father studied his face for a long moment. "What more could I want from life than what I've got? Your mother. You. A successful career helping other people. What more could *you* want?"

What more could he want? He had a successful practice. Plenty of money. Power? Recognition? He was always looking for more. Why?

Their food arrived, but during dinner, though he asked about the particulars of their trip and other things, the question kept haunting him.

"I have an interesting case I'm working on," he signed, feeling more at ease sharing private information using sign rather than spoken language. "It's different from any other I've been asked to evaluate before."

"How so?" his mother signed.

"There are some anomalies in the patient's skull. And her hearing range is very unusual."

Had he not been looking directly at his parents, he might have missed the look that passed between them.

"What sort of anomalies?" his father asked.

"She has an extra sinus in her forehead. And her hearing ranges are very unusual and widely separated."

"Where is she from?"

"Alaska. Or at least that is where she was raised. She has no family medical history because she was abandoned as a child."

"Poor thing." His mother's signing movements became choppy with distress.

"Do you provide psychological counseling for your patients before and after surgery?" his father asked.

"Before surgery we do a psychological evaluation to make certain they can handle the procedure. We refer them to a counselor afterwards, but it is up to them whether they attend sessions. Why?"

"Because the transition from the silence of a non-hearing world to one of sound can be overwhelming, nerve-shattering. Would it be a conflict of interest for you to refer this patient to me?"

"Why this patient, Dad?"

"Because I deal with displaced non-hearing patients, and she may have other issues besides the normal struggles faced by a regular patient."

"How old was she when she was abandoned?" his mother asked.

"An infant, I believe."

"And what does she do now?"

"She's a graphic artist for a design corporation."

His mother and father nodded.

Why were they showing such interest in this one patient? But then, because the practice of medicine had such strict privacy rules, he rarely discussed his work with them. Why had he brought up the case at all?

Because he was so intrigued by the physical findings, and they continued to pop into his thoughts.

"I'll ask her who she would prefer to speak with, you or our regular counselor," he said.

His dad nodded.

The conversation turned to his parents' trip, the care of their home, the payment of bills while they were away. They lingered over dessert, and he paid the check.

When they stood in the entrance foyer of the hotel, his mother approached him. She smoothed the lapels of his suit, and for a moment rested her head against his chest. She seemed tiny, fragile, and a sharp twinge of alarm pierced him. His arms tightened around her for a moment.

"You didn't tell me why you suddenly decided to take this trip," he signed to his father.

"We've been away from our roots for too long. We decided we'd like to see the many changes that must have taken place since we left. It's always been our dream to return one day, and what better occasion than our anniversary?"

"While we're away, I want you to promise me you'll spend time socially with other people, Graham," his mother signed. "You need something more personal in your life.

Surely there's more you want than just your patients and work." She smiled and threaded her hand through his father's arm, "There's so much to explore and experience."

What more did he want?

A challenge. Something different. He craved an element of surprise or interest in his life. His thoughts returned to Katrina Larson and her unusual X-ray and CT results.

She might lead him to exactly what he was looking for.

Chapter 3

Drew pushed the elevator button and waited for the doors to open. Roma cuddled close to him and nuzzled his neck. "I've had a wonderful time."

"I'm glad." He'd taken Roma to dinner, dancing, wooed her, made all the seductive moves to signal his contrition for ignoring her. Even though they'd been dating nearly a month, it had been more than a week since he'd seen her. He'd been too distracted by his search for the blonde. He was intelligent enough to realize women expected to be courted a little, even if they had every intention of taking their clothes off at the end of the evening.

Roma's pique at his behavior had eased. Now, here they were, at her apartment.

But was this really where he wanted to be?

All night thoughts of the blonde at the club had intruded. Why couldn't he get her out of his mind? It had been several days since their encounter and still he couldn't forget about her.

Roma kissed his throat and nipped at his ear. Though his body responded, his heart kept up its usual steady rhythm, and his thoughts strayed to the other woman.

Why couldn't he find the blonde? No one seemed to know anything about her.

The elevator doors opened and they stepped in. Roma turned her voluptuous curves against him and proceeded to wrap herself around him like a honeysuckle vine. He'd led her down this path all night, and now they'd arrived back at her apartment he needed to follow through. He shoved thoughts of everything but her from his mind and pressed his lips against hers. And waited for the rush of excitement, of arousal, to wash over him.

The elevator stopped on her floor, and they separated just enough to walk down the hall to her apartment. He took the keys and unlocked it.

"You know what I like most about you, Drew?" she asked as she curled her fingers around the waistband of his pants and, walking backwards, tugged him toward her bedroom.

He tossed the keys on a long table next to the door as they passed. "What?"

"You always know what you want. You take charge, and you go after it."

With the backs of her fingers already fluttering against his abdomen beneath his fly, he could say the same for her.

They fell across the bed together. Roma's legs parted to cradle Drew's hips. Her body, slender and graceful, moved beneath his in an eager simulation of lovemaking.

Drew kissed her, and her lips opened in response, inviting the thrust of his tongue. Her lush mouth moved hungrily beneath his, and she ran questing hands beneath his shirt, caressing his back. Her hips undulated against him.

He tugged the straps of her dress down, and she shimmied free of the bodice. Light from the hall lanced across the bed, highlighting her pale skin. Her warm mahogany brown hair spread across the blue flowered comforter as though she reclined in a bed of tropical flowers, and her exotic, floral perfume played into that fantasy.

The memory of another feminine scent, a blend of the sea and something fresh and floral, intruded, overpowering Roma's. He pushed the thought away. He'd been seeking her fragrance for days, waiting for her to return to the club, but she hadn't. The woman moving beneath him was as good a substitute as any.

He cupped her breast and bent his head to taste the dark peak and suckle it. Her soft moan kicked his desire higher. When her hand slid between them, finding and lowering his zipper, his body quickened, eager for her touch.

Her fingers closed around his shaft. "Sing to me, Drew," Roma pleaded.

He froze and lifted his head to look down at her. "No."

"You have to."

"I can give you just as much pleasure without it," he said.

Her features crumpled into a pout. "Please." She stroked his cock, trying to tempt him.

He needed to be a regular man with her, not the crooner who fed women's needs with his voice night after night. "I'd rather not."

The sensual pout turned into a frown. "Why?"

"I sing for hundreds of women, Roma. I want to be a normal lover with you."

She rose to touch her lips to the sensitive area between his neck and shoulder and applied suction. His cock swelled and grew harder.

"But you aren't just a lover, are you? You're more than that. I want you to sing to me as you do to them, Drew."

His heart stuttered at her words. Did she know he wasn't human?

"What do you mean, Roma?"

"You know your voice drives women crazy. You're going to be a star one day."

With her hand gripping him and pumping with well-practiced pressure, the urge to give her what she wanted was strong.

But she was getting too close to discovering his secret. He needed to make up his mind. He either trusted her enough to tell her, or he had to end this.

But even if he broke it off with her, where would his quest end? And how? He could go on fulfilling women's superficial needs with his voice, and his own with their bodies, for the rest of his life, but he would never know what it meant to be desired—loved—as a normal man. Well, as close to a normal man as his species could manage.

Blue-green eyes the color of the Mediterranean Sea flashed though his mind. Would he have to hide what he was from the mystery woman? If he ever found her.

"What does it feel like when I sing to you?" he asked.

"As though I'm going to come without needing a touch. It holds me on the brink and makes me so hot I can't sit still."

He nibbled her ear lobe. "And with my touch?"

"I've never had such strong orgasms."

"And when I don't sing?" His lips grazed her throat.

"You still give me what I need." She cupped his balls and gave them a light squeeze.

"But it isn't as intense?"

"No."

What if he turned the full power of his Siren on her? She'd become a slave to her desires and make him her master. Humans were so fragile, physically, psychologically—in every way. He couldn't live his life tiptoeing around his mate. He needed someone strong enough to welcome and match the full brunt of his desire. And he wasn't going to find it looking in the human population. But where?

When the blonde came to mind again, he paused to look down at the woman beneath him. He had already moved on from her.

But he could give Roma what she wanted one last time before he ended things between them.

He bent his head and hummed into her ear as softly as he could. He slid his hand down her body to her thong panties, traced the fragile string and tiny swatch of fabric covering her sex back and forth with a fingertip until it grew wet with her juices. She lifted her hips and strained toward his touch, the scent of her arousal rising to him.

He covered her lips with his own and released a tone close to a growl. At the same time he snapped the string of fabric covering her and slowly worked first one finger, then another, inside her. He caught her rhythm, his fingers stroking deep, finding the spot that brought her the most pleasure.

With each new note he hummed, Roma's hips twisted and pumped more furiously. He lifted his lips from hers to brush open-mouthed kisses between her breasts and down over her stomach, allowing the vibration beneath his voice to build until it touched the very heart of her sex. She arched beneath him, her body jerking as though it had been touched by an electric current, and she cried out.

He ended his song, but her abdominal and vaginal muscles continued to contract for several moments. He waited until the aftershocks of her orgasm had passed, then withdrew his hand.

She lay panting, a fine sheen of sweat covering her skin. With color flooding her cheeks and her breasts heaving from her climax, she looked like a sex goddess.

Drew pulled away, rolled off the bed and regained his feet. He pushed his erect penis back into his briefs and zipped his pants.

Roma raised herself on her elbows, showing her large, rose-tipped breasts to their best advantage. "What is it?"

"Did you want me before you heard me sing, Roma?"

"Of course I wanted you," she said. "I can't believe you're even asking me. All you have to do is hum and you can have any woman within hearing distance."

Exactly.

He'd spent more time with her than he had any other woman. After weeks of dating, instead of caring about him, she'd become addicted to the sound of his voice, as were all the other women who attended his shows. But he needed more. He wanted a woman who'd never heard him sing a note. Because once they did—he didn't stand a chance of inspiring love, only desire.

His gift wasn't a gift at all. Where human females were involved, it was a curse.

He'd had enough. "I won't be calling you again, Roma. What I was searching for with you…isn't here."

Roma scrambled from the bed. She held the crumpled dress she'd only half removed against her and rushed to intercept him. Her hair tumbled over her shoulder only partially covering her breast. "Where are you going, Drew? We need to talk about this."

"I don't think there's anything to say. You enjoy the sex. But you don't have real feelings for me. We've been enjoying each other's company. But I want more. And if there was a possibility of that happening with you, we'd both know by now."

She gasped, eyes wide with panic. "But you can't just end it like this."

He didn't bother to answer, just continued toward the door.

"You can't leave like this," she screamed.

Yes, he could. Next time she could get her fix at the show and pay money for it, like all the rest.

He exited Roma's apartment building and stormed into the parking lot. The night air was crisp, and he flipped up the collar of his lightweight jacket. His sexual frustration took a second seat to the anger building inside him with every step. When he reached his car, he slammed his fist down on the hood.

"Goddammit!" Why couldn't he get this right? He braced his elbows on the top of the car and jammed his fingers through his hair.

If he could become part of a community of other preternatural beings he wouldn't be facing this constant search for acceptance. But he'd lived on land his entire life, and rarely met others, and none of his own species. There were none.

His own otherworldly powers made it easy for him to sense things in others, but he couldn't recognize their gifts, or what they might be. And it wasn't likely they'd be eager to identify themselves when they crossed paths with him. This need to stay hidden, to blend into human society, put constant restraints on their interactions.

Since he was half Brazilian dolphin shapeshifter, called *Encantado*, and half Siren, with Mer mixed in with both, his talents were an odd combination. They had seemed to evolve as he matured. Because he was a mixed-breed, the supernatural community refused to embrace him. Those who were half human looked down on him too.

As far as he knew, there were no other beings who had his same or even similar mix of species. He was a freak. And thanks to the rampant prejudice in the supernatural community, his only option for a mate was a human female. But humans were the ones he affected most strongly with his gift. He couldn't bear the thought of going through life never speaking, never singing.

Ah, hell. Why did he care so damn much?

Because he wanted what his parents had. His parents had left their communities, their families, to be together.

They had come to America because this country truly was a melting pot, and they could blend in with humans. He was a living expression of their love. He never doubted they loved him. But they also worried about what he might become if he continued to go through life alone.

He'd never had a reason or a desire to fix the issue until recently. If he was honest with himself, he'd admit he never truly wanted to build a relationship with Roma. He'd been wary and watchful, needing to see how things progressed before committing himself. He hadn't allowed his emotions to become involved. Not yet.

He'd been a plaything for her. The realization stung his pride.

Was there something wrong with him that he couldn't be wanted just for himself? Why couldn't he connect to women emotionally? Since neither his Siren nor his Encantado heritage promised anything close to monogamy, he might never experience that kind of closeness. Did the *Encantado* part of his genetics prevent him and the women he hooked up with from bonding? His mother's Latin heritage was proving more and more difficult to live with...and control.

The vision of a heart-shaped face and wide-set eyes glaring at him warily tempted him. Her scent alone had driven him to jump off the stage and pursue her. What would happen if he experienced more of her unique essence?

She was a supernatural being, but what kind?

And would she talk to him? The high-pitched sound that had shattered the door and shaken every piece of glass in the club had come from her. He was certain of it. Though he could emit sounds painful to human ears, he didn't use them. His parents had always taught him not to use his gift to cause harm.

He never should have grabbed the blonde. He'd startled her and he'd also read fear in her eyes. Why would she be afraid of him?

And if she was afraid of him, how could he ever persuade her to speak to him?

Drew opened the door of his Camry and got in. He gripped the steering wheel with both hands. Her elusive perfume, like the sea and some kind of flower, called to him again. The memory drifted around the edges of his senses.

He had to find her.

But how?

He'd searched for her at the club every night, and for the women she came with. But he'd been so focused on her, he'd only glanced at them.

He started the car, pulled out of the lot, and turned toward the club.

If he could catch a hint of her scent at the club, maybe he could track her. Why hadn't he thought of that before?

Unfortunately, at least a few thousand women had been through the club since the blonde had been there. Would he be able to pick up her scent again?

He had to try.

Chapter 4

Giving Cheryl a ride home was always an adventure. She never knew what domestic chaos would greet her when she crossed the threshold of her friend's apartment.

Katrina stood in stunned silence at the door of Cheryl's bedroom. It was worse than the last time she'd visited. Clothes, shoes, and accessories covered every surface but the bed. It looked as though the closet had projectile-vomited colorful fabric all over the room. And every drawer had taken part as well. "I'd heard rumors recently about this room, but didn't believe it. I think I'll take photos and post them on several social media sites."

Cheryl twisted around to face her, mouth open and eyes wide. After a moment's pause, she threw her head back and laughed. "You wouldn't dare."

What did she sound like when she laughed like that?

Katrina could read how deep Cheryl's amusement was through her body language and facial expression, but even after she had the cochlear implant surgery she wouldn't get the full effect of the human voice. It sounded mechanical, almost robotic, to hear through the device, or so she'd been told. But what did *mechanical* or *robotic* sound like?

She remembered the songs of dolphins and whales traveling thousands of miles through the water, the base rumble of their call when they sought a mate, and a hundred other marine symphonies, vibrating at frequencies she could hear.

But she could never return to the sea. One of the helpers at the orphanage had made certain of that.

And on land she couldn't hear her best friend's laughter.

Both thoughts triggered an ache like a bruise that never healed.

Cheryl removed the dress she'd just tried on and tossed it onto a chair in the corner of the room. Katrina shook her head. Did she even have this many clothes?

"How do you reach the bed when you bring someone home?"

Cheryl shot a saucy smile over her shoulder. "We manage."

Katrina braced herself and braved the room. A faint blended scent of perfume and nail polish hung in the air. She tiptoed around a basket of shoes with a multi-colored shawl draped over it, picked up a lacy blouse in her path, and laid it on the bed. Traveling from the military precision of the living room into the visual pandemonium of the bedroom was like going through deep culture shock. In one room everything was in place, and then the door opened to...chaos.

She sat down on Cheryl's bed and folded the blouse. "Where is your date taking you?" she asked.

Cheryl shimmied out of a short mini skirt and turned to

face her. "Out for dinner and a club."

An anxious knot cramped Katrina's stomach. The word *club* had a negative connotation for her ever since she'd fled The Next Best Thing.

Cheryl reached for a black, woven, see-through blouse and held it up. "What do you think? This and my black leather skirt?"

Reed-thin, with flame red hair, buttermilk white skin and legs that went on forever, Cheryl had the build for every style introduced since time began. How could she *not* look good in everything she put on? Maybe her perfect figure was behind her compulsive clothes buying.

"I think you'll look like a lit candle, and he'll think you're gorgeous."

Cheryl pursed her lips. "You say the sweetest things. If I were gay, I'd have a crush on you."

Katrina laughed. If she were gay she wouldn't be having these uncontrollable longings for a dangerous, incredibly good-looking male stranger. She threaded restless fingers through her hair.

Cheryl gathered the clothes she intended to wear and tossed them atop the pile in the chair. She shimmied into a t-shirt and a brief pair of silk boxers, then sauntered over to flop back onto the bed.

Her friend's lack of self-consciousness only underlined her own issues. Katrina slipped off her shoes and stretched her toes. Her scarred feet looked red and raw. The leg makeup she applied every morning had worn off over the course of the day.

Cheryl touched her arm. "You've been kinda strange

since the other night," Her friends usual good-natured features settling into a thoughtful pout, her green eyes searching.

"What do you mean?" Katrina stalled to gain time for an excuse to come to her.

"You know what I'm talking about."

Katrina lowered her eyes to the blouse now crushed between her hands.

She hadn't quivered with delight or had an orgasm from the sound of Drew Saunders' voice like the other women. It had been all they could talk about the next day at work.

But she had heard a few of the tones he projected. She had to put the experience out of her head. She'd grown used to the silent world she lived in now. She didn't want him tempting her with something she'd learned to live without. The cochlear implant would give her hearing without the added risks the Merman represented. She had to forget about him.

But during the few moments she'd stood face-to-face with him, and he'd directed all his raw sexuality at her...She clenched her hand against the empty ache the memory triggered. Had she ever experienced such an instant—

Cheryl squeezed her arm, to regain her attention. "It was really freaky having the door explode like that. We were talking all night about what the sound could have been. It had to be feedback from the amps, but I swear I've never heard anything like it. It left all of our ears ringing. Could you hear it?"

"Yes, I heard it." She should never have screamed at him like that. But she'd felt so overwhelmed just standing next to him. All the passion he projected...and he'd been aroused. She could feel it. And he'd smelled tempting, wonderful, like...*home*. She'd wanted to bury her nose against his shoulder and breathe him in. God, she was primed sexually just thinking of him.

She had to be careful. Mermaids bonded for life, and if she was unlucky enough to bond to the wrong person, she'd spend her whole life longing for love and affection from someone who couldn't return her feelings. That knowledge made her cautious with the men she dated. And Drew Saunders triggered her self-protective instincts times ten.

"You really heard that sound?" Cheryl's brows rose. "I don't know why I'm surprised. I bet they heard it across the street. He was talking to you when it happened. What did he say to you?"

"He asked me why I was leaving."

"Why did you leave?"

She drew a deep breath. "I didn't like the way he manipulated you and the others."

"Honey, that wasn't manipulation. That was pure heaven. Amped-up sex for the ears."

"But it's empty gratification, Cheryl. Wouldn't you rather feel the touch of someone who really cares about you than pleasure for pleasure's sake?"

"Well, yeah, but I'd take what he gives in a pinch. His voice is phenomenal. And he ain't hard to look at. You have to admit that."

Katrina's heart raced and her stomach suddenly clenched with nervous spasms. He stood at least ten inches taller than she, and his dark hair, cut short, lay against his head like a seal's pelt. His strong jaw and cleft chin were darkened with just enough scruff to look sexy as hell. His pale, gray-blue eyes, set beneath a strong brow ridge and surrounded by thick, dark lashes, had looked right into hers and she'd... She couldn't go there. She couldn't breathe. "Is that where your date is taking you tonight?" she managed.

"I don't know."

"I wish you wouldn't go back there."

Cheryl studied her face, her expression, for once, serious. "It really freaked you out, didn't it?"

Though they'd been friends a long time, and she knew Cheryl loved and accepted her, she still didn't grasp what being deaf meant. "When you can't hear and have to depend on lip reading for information, you key into body language, facial expression, all sorts of clues...I found it...demeaning to you all."

Cheryl's eyes widened. "If you could hear him sing you wouldn't feel that way, Katrina. His voice is something special. He'll be a star one day."

Though she couldn't hear him, she'd experienced his power in a different way. He had drawn her in as much as he had the rest. He just hadn't rung her bells physically as he had the human females. It took more than sound for *it* to happen for her. But what she'd experienced was still powerful. It had been nearly two weeks and she still longed for—

Cheryl rolled onto her side and propped herself up on an elbow. "Why don't you call Sid, and we'll go out together?"

Katrina shook her head. "He and I decided to take a

break from each other three weeks ago."

"Is it because you want the implant?"

"Yes." And because he was a cheating asshole. He'd been beyond angry she wanted the implant, and viewed it as a betrayal. The woman he'd cheated with had been payback. If only she could banish the sight of his bare butt pumping away like there was no tomorrow. It had been humiliating and degrading for both her and the other woman. She couldn't bring herself to even talk about it. The experience had taught her a valuable lesson.

Human men could not be trusted any more than their Mer counterparts.

Sid embraced his deafness as though it were a special calling. But while it was fine for him to be satisfied with his life, she wanted more. She'd given up so much already. "He thinks because I can function without it, I shouldn't have the surgery."

"Men can be such selfish assholes sometimes."

No argument there. Cheryl's attitude almost tempted a smile from Katrina.

"When is your meeting with the doctors?"

"Tomorrow."

Cheryl laid a hand on her arm, this time in comfort. "Would you like me to go with you?"

Katrina smiled at Cheryl's thoughtfulness, but shook her head. "I'll be fine. They're going to take me through my test results, go over the dangers of the surgery, the pros and cons, and then I'll have to make the final decision." She gave Cheryl's hand a squeeze, and rose. "I'm going. You need to get ready for your date. I have a project I need to finish." She dropped the blouse in Cheryl's lap.

"All work and no play makes Katrina a dull girl." Cheryl bounced off the bed. "You could go out with me and Howard."

"Howard?"

Cheryl made a shooing motion with one hand. "I know his name gives the impression he's a nerd, but he's not." She grinned and did a suggestive roll of her hips. "He rocks my world."

Katrina laughed. "I'm happy for you. Thanks for the invitation, but I think I'll finish the website design for the restaurant and I still have the office supply store site to do a few tweaks on. I'll text you after my doctor's appointment tomorrow to keep you posted."

"Okay. If you change your mind about tonight, text me, and we'll meet you somewhere for a meal."

Katrina nodded. "I will."

She exited the apartment and strolled down the sidewalk to the parking lot. She studied the huge century plant that unfolded like a prehistoric wonder in one of the landscaped beds outside the restaurant next door. A bus rumbled by, replacing the pleasant scent of grilled food with the stink of its exhaust, and she wrinkled her nose.

Inside her car, she paused to think about Cheryl's attitude regarding what had happened at the club. Was Drew Saunders' seduction of the audience truly not as big a deal as she had made of it? The experience hadn't changed Cheryl's attitude toward her new boyfriend.

Katrina bit her lip. Had she overreacted?

The longing to see Drew Saunders rose up so powerfully it brought tears to her eyes. Certainly she wanted to hear those underlying tones he projected when he sang, but if he was from a similar Shoal... She wanted to see him again. To question him.

He couldn't be Mer. If he were, he'd be deaf like her.

But he smelled like...like salt, the sea, and Merman...but something else, too.

Maybe she could go, but stay outside, close by the bar. No one would notice if she hung out at one of the open-air restaurants in the Gaslamp Quarter. It was a popular area, and there were always crowds.

She rested her forehead against the steering wheel while she fought the need to go there now. This very moment. She swallowed against the knot in her throat, raised her head, and turned the key in the ignition.

An hour later, her clothes changed, her makeup freshened, she closed her apartment door and locked it. It was easier to take a taxi than find a parking space. The cab was already waiting when she exited the apartment building's front door. She slid inside and gave the driver directions to The Next Best Thing.

Twenty minutes later, she slipped out of the car into the heart of the Gaslamp Quarter. A line stretched down the street in front of the nightclub. She inhaled the scents of food, exhaust, and the heavy perfume of a scantily clad woman passing by.

What had she expected, that he'd be out on the street? Biting her lip, she turned her back to the standing crowd outside the club and studied the restaurants in front of her.

Someone grabbed her shoulder.

She startled and squeaked as strong hands turned her toward The Next Big Thing.

Chapter 5

Drew massaged his pounding temples with one hand. A combination of frustration and lack of sleep had brought on the headache. Using the club as the central point, he'd worked his way out in a circle, and cruised the city with the window down, searching for his mystery woman until dawn. He'd hoped to catch a hint of her fragrance. Nothing.

Though it was two hours before show time, Simon had called, urging him to come in early so they could discuss something. Drew turned onto Market Street, and then whipped the steering wheel to avoid a sedan as it swerved into his lane. "Damnit." A rare parking space opened up right in front of him, and he whipped the car into it and parked, locked up, then hoofed it up the block, then over.

Entering the club five minutes before their meeting time, he paused at the door to allow his eyes to adjust to the dimness inside. Late afternoon patrons lined the bar and sat in small groups at tables nearby. The scent of fine whiskey and strong coffee hung in the air. Tempted to order an Irish coffee, Drew paused at the bar and asked Ron, one of the bartenders, for some aspirin and a bottle of water instead. He kicked back the pills and washed them down with the water before he leaped up on the stage.

He strode down the back hallway to the office and thumped the door with more strength than necessary. When it swung open, he was surprised to find Connor Walsh, the band's agent, already there. Tony tilted his chair back against Sam's desk, the front legs of his seat in the air. Seeing Drew, he leaned forward and dropped them to the floor. His dark curly hair looked mussed, as though he'd been running his fingers through it. His Italian features had been set in a frown, but cleared when he spotted Drew.

Rand Michaels was hunched forward in his chair, his hands linked between his knees. His almost-perpetual dissatisfied scowl darkened his face and narrowed his eyes.

Simon sat in a chair directly behind the door. His features remained neutral, but a pulse beat in his throat like his heart was doing a rumba. His smile was weak when he nodded at Drew. "Hey."

This meeting felt like an ambush. Tension raced through Drew's body as he studied Connor's expression.

"We have a phenomenal offer on the table, Drew," Connor said, breaking the silence. "All you have to do is sign on the dotted line."

His earlier frustration and the headache combined to make him irascible. "I'm not signing anything until I hear the details."

Connor sidled closer. "You won't get a better recording deal than this one, Drew. Your insistence on waiting has worked to our advantage. It's pitted the companies against each other and caused a bidding war.

Drew's heart kicked into overdrive and excitement zinged through him. He hadn't seen any of this coming. If only there was some way to test how a recording of his voice might affect the listening public. "Which record company is ahead?"

"Capitol Records. They've promised a higher percentage in royalties, plus a bonus when the CD goes gold or platinum. They threw in some other incentives in merchandising and marketing to sweeten the pot."

Sam's chair was the only one available. Drew leaned back against the desk instead of taking it. "I'm listening."

Connor went over the contract step by step, proving he wasn't just a pretty face. The man knew his stuff.

The deal was sweet. But could he control how much of his special magic recorded onto a CD? And if he couldn't, the consequences might be… It was hard to imagine, and defied rational analysis. He remained silent, thinking things through.

Rand exploded from his seat and shoved his face close to Drew's. "God damnit, man. What is your problem? What do you even have to think about? You can't say no to this. This is what we've worked for since we put the band together. You have to do it."

Drew breathed through the urge to knock Rand on his ass. Humans were so fragile, and if he broke this one he'd go to jail. Sacrificing his freedom because their drummer was an asshole was not an option.

He focused on a spot between Rand's brows while he attempted to tamp down the rage threatening to tear loose.

He couldn't stifle the rush of heat fanning out around them. "Get out of my face."

The controlled, quiet intensity of his voice resonated through the room.

Out of the corner of his eye he saw Connor back away.

Drew's eyes shifted to Rand's, and for a long moment he allowed the other man to see the cold, clear anger he held in check.

Sweat beaded Rand's forehead, and his angry demeanor dropped away as suddenly as it had erupted. He eyed Drew warily as he stepped back.

Drew shrugged to ease the tension from his shoulders and directed his attention to Connor.

"When do we meet with the execs?"

There was a collective sigh of relief from everyone. He allowed himself a wry chuckle. Were they relieved he was going to sign a contract, or because he hadn't killed Rand?

Connor smiled. "Thursday. Day after tomorrow."

Tony slapped his shoulder. "Thanks, Drew."

Damn, he'd been an asshole for not showing how excited he was about the whole thing. He smiled. "We've all worked hard for this."

Simon stepped forward to shake his hand, his thin face homely until he smiled. He'd been working in the music business longer than the rest of them, and if anyone deserved this, Simon did.

Drew smiled. "All your hard work has paid off, man. You may even get the opportunity to do some solo work on the guitar."

Simon's grin widened. "Baby steps, man. I'll be happy

just to get my name on the first album."

But they still had a problem to deal with. Drew's gaze settled on Rand again. "You know what this means, don't you?"

"Yeah, more money. Real money," Rand said with a smirk.

"I'm not talking about the money. I'm talking about the music."

Rand was a brilliant musician. He could write music and maintain a steady beat for hours. He had an instinctive understanding of how to add in the special tempos of his instrument. But his control over his temper was non-existent. It seemed no one had ever called him on it.

With the ego boost from more fame and fortune, he could become a huge liability for the rest of the group.

Drew kept his voice quiet, but emphasized every word. "To get to the money, you have to produce a quality product. And you can't shoot for star quality if you're lost in your own hype. It interferes with creating the music. In other words, you're going to have to adjust your attitude. The rest of us are no longer going to enable you by cleaning up after you, Rand. No more bailing you out after fights, DUIs, or public intoxication busts. No more putting up with your temper tantrums. I'm not going into this with someone who can't be depended on to do the work."

A sullen, ugly look crossed Rand's face. "I'll do the work."

For a while he'd do it, then he'd screw up and he'd be gone.

As though he read Drew's thoughts, Rand's fists

clenched at his sides. "You're not cutting me out of this deal."

"No." He could step in and take the man's anger from him, but human psyches were fragile, and it might rob him of other things as well. Things he directed into his music that made his playing special.

Rand's relief flickered across his features.

"You'll be the one to cut yourself out, the first time you miss a gig or a recording session because you're sitting in jail after a fight, or because you're drunk. Your anger will be what ends this for you, Rand. So either direct it into your music, or get help. But you're not going to fuck this up for the rest of us."

Tony laid a hand on Drew's shoulder in support. Simon stepped close as well.

The drummer looked from one to the other, his lips compressed in anger. Then his expression altered when he met Simon's stare, the one member of the band he truly respected.

"You're a talented musician, Rand," Simon said. "But this is the big leagues, not a garage band or small club stuff. It will be a circus. And it will be up to you to hold it together."

Rand nodded. "I won't screw it up, old man."

It was even-tempered Tony who offered Rand his hand first. Then hand shaking and shoulder pounding moved around the circle. Drew dragged pretty boy Connor into the huddle. "You've done a great job for us."

"Thanks." Connor smiled. "But it was your nerves of steel that brought things around to where we wanted them.

Were you really that reluctant to sign a contract?"

No. Yes. What was he supposed to say? "The other deals didn't feel right."

Connor shook his head. "I wouldn't want to play poker with you, Drew. You have no tells, and you don't flinch."

Drew grinned. He'd heard it before. "I didn't go into this for the money, Connor. I went into it because I'm good at it, and I like to make music. It was what I was born to do." No lie there. It was as much a part of him as the color of his eyes. "So far it's the only thing that's truly important to me."

"I want to be around when that changes," Rand said. "You'll finally be as human as the rest of us."

That could never happen. Or could it? Once again the blonde intruded into his thoughts. He tossed a smile Rand's way. "I'll never let you know if or when it does. You'll rag me from now till doomsday."

"Damn right," Simon said, with so much feeling even Drew laughed.

As they filed out of the office Simon said, "Next time you're playing chicken with our band business, Drew, you need to fill the rest of us in."

"It was only by accident," he admitted.

Simon's steps faltered and he stared at him. "Jesus, man."

"Holy shit!" Tony exclaimed.

Drew laughed. "Like you said, it's going to be a circus. I wasn't sure I wanted to be a part of it."

"But you're going to sign the contract now," Simon said with a troubled frown.

"Yeah. You guys deserve it. And as long as I can make music…" He shrugged.

"How 'bout we celebrate the contract with a drink?" Rand interrupted.

"Not before the show, Rand," Tony said.

Drew almost smiled. If he'd known all it would take was his standing up to Rand and reading him the riot act, he'd have done it months ago. He flipped on his keyboard. "I'm going over the new song we've been working on."

"Jesus, guys. We're gonna be rich, and you don't even want to celebrate." Rand stared longingly at the bar.

"Yes, we do, Rand. But not before the show," Simon said.

"Jesus!" Rand shook his head.

"After the show I'll buy a bottle of champagne and we'll do it right," Drew suggested.

Rand grimaced. "How 'bout a bottle of bourbon instead?"

Drew grinned. There did seem something wrong with the image of Rand sipping from a champagne flute. "All right. A bottle of bourbon."

A couple came into the club, bringing with them a flash of sunlight that reflected off the mirrors at the bar.

Drew caught a faint whiff of the scent that had haunted him for days. He twisted on his heel and pulled it deep into his lungs before the door swung shut.

"What is it, Drew?" Tony asked.

"I just remembered something I left in the car. I'll be right back. Go ahead and warm up without me."

With the urge to run dogging every step, he forced himself to stroll to the door and out onto the street.

Chapter 6

The luscious aroma of grilling meat followed them all the way through the restaurant as the waitress showed them to an outside table, where the spring night was still warm enough to be comfortable. A short brick wall and decorative black wrought iron railing separated the exterior courtyard of the restaurant from the street.

Katrina took the chair on Cheryl's left, while her date, Howard, sat on her right. Six feet tall, with dark shaggy hair and green eyes, he had a rangy build and a quick, attractive smile. Exactly Cheryl's type.

"I'm so glad we ran into you," Cheryl said. "I was going to text you before we went into the restaurant."

"I just couldn't stay home. But I didn't mean to interfere with your date." Katrina shot Howard an apologetic look.

He gave her a friendly, relaxed smile. "No problem, we're eating dinner and going to the club across the street. If we can get in."

Katrina glanced at Cheryl and raised a questioning brow. At Cheryl's chagrin, Katrina looked away. She bit her lip.

Her stomach jittered with nerves. "I thought I'd give the band another chance myself."

Cheryl touched her arm, and she looked up.

Katrina added, "I can't hear them, but I can check out the lead singer."

Cheryl laughed.

Katrina picked up the menu and studied it to give the couple some alone time. By not reading their lips, she could tune out their conversation, and avoid intruding too much on her friend's date.

On the light breeze a scent rolled over her, wonderful, light, like the sea and cinnamon. She closed her eyes, savoring it, as she gripped the menu. He was close. She glanced up and registered Cheryl's expression of surprise, and the way she focused on someone standing behind Katrina's left shoulder. She read the words, "She's deaf. She can't hear you," when Cheryl spoke.

He brushed a hand over Katrina's shoulder, and she tensed. Her body warmed to his presence. The Mermaid part of her genetics responded, running rampant, sending out an answering fragrance. She swallowed, though her throat had gone dry as sun-baked sand.

As he came into view, his body heat reached out to caress her. She shivered. She raised her eyes and paused to study his jaw, dusted by a five o'clock shadow. She tilted her head back. His gray eyes, surrounded by dark, thick lashes, had a ring of midnight blue around the iris and a starburst of golden brown around the pupil.

She followed his movements as he took the chair next to her. He studied her as thoroughly she did him.

"Do you read lips?" he asked.

She nodded, unable to speak.

"I've been looking for you," he said. "Waiting for you to come back to the club."

His bottom lip, fuller than the top, grabbed her attention. She found the shape of his mouth so inviting, she had to fight the desire to kiss him. Her heart beat as though she'd swum a mile. Blood rushed through her veins in a tide.

"I'm glad I found you." His movements slow, he rested his fingertips on her wrist and lightly brushed them over a small patch of skin there. He might as well have caressed her whole arm, because the sensation traveled over her skin like a brush fire. The same tempting sensation had inspired her to scream at him before. Now she worked to suppress a gasp.

She bit her lip and dragged her arm away from his touch.

Frustration flickered across his features.

"Will you come to the show tonight? You and your friends." He nodded to Cheryl and Howard. "I'd like you to be there so we can talk afterwards."

Talk. Her heart sunk.

Would he think her voice strange? Though she'd practiced years to gain intonation and clarity in her vocalizations, she was still tormented by fears of what people might think about her speech.

And what would they talk about? How he seduced the women who came to his show? What species they each were? And would he admit what he was? Or would they try to lock the information away from each other?

"Please," he said when she remained silent.

"All right." She nodded, praying those two simple words sounded normal.

He smiled with such charm heat rushed up to settle in her cheeks.

"I'll have a table waiting for you close to the stage." He took her hand and held it in his. "What's your name?"

Her throat nearly closed with the rush of sensation tickling up her arm and across her breasts like a caress. "Katrina." Was he attempting to seduce her with his Mer capabilities as thoroughly as he did the human women with his voice? Or was it mutual?

"It's nice to meet you, Katrina. I'm Andrew, but everyone calls me Drew." He swallowed, and his strong throat worked as though he was having as much trouble suppressing his reaction to her as she did to him. "You're not going to run away again, are you?" he asked, worry evident in the intensity of his look.

The idea fluttered around the perimeter of her thoughts. But would she be able to fight the urge to see him again with any more determination than she had before? Probably not. "No, I won't run away."

His expression relaxed into a smile. "I have to go practice. My band is waiting for me." His body language clearly showed his reluctance to release her hand and rise to his feet. "Come over right after you finish eating. I'll get you settled and introduce you to the other band members before the crowd gets too out of hand."

She nodded.

He turned his attention to Cheryl and Howard. While he introduced himself and shook their hands, Katrina fought to regain her composure and shore up her defenses.

"Call me on my cell when you're ready to come over. I'll have the bouncer meet you at the door and bring you in," he said to Howard, handing him a card.

By the time his attention swung back to her, she'd found a steadier place.

"I'll see you in a short while." He smiled at her, all his simmering intensity focused on her.

She couldn't get her voice to work so she nodded, but she watched him weave his way through the surrounding tables and saunter back into the restaurant. He reappeared at the front entrance, and able to see them through the outside railing, raised a hand in acknowledgement before he jogged across the street to The Next Big Thing.

Cheryl grabbed her arm, her features alight. "Oh my God! That's the most romantic thing I've ever seen. He's been *looking* for you!" Her smile died with the suddenness of a flipped switch. "Oh, shit. I hope he's not a stalker."

Drew hit a jarring chord, then swore. Tony and Simon stopped playing and turned to look at him, their surprised expressions almost identical.

"Sorry."

He had always been able to compartmentalize his life, his thought, his feelings, but he found it impossible to do so now. His heart still jogged in his chest in an accelerated rhythm. The Mer fragrance she emanated still wound through his head. He could barely concentrate for worrying about whether or not she'd show.

Her name was Katrina. Why the hell hadn't he asked her last name? If she decided to bolt, he wouldn't be able to find her.

He should have called Simon, made some excuse and stayed with her. But if he'd acted too eager, he might have freaked her out.

Shit. He was acting like a kid with his first crush. He needed to regain some control.

He'd never responded to any woman like this. Was it just Mermaid genetics taking over them both? Or was there a genuine attraction?

Hell, he'd longed to find woman who couldn't hear him sing, and now he'd found one. What were the odds? But now he felt too worked up over all the preternatural shit that went along with being attracted to someone *special* to concentrate on anything else.

He needed to get his head into the song and block out everything else. "Simon, how about you to play the eight bar intro solo, then the rest of us will come in? Let's see how it works."

"Okay."

The lone cry of the guitar brought a drama to the beginning of the song the keyboard couldn't touch.

When they'd played the composition all the way through, Tony said, "Good call, Drew."

"We'll work on it some more tomorrow. I like the wailing sound of the guitar in spots. We may want to play it up, but I need to think about it. Time to gear up for the show tonight." His cell phone buzzed in his pocket, and he jerked it out.

"Hey, this is Howard. We're on our way," a male voice said.

"Okay, thanks." His face felt hot and excitement roiled through him. He flipped his keyboard off. The doors would be opening to the public in thirty minutes. He'd have twenty to sit and talk with Katrina and her friends. He rushed to find Clyde's number. The bouncer answered. He gave him a description of Katrina and her friends. "I'll be in the club waiting for them."

"I'll send them on in," Clyde said.

Catching Rand's curious look, Drew said, "I have some friends coming tonight. I have to get them settled before I change."

"We didn't know you had any friends besides us," Rand chided.

Tony and Simon laughed.

Drew shook his head. Rand wasn't too far wrong. He found it hard to connect with humans. Had they not had music in common, he probably wouldn't have built a relationship with any of the band members. It wasn't a deficiency in them, but himself. He recognized that. "Well, I have been focused on the band, but I'm trying to broaden my horizons."

"It's a woman," Tony stated.

Drew laughed. "Yeah, it is." It wouldn't be fair to her, or the guys, if he didn't warn them about her condition. "Katrina is deaf, and I want to make sure she's seated close to the stage so she can lip read our songs."

"Hey, that's cool," Simon said. "Not that she's deaf, but that you want her to be able to enjoy the music. Can she hear anything at all?"

"I'm not sure. But she'll be able to feel the vibration and beat of the instruments. When I introduce you to her, be sure to speak directly to her so she can read what you're saying. And please don't shout."

"You're gonna *introduce* her to us? This must be serious," Tony said.

That remained to be seen. With her lush, caramel-streaked hair and teal eyes, she was beautiful, and they'd be tempted to move in on her if he didn't brand her as his. Just the idea triggered an unfamiliar territorial flare of emotion.

Clyde appeared at the door with Cheryl and Howard, Katrina right behind them. The slow way she placed her feet as she walked echoed the uncertainty he read in her face. Being unable to hear in situations like this had to be difficult for her.

Drew jumped off the stage to greet them, and the rest of the band followed.

"Thanks for coming," Drew said as he shook first Cheryl's hand, then Howard's. He turned his attention to Katrina. Soft color touched her cheeks and she glanced away. Drew smiled. Her body language and shyness told him she was definitely attracted to him.

He introduced her to the band members one at a time. For once, Rand was on his best behavior and actually smiled. Cheryl asked a question about the amps on the stage. The guys pulled out chairs, and she and her date were soon being entertained.

"Where would you like to sit, so you can see the stage clearly?" Drew asked. He found it difficult to take his eyes off Katrina. The smooth slope of her shoulder bared by the spaghetti straps of her sea green dress begged to be caressed, kissed.

"May we sit here?" she laid a hand on the back of a chair positioned at a table to the right of center stage.

Her voice, though flat on certain syllables, sounded close to any hearing person's. He was fast growing used to it. "Sure." He held her chair out and waited for her to sit. He took the one to her right and turned it so she could read his lips. "Can I get you something to drink?"

She shook her head.

"Have you always lived in San Diego?" he asked.

"Only for about eight years. I moved here from Alaska to go to college, and a graphic design company hired me right out of school."

"Alaska?"

"Yes. I was abandoned at an orphanage there at birth."

Abandoned! How had a preternatural child survived in a human orphanage? How had they reacted to her abilities? And the sudden changes that took place during puberty? Damn.

"I'm sorry you had to go through that. I've been very fortunate. My parents are still alive and together, and they live close by. They immigrated to America from Canada when I was two."

"I would like to meet them when we know each other a little better."

"I think my family and you may have some things in

common." Speaking in code was a pain in the ass, but to say things straight out could be dangerous. It wasn't done in the preternatural community.

Her sea-blue gaze rose to his. "How can you tell?"

He leaned forward to take her hands in his. "We'll talk more about it after the show tonight."

The hard beat of shoe heels on the tile floor acted as a warning. He looked up. Roma bore down on him with the determination of a runaway speedboat. She had continued to pursue him like a lovesick groupie, even though he'd broken off the relationship a week before.

"What the hell is going on, Drew? Clyde tried to keep me out on the street," her strident tones screeched across the room like a gull's cry.

Chapter 7

Katrina turned her head to keep from reading what Drew and the woman were saying. It was clearly a private conversation, because he'd tugged her toward the front door and turned his back to the rest of the people in the room.

Was everyone listening to them? She cringed at the thought.

His band members excused themselves and disappeared behind the stage to get ready for the show. Howard avoided Katrina's eyes as he and Cheryl joined her at the table.

Cheryl slipped into the chair next to her and placed a hand on her arm. "Do you want to leave?"

Drew and that woman had something between them. But could those feelings be as strong as the attraction he and she were feeling? She'd never come close to this intensity with the humans she'd dated, and they'd barely met. With Mitchell, her one Merman encounter, there'd never been this unquenchable thirst for more. Her attention strayed to the front door where he and the woman were engaged in a heated argument. "No, I'm not leaving. I told

Drew I wouldn't run away again."

Cheryl grinned. "Good for you." She glanced over Katrina's shoulder. "From what I'm getting, he ended it over a week ago, but she's not getting the message. Or rather she's determined it isn't gonna happen."

Katrina shook her head. "Don't eavesdrop."

"You are too good a person. If I were you, I'd be hanging on every word."

"You're already doing that for me."

Cheryl laughed.

"He'll do what he has to do. But I won't jump into the deep end of the pool right after I watch him break up with someone else."

Cheryl studied her face. "If he hurts you, so help me, I'll rip his heart out."

"Thanks. But you won't have to. I can manage that all by myself."

If only her friend knew. She was able to literally rip Drew's heart out, but she wouldn't. Part of passing for human was being careful not to act as if she was anything else. She wouldn't allow her Mermaid instincts to rule her any more than she would her human ones. Her life depended on it.

Cheryl grinned. Her head came up as though something had captured her attention. "She's leaving."

When Drew returned to the table his features were taut. "Clyde's letting people in, and it's going to be a madhouse soon." He offered Katrina his hand. "Can I speak to you privately for a few minutes?"

She placed her hand in his. He tugged her to her feet

and toward the steps leading up on stage. He guided her behind the backdrop and down a narrow hall to a small dressing room littered with clothes and water bottles. Drew ignored the mess and turned to face her. "I'm sorry you had to witness the scene out there."

"Is she all right?" she asked.

"Upset. I ended our relationship and she's having difficulty accepting it."

"And you?"

"I shouldn't have gotten involved with her in the first place. We were too different." His expression of regret lent weight to his words.

What had he expected? "If she became involved with you because of what you can do with your voice, it was a lie."

Drew's features blanked and his body took on a stillness only the preternatural could attain. If she'd had any doubt he wasn't human, she'd have known from his stance.

She rushed on. "I know what you're doing when you sing. I know what kind of effect you have on the human women, and it's wrong. You have to stop."

"It isn't that easy, Katrina. It's part of what I am."

She swallowed. "And what would that be?"

"I'm the same as you, with a little something extra thrown in for good measure."

So he was of Mer decent, but something else as well, just as she'd thought. That something extra must be why he wasn't deaf.

"We've signed a recording contract today because of what I can do."

Her stomach muscles tensed and she put her hand over her midriff. That could be...*disastrous*.

He stepped close and cupped her hips. The heat from his body, the scent of his skin enveloped her. "Can you hear anything when I sing?"

"Not like the others," she admitted reluctantly.

"But you do hear something?"

"Just an undercurrent. It doesn't affect me like it does them."

The tension in his features, relaxed. "Good."

She swallowed against the dryness in her throat. "You can control it, can't you?" She focused on the swirls of hair feathering his skin at the open throat of his shirt. She wanted to nestle against him and soak up his essence.

"You smell so good." Drew's throat worked as he swallowed. His irises expanded and his tricolored eyes darkened with heat. "I can control some of it, but not all."

The scent of his arousal intensified her need as powerfully as his voice did the human women he entertained. "I felt uncomfortable witnessing what you did to the other women."

"Was that why you left?" He brushed her hair back over her shoulder, his fingers lingering against her bare skin as he traced the spaghetti strap over her shoulder.

Though his touch was light, the sensation it created trailed down to her breast. Her nipples tightened. Need writhed inside her, stealing her voice. Incapable of speech, she nodded.

"I don't force it on the audience. They keep coming back of their own volition."

"It's an intimate intrusion," she managed around the tightness of her throat. "And you're using them."

"No more than they're using me. It's a symbiotic relationship."

Why couldn't he understand what she was saying?

Realization hit her with the force of a tidal wave. Because it wasn't in his nature to think he was doing anything wrong. *He was a Siren.*

In an attempt to break away from the sensual spell he wove, she spun away and put one of the straight-backed folding chairs between them.

His features, so definably masculine, became harsh. "What is it?"

"Can both your parents hear?"

"Yes."

"Did your father seduce your mother with his voice? Or was it the other way around?" God, she hated this frustrating backward two-step preternatural beings did when it came to sharing information about themselves or their families.

"My mother doesn't sing. Not the way I do."

"It was your father, then?"

"Not entirely. They're both…" He hesitated, "…special."

What did he mean by that? Why couldn't he come out and tell her?

He turned his head to look at the door. "The guys are calling me. I have to go change and get on stage. Are you going to stay for the show?"

She had promised him she would. But the need to put

as much distance between them as possible stretched and clawed at her. Sirens weren't exactly known for their deep relationships, or their faithfulness, only for their gift of seduction. And Drew had a strong gift.

If she stayed, would she be strong enough to resist him? Did she even want to?

Yes, she had to resist.

All the things that might happen if they gave in to one another raced through her mind. The good and the bad.

The response he triggered merely by standing close should be enough to warn her off. Her entire body ached with the need to press herself against him as tightly as she could get and let nature take its course.

He stepped forward until his knees rested against the chair seat. "Your scent is delicious, Katrina. I can almost taste it."

His words painted a picture of his dark head between her thighs, his mouth on her. She tried hard to block it off. A sexual heat raced down from her head to her fingers and toes.

Drew's cheeks flushed and his eyes darkened. "We have to discover where this can go."

Her fingers tightened on the slick metal back of the chair, bearing down on it until the metal became hot and pliable. "We both know where it can go. It could be a disaster."

"Or a blessing," he countered. "Just give us a chance to get to know each other."

She closed her eyes against the sensual persuasion of his masculine features, his muscular body, and tried to block out the scent of his need.

If Sid, in his human selfishness, couldn't remain faithful to her, Drew Saunders in all his Siren glory certainly couldn't. She needed her head examined. She was probably going to regret this.

"All right. I'll stay."

Chapter 8

Drew had never been more aware of how an audience reacted to his voice. With Katrina watching, listening to every note, he attempted to direct only those tones she responded to. And he knew when she could hear him. The rise and fall of her scent directed him.

But her concern about what he was doing made him hyper-aware of how the other women responded, too. He realized when his tone affected her, it didn't them. The irony had him shaking his head.

"What's going on?" Simon asked as soon as they started their first ten-minute break. "You seem off your game tonight."

"He's a little distracted because of the new squeeze," Rand pointed out. "He's barely taken his eyes off her since she sat down. The other women are noticing it, too."

Drew frowned and scanned the audience. What Rand said was true. Several women sitting close to Katrina were eyeing her with open hostility. He shook his head. He was going to have to take care of business and do his job whether she liked it or not. The guys were depending on him. And to be honest, he'd grown to expect a certain response to his performances. His audience had as well.

Ten minutes later, he took the stage determined to give the women what they wanted. The change in his listeners was immediate, and the band settled into their regular performance rhythm.

Two hours later, when the last note was played, Drew turned off his keyboard. He hurried back stage to clean up before joining Katrina and her friends. The sound of recorded music throbbed through the walls as the DJ took over for the final two hours the club remained open. He washed his face and hands, changed out of his sweaty shirt, and got a bottle of water from the dressing room fridge before returning to the club floor. He was met by a barrage of claps and squeals when he stepped off the stage and waved to the women sitting at the tables close by, but homed in on the one where Katrina sat.

He invited them backstage to the dressing room, where Rand had gone to another room and returned with two more chairs. Drew guided Katrina to the small sofa and sat down beside her.

"The show was great," Cheryl said, as she settled in one of the chairs. "Your voice is amazing."

"Thanks. The rest of the guys will be joining us in a moment. We've been offered a recording contract, and we're celebrating."

"That's wonderful," Cheryl said with a smile.

"Not surprised at all. You guys are really good," Howard said.

"Thanks. We've been working toward this for a long

time."

"When did you get together?" Katrina asked.

"Simon and I met in college. We created a couple of bands back then, but they never went anywhere. Then when Tony and Rand joined us, things started clicking. We had finally found our sound. And the writing was coming along."

"But you've always sung."

"Yes. It's like breathing to me."

She nodded. "Like swimming is to Mermaids."

"Yeah."

Her blue-green gaze focused on his face. An instant rush of blood shot to his groin and he hardened. If making eye contact could do this to him, what would happen if they went further? The change in her scent and the heat circulating around her body alerted him to her response.

"I used to swim. I don't do it anymore."

Shock parted his lips, and he swallowed, hard, in sympathy. How tragic for a being who was meant to embrace water to decide to avoid it? What had forced her to make such a decision?

Drew leaned close and rested an arm along the back of the couch. "Why, Katrina?" he mouthed without sound just for her.

"Something happened and I had to stop."

One of the waitresses tapped on the dressing room door and Rand stood to answer it. The next moments were taken up with ordering drinks. He'd never felt less like drinking, but he had promised a bottle of bourbon to the guys, and ordered champagne for the ladies.

When their waitress, Sandra, returned with both bottles and glasses, Rand poured their drinks and handed them out.

"To the band," Drew said, lifting his glass in a toast.

They all drank.

"To being knee-deep in chicks and money," Rand said next.

The guys laughed. Drew noticed Katrina and Cheryl looked at each other and Cheryl rolled her eyes.

Rand refilled his glass.

"To the music," Simon said and raised his drink and everyone followed suit.

Everyone turned toward Tony. He was the quietest member of the band, almost shy. "To staying friends throughout this whole thing. I don't want the business of making music and money to come between us."

"Hear, hear," Drew said in agreement.

Simon added, "I agree."

"Right on, man," Rand said.

Outside the dressing room, they could hear the DJ onstage introducing himself and ramping up the volume of music.

"We can take this celebration on the road, guys," Rand suggested.

"I'll drop you two boys wherever you want to go," Simon said. "I need to get home to Briana."

"You are so pussy-whipped, Simon," Rand complained.

"Yeah. Ain't it great?" Simon shot back with a grin.

Everyone laughed.

Drew turned to Katrina. "Will you allow me to take you home?"

She studied him for a long moment, her expression solemn. "It might not be a good idea for us to go down this path."

"Or it could be the best move either of us has ever made. We won't know unless we explore it." He had to convince her.

Her eyes dropped away. "Or it might be dangerous for us both."

He tilted her face up so she would catch what he said. "You mean the possibility of bonding?"

"Yes."

Could he bond with a Mermaid?

He didn't know. *He'd never been with one.* But they were both part Mer.

Was that why he was experiencing such a strong sexual attraction to her? It was all he could do to keep his hands off of her. He plucked a stray strand of sun-streaked, wavy honey hair from her shoulder and discovered its soft texture. He wanted to cup her heart-shaped face and kiss her until neither one of them could breathe. Now, drawing in her delicious Mer scent every time he inhaled, he could understand how his response to her clouded his reason.

Yes. He could bond with her.

The realization did nothing to diminish his arousal. In fact, it made it more intense. His heart beat hard in his throat and his skin felt hot.

As their eyes met, her pupils expanded. He grasped her wrist and felt the heavy beat of her pulse beneath his fingers.

"We need to talk," he said.

"Because of our Mer genetics, you know it's more complicated than that."

A slow smile spread across his face and expanded into an all-out grin. A rosy blush suffused her face. He leaned over and brushed a kiss across her cheekbone, unable to resist the opportunity to get close. He lingered long enough to press his cheek to hers. She rested a hand against his chest and the heat between them flared to firestorm level.

Had he ever been this turned on by a woman? "I do have more self-control than you're giving me credit for," he said, his voice husky. "What about you?" His thumb ran lightly over her pulse.

She looked away, but her chin went up. "My self-control is fine, thank you."

He grinned.

Cheryl and Howard rose to leave and Katrina started to get up.

Drew's fingers tightened carefully around the wrist he still grasped. "Let me take you home. I promise to be on my best behavior."

She searched his face, then a slight smile tweaked her lips. "I have a doctor's appointment in the morning, and a meeting with a client right after. I have to get to bed. It would only be a ride home."

"Okay," he nodded. At least he'd get to spend a few more minutes with her.

"Is that all the celebrating we're going to do?" Rand whined, his features twisted in a sulky scowl.

Simon threw an arm around his shoulders. "Rand, my man, down that hall over there…" he pointed at the dressing room door "hundreds of female fans are waiting for you. Would you rather be celebrating with us, or with them?"

"I see your point. Tony, you gonna be my wing man?" Rand asked.

"If you're waiting on me, bro, you're backing up." Tony gripped his leather jacket and the bottle of bourbon. He was halfway to the door before Rand jumped to his feet and beat a path after him.

Katrina laughed aloud.

Drew smiled. The flat tones she hit in her speaking voice were absent. It was the most beautiful sound he'd ever heard.

Chapter 9

O ut on the street, Drew was mobbed by several fans who'd been inside the club. While he signed T-shirts with the band's logo on them and napkins from the club, Cheryl grabbed Katrina's hand and dragged her aside for a short tête-à-tête. "Go forth, sistah, and get laid. This guy is so into you, I thought he might combust sitting next to you."

Katrina laughed, then sobered. "He broke up with his last girl friend only days ago. I don't intend to sleep with him the first time we talk."

"Well, from his body language he's more into you than he ever was her." Cheryl turned serious. "On second thought, be careful. And call me later."

Katrina laughed again and shook her head. "Yes, Mother." She hugged her. "I'll be fine. He's just going to drop me at my apartment."

"That's what they all say." Cheryl flipped her thick red hair over her shoulder. "There's a kind of wild sexuality about him that's almost impossible to resist. If you really want him to keep coming back, you may want to hold him off for a little while."

If she only knew. "Consider it done."

Drew broke away from the fans surrounding him and strode toward her. The way he focused on her was almost frightening. If he pushed, would she be able to resist?

Katrina gave Howard's arm a pat and murmured good night as she passed him.

Drew held out his hand. The glide of skin against skin as their palms melded set off a sensual storm inside her. They walked hand in hand down two blocks to where his car was parked.

The interior of the vehicle seemed intimate and isolating after their conversation at The Next Best Thing. Unable to read his lips in the dark, Katrina's anxiety spiked and tension knotted her stomach.

Drew reached up and turned on the overhead light. "You didn't tell me where you live."

Katrina smiled at his understanding and drew a relaxing breath before giving him the address. He pulled out into the slow line of traffic.

She was struck by the irony of being so powerfully drawn to a man who used his voice to make a living, when she couldn't hear him.

Drawn to a man who used his voice to seduce other women.

She bit her lip. How could this possibly go anywhere when they had two such huge obstacles to overcome? "Did you try to seduce me with your voice?"

Drew glanced in her direction and waited until he'd come to a stop at a street sign before turning his head to answer. "I was interested in knowing which tones or notes you could hear. You can't blame me for being curious."

"My hearing range is very limited. I hear nothing at the octaves where normal people speak."

"But you can hear underwater because you're an aquatic creature."

"Yes." She was not quite normal, even underwater. And she could never go back there again. Her earlier caretakers at the orphanage had seen to that. Her feet itched just thinking about it.

Traffic cleared and, as he pulled out, Drew reached up and flicked off the overhead light.

Twenty minutes later they pulled into the parking lot next to her apartment building. The streetlight lanced across Drew's face, the contrasting shadows limning his strong jaw and the five o'clock shadow darkening it. His lips, not too thick or too thin, looked perfect for kissing.

Katrina drew a deep breath to calm her reaction.

He flipped on the overhead light. "Shall I walk you to your door?"

Katrina studied the dark sweep of lashes surrounding his unusual tri-colored eyes.

What they were toying with could backfire on them both. Could lead to misery. But if they didn't explore it, they might be giving up on something rare and special.

The fact that he seduced women, used them every time he opened his mouth, gave her pause. He'd tried to discover how to do the same to her. She'd become aware of what he was doing about the time the band had taken their first ten-minute break. Had he stopped because he realized he couldn't use his voice to get to her? *Not much, anyway.*

Drew's expression grew serious. "I've been wanting to meet someone I can't seduce with my voice for a long time. I won't try any tricks."

Katrina studied his strong, masculine features. Could she trust him?

She swallowed against the wild beat of her heart. Could she trust herself? *Probably not.* She needed to say no. Just to be certain. She looked up to see him waiting for her answer. Would he kiss her goodnight? She cleared her throat. "All right."

Drew unhooked his seatbelt and was out of the car and coming around to open her door before she had gathered her purse from the floor.

His hand rested on the small of her back as she keyed in the security code to enter the apartment building, but tucked his hands in his pockets riding the elevator to the third floor. The swirled pattern on the rubberized tile in the hall always made her a little dizzy, so she focused on the doors they passed.

Katrina's nerves spiked as she reached her door, and she fumbled getting out her keys. Drew took them from her and unlocked the door, then gave them back.

She pushed open the door, flipped on the light, then turned to look up at him.

"How long have you lived here?" he asked.

"Four years."

His eyes moved past her to her desk in the living room. "What do you do for a living?"

"I'm a graphic artist for Harley Graphic Designs." Had she remained among her people, she'd have never known how to use a computer creatively, but then she'd have never understood she was missing anything, either. "Do you miss…home, or have you always been on land?" she asked.

He braced an arm upon the door facing. "I've been landlocked for years. And I'm not welcome in those circles. They think I'm too much a mixed breed."

"I am, too. But I wanted to know what it was like." And she'd hoped to find her family. Instead she'd found she could no longer adapt. In fact, deep water was now dangerous for her.

"Will you go out to dinner with me tomorrow night? I want time for us to talk." He smoothed back a long strand of blonde hair, his fingertips lingering against the small patch of skin behind her ear.

Though his touch was innocent, every cell in her body seemed to reach out for it. She gulped air, feeling breathless. "It isn't a good idea for us to see each other, Drew."

"We'll eat a meal and talk. What time do you get off?" he pressed.

Why did this have to be so hard? "Around five thirty."

"I'll be waiting for you here."

Though the voice in her head was saying, *this is not a good idea*, the rest of her said, "Okay."

"Do you have a cell phone?"

"Yes."

"May I have your number?"

She laughed. "I'm not normally this obtuse. It's–I never expected to meet someone like—you…me. I've only met two others, and they…"

"Couldn't wait to get away?" he suggested.

"Yes." So, he'd experienced the same thing.

"It seems our kind chooses a solitary existence when we're outside of our normal habitat. Maybe it's because to be with others tends to make the longing for home worse."

Would spending time with him cause her to wish for something she couldn't have? *Of course it would.* "Then maybe this is a mistake."

Drew stepped close, cupped the back of her head and kissed her.

The gentle pressure of his mouth was intent but not forceful. Her first seconds of resistance washed away upon the tide of longing and need rushing through her. The heat from his body wrapped her in warmth, drawing her in. Her bag fell from her shoulder and hit the floor.

She slid her arms around his waist and leaned into him. She inhaled in his unique Merman scent.

When his tongue slipped between her lips she groaned. He tasted like expensive bourbon and him. Her tongue tangled with his while Drew's arms tightened around her, holding her closer. She felt his response and fought the urge to rise on tiptoe to better fit her body to his.

Drew gently broke the kiss, and she opened her eyes to look up at him. A gasp escaped. The normal human planes of his face had transitioned to something more angular and rugged, his cheekbones flatter and more prominent, his eyes holding a preternatural glow. He looked...foreign, majestic and...desirable.

"What is it?" he asked.

Movement down the hall caught her attention. A man and woman approached, neighbors who lived in three-nineteen. They couldn't see him like this. She grasped Drew's arm and tugged him into her apartment and shut the door.

His expression, both bemused and surprised, had her shaking her head. How had he not felt the change? She pointed at a mirror over the couch. "Look at yourself."

The light over the door signaled her doorbell had rung. She motioned Drew to step out of sight, and then opened the door.

Mrs. Stein, the woman she'd seen coming down the hall, held out Katrina's purse, her gray brows raised. "I don't think you want to leave this out here in the hall."

Katrina's cheeks burned and she forced a laugh. "No, that wouldn't be a good idea. Thank you."

"Good night," Mrs. Stein said with a nod and strolled down the hall.

Katrina closed the door and leaned back against it, her attention returning to Drew where he stood in front of the couch and stared into the mirror.

Drew touched his cheekbones, his brow, his jaw. It was still his face, but it had transformed. He'd been so worked up with wanting Katrina he hadn't felt a thing.

"Has this ever happened before?" she asked.

"Not outside of being submerged in water." He grimaced. *Great way to start out with her.* He was coming out of the preternatural closet, and there wasn't a damn thing he could do about it. "I don't frighten you, do I?"

Katrina laughed. "No. You just startled me. You're

handsome either way."

A slow smile spread across his face. "We could continue what we were doing and see how far this goes."

Color rushed into her cheeks. She approached him and reached up to touch one raised cheekbone. "It doesn't hurt, does it?"

Liquid warmth spread across his skin, and he rested his hand beneath her elbow to encourage the contact. "No." Not the transition, but his rock-hard erection was giving him some discomfort.

Her throat worked as she swallowed. "You can't leave as long as—" She gestured to the source of his discomfort.

Or they could make love and see if sexual release would make the transition go away. He took a calming breath.

"Have you ever been with anyone like me?" she asked.

"No."

"I've only been with two human males, and a Merman, although that was years ago."

How many women had he been with? He wasn't sure he'd be able to give her an accurate count. What would she think of him if he told her?

She could be his first preternatural lover. The thought sent a fresh wave of blood to his cock. He bit back a groan. "I promised I'd be on my best behavior. So I'm trying not to touch you. But you're making it very hard for me."

Her pupils expanded, making her ocean blue eyes darken to teal. Her Mermaid scent intensified. "I don't mean to. I'm just trying to get to know you."

They could learn a great deal about each other in bed. He raked his fingers through his hair. He needed a distraction. Her computer. "You could show me what you're working on. Practice tomorrow's presentation to your client."

She smiled. "Do you really want to see it?"

"You watched me perform for the last three hours. I'd like to see what you do."

"Right now I'm working on several websites. The one I'm presenting tomorrow is for a small office supply company. They sell everything from office furniture to envelopes. Anything you might need to run a small business. I'm setting up their online ordering system. It isn't very sexy, but it might earn me a promotion and more money."

Drew's attention swung to the round oak table with four chairs off to the right. The living room and kitchen were one long room decorated in soothing tones of blue with touches of yellow, lime green, raspberry, and purple. The vibrant colors reminded him of coral reefs and their colorful, often iridescent inhabitants. Had she been there?

"I'll get a chair," he said, crossing the space to lift the seat and carry it to her desk.

They both settled before the computer and Katrina opened a file on the desktop. The website was set up with the logo for the company on every page in metallic colors. The site was well arranged, colorful, loaded very quickly, and had some interactive features that were innovative.

Drew touched her arm to get her attention. His fingers lingered despite his vow to take it slow. "How long have you worked on this?"

"Nearly three months." She touched his hand where it

rested on her arm. "I have all their products listed, and everything ready to sell online. All I have to do is upload the command to make it go live. I hope they'll be pleased with it."

"I'm sure they will. When is your presentation?"

"Eleven tomorrow morning." She leaned back and rested her hands in her lap.

"We'll celebrate both of our successes tomorrow at dinner."

"The woman who showed up at the club tonight, how long have you been apart?"

"A little over a week. After I saw you at the club, I spent several days looking for you. I even tried to track your scent. She and I went out once during that time, and I broke it off afterwards."

"Not because of me." She shook her head.

"No." How could he explain? "Dating human women isn't going to work for me. If it were going to, I would have already found a mate and fathered children." His voice grew husky. "My reaction to human females isn't anything like it is with you." If this didn't work out, would this experience forever leave him craving more?

He rested his arm on the back of her chair and turned so his knee brushed hers. "Human women are very fragile. I've always been careful."

He'd also been wary of dropping his guard in case he might expose what he was. The partial transition Katrina had triggered proved he'd been right to be cautious. "It's exciting to know I don't have to hide what I am from you." Not all of it, anyway. There were parts of his genealogy he wasn't willing to share with her. If things progressed between them, eventually he'd share it all, but not yet.

"I understand. When I was sixteen, I left the orphanage to hunt for my parents. I encountered quite a few unusual…folks."

"Were you able to find your parents?"

"Not then, but I found my father later." She shook her head. "It was stressful and disappointing."

"I'm sorry." He grasped her wrist and ran a soothing thumb over her skin.

"Are you still in touch with yours?" she asked.

"Yes. They live close by. My father is a fertility specialist. My mother works raising money for the opera."

She smiled. "Singing and fertility. We can't help ourselves, can we? I'd have gone into something closer to the water if I could have."

"What happened?"

Her expression grew solemn. "That's a long story, and better left for another time."

Drew sighed. He was tempted to draw her close for some comfort, but he didn't trust himself. Didn't trust how she would perceive it.

She brushed his cheek with her fingertips. "Your face has gone back to normal."

He wanted to grasp her hand and hold it against his skin so he could revel in her touch.

"Does that mean you're kicking me out?"

Her cheeks pinkened. "Drew—"

"I'm teasing. I know you have to get up early. I'd better leave so you can get some rest. You'll want to be fresh for your presentation." He rose.

She followed him to the door.

He turned to face her. "I'll see you tomorrow."

Her blue-green eyes moved over his face. "It's only a few hours."

It seemed a great deal longer. God, had he ever felt this way about a woman before? Every cell in his body reached for her.

Not trusting himself to kiss her again, he grasped her hand and bent his head to press his lips to the inside of her wrist. Her cheeks flushed again as he looked up into her face. "Good night."

He at least got the satisfaction of hearing the huskiness in her voice as she murmured good night.

He turned to leave.

"Drew?"

Had his hearing not been so acute he'd have missed her soft inquiry. He turned to look over his shoulder.

Katrina bit her lip, and her throat worked as she swallowed. "This isn't a good idea."

There had been a time, when he'd first gained control of his powers, that he'd immersed himself in a sea of feminine bodies and sex. The phase had run its course in a little over a year. Even though he'd been more circumspect about his behavior since, there'd still been lots of women and even more sex.

But had there ever been a *real* connection between him and a woman? And if she bonded with him, would he follow through with the commitment it would represent? Was he even capable of making someone happy outside of the bedroom for an extended time?

But her concerns should be his, too.

In his thirty years, he'd been either lost in meaningless relationships based on physical pleasure, or working toward his music career. Until now.

But now he'd seen what might be possible with her, how could he take a step back? This might be his only opportunity.

And if exploring more than a physical joining with her was what it took to get there…

He saw the struggle in her face.

"You might find it too much. I mean—if our being close throws you into transition and all we did was…" Her cheeks reddened again. "What if it happens in public?"

"I'll learn to control it. Do you know how rare it is to find someone you can feel this attracted to? Someone you have this much in common with?"

If he could beat back his own nature and give this, whatever it was, a chance to breathe, they might both find out they could have something extraordinary together. "All I'm asking for is a chance." He'd never had to beg a woman to let him in before. It was a little humbling to do so now.

He knew he'd said the right thing when her features softened.

"All right. I'll see you tomorrow."

Chapter 10

Katrina clutched the narrow cushion on either side of her legs, the chair's upholstery sturdy and textured enough to chafe her fingertips. The room was more an office than an examining room, with several comfortable chairs and a table serving as a desk. Nerves triggered a cold sweat beneath each arm, while her feet had turned to blocks of ice. What was taking so long?

Sensing movement behind her through a sudden drift of air from an opening door, she turned to look over her shoulder. Dr. Turner entered the room, his bland features lightened by a smile.

"Good morning, Katrina. I'm sorry you had to wait." Turner used both sign language and spoke to make certain she understood.

"That's okay." Her attention shifted to the tall, broad-shouldered man who followed him into the room. He had blond hair and a compelling face, not exactly handsome, but very masculine. The intensity in his green gaze when it settled on her made her uncomfortable.

Turner motioned with his hand to gain her attention.

"This is Dr. Graham Powell, my partner here at Auditory Solutions. He'll be your surgeon."

Surprised Katrina bit her lip. "I thought you would be doing it."

"Dr. Powell does all our implants," Dr. Turner explained. "I do the workups for them, and other types of surgery."

Why had he not told her this before? Or maybe he had and she'd missed it. Her stomach muscles tightened in frustration and unease. She'd developed a rapport with Dr. Turner. This other doctor was an unknown.

Her attention shifted to the taller man as he drew a chair closer to her and sat down. He signed and said, "Hello."

Katrina studied Dr. Powell's face. "Hello."

"I've been doing this for many years, Ms. Larson. You'll be in good hands." He signed with confidence and speed.

"How many years?" Having this unexpected change thrown at her made her wary.

"Nearly ten now," he answered.

"You sign like someone who has done it for a long time."

"My whole life. Both my parents are deaf."

"You do it very well."

A brief smile gave his overly masculine face an unexpected charm. "And your speech and intonation are very good. They will get better with the implant. Have you always been deaf?"

Katrina hesitated. "As long as I can remember."

"And your parents?" he probed.

"I was abandoned at birth and placed in an orphanage

in Alaska. I moved here for college."

His brows rose. "They never found your family?"

Katrina shook her head. How could she explain that her Merman father had purposely seduced the human woman on a whim and then abandoned her? Was that why she was so wary of becoming involved with Drew?

All the Mermen she had met were seductive, handsome, and arrogant. And completely without a conscience. Until they bonded.

Dr. Powell pushed forward into the surgical preliminaries. "You have some unusual anomalies in the size and spacing of the internal hearing apparatus, Miss Larson. They're a little larger than normal, which may be why you have difficulties. I saw no damage to the auditory nerve and I can't explain why you can hear sound below and above normal hearing range but nothing in between. But I believe with the implant we can train your brain to recognize those octaves."

He stood and shifted closer. "May I demonstrate and explain to you what will happen during surgery?"

"Okay."

He tucked her long hair behind her ear, the gesture strangely intimate. He stood to one side but faced her. "I'll be making an incision here." He traced a line behind her ear where the scar would be hidden. "Then curve it around here. We'll make a pocket for the device beneath the muscle and shave an area of the mastoid to fit the device here." He touched her skull with his fingertips, sending a chill through her.

He continued. "Through a small hole into the middle

ear, I'll thread the wires through your cochlea, so the auditory nerve can receive stimuli through the device."

"The magnet which will hold the external transmitter will go here." He slid his touch up above her ear. "You'll be discharged the same day to go home. A week after surgery, you'll come back in and I'll remove your sutures."

"How long will it be before I get the external device?" Though she'd read up on the procedure she wanted to confirm her research.

"Between three and four weeks. You may have to do some auditory therapy so your brain can learn to process the new input."

If her physiology was different it might not work. But she'd never know if she didn't try.

Would it permanently damage the cochlea of her left ear when he placed the wiring into it? There was no way to ask without it sounding strange. She suspected she'd be giving up half her underwater hearing so she could hear on land.

She'd been through all the pros and cons before, but now she was faced with going under the knife and having the hearing ability she did have halved. Anxiety kicked in. "There's no guarantee this will work." She'd tried to keep her hopes under control but it was difficult.

"Nothing is ever a hundred percent. But I believe you will be able to hear something with the device," Dr. Powell said.

Dr. Turner leaned forward and touched her arm. "Shall we set up the surgery? Or would you like a few more days to think about it?"

Dr. Powell's glance in his direction was subtle, but

Katrina caught it. Impatience flickered across his features. Was he eager for her to have the procedure because he was a strong proponent of it, or hungry for the money it would bring into their practice? This wasn't cheap, even with insurance. She'd worked for eight years and saved every dime she could to pay for it.

Katrina fisted her hands in her lap. She lived on land. With the damage to her flukes, she couldn't return to the sea on a permanent basis. And even if she could, she wasn't sure she would. She had to do everything she could to function in this environment. She gnawed her lip. "Go ahead and set it up." She could always cancel if she changed her mind.

Dr. Powell signed. "I'd like to do some additional scans of your skull. You will not be charged for them."

She studied his expression. It was so hard to trust strangers, and she sensed Powell had an ulterior motive. "For what purpose?"

"Research alone. I'm studying some of the genetic anomalies that cause deafness. Yours is one of the more interesting cases. Perhaps if we discover exactly why you can't hear, it might help someone else in future."

Was there anything else he could discover by looking at additional scans? What were the physiological differences between her and a human woman? Or would he just think she had some genetic issues?

"We could do it later today, if you have time."

Feeling pressured she countered with, "I'm sorry. I have a business meeting that will take up most of the afternoon."

"Then what day would be convenient for you?"

Why was he so interested in this? "What exactly was different in my scans from anyone else's?"

The two doctors glanced at one another. "The internal mechanisms of your inner ear are larger than normal, as are the auditory nerves. What's more unusual is you have an extra...sinus in the forefront of your skull. We've never seen anything like it before."

"How big a sinus?" She bit her lip again.

"Eight centimeters by five. Or roughly a three inches by two. It's shallow but it's there."

Oh shit! It had to have something to do with being Mer. "Is it connected to my ears in some way?"

"No," Dr. Turner answered.

Once again Powell shifted and glanced in Turner's direction.

"Then how would it have a bearing on my hearing?"

Powell's fingers flew as he signed. "We don't know. That's why we wanted to study it further."

Katrina focused on Powell, every instinct alive with wariness. "No."

For a moment his features blanked in surprise. "We would be willing to reimburse you for any inconvenience, Ms. Larson."

"Inconvenience has nothing to do with it, Dr. Powell. Since it has no direct effect on my hearing, and it isn't causing me a problem, I'm not interested in knowing more about it."

He cocked his head and his eyes narrowed in confusion. "Why not?"

"Because having my birth defects pointed out to me and

discussed in some kind of scientific article feels like an invasion of privacy and one more hurdle to overcome."

He frowned. "Your name would not be used. The data would only be used for research purposes."

"If this added space has nothing to do with my hearing, why would you be so interested in it?"

"Because it's an unknown, and any time there's something unknown about human physiology, we can't know without further study if it might have a bearing on your health later on."

Katrina hesitated so he wouldn't feel she was rushing to judgment. "I'll take my chances."

Powell's lips compressed and the planes of his face clenched in impatience.

Katrina rose from her chair. "Do you still want to do my surgery, Dr. Powell?" She wasn't sure she wanted him to do it now. Once she was on the table, what might he do? She'd have to give it some serious thought. There were few experts in this speciality in the area. To change doctors at this stage of the process would set her back months.

Powell's expression turned distant, professional. "Certainly. The surgery isn't contingent upon the scans for the study. But I would have subsidized the cost for your participation."

He really wasn't used to having anyone stand in his way.

"That would be very generous, but no thank you." Katrina gathered her purse.

Dr. Turner touched her arm to get her attention. "Our staff will contact you when we have the surgery scheduled."

"Thanks, Dr. Turner." Katrina studied Dr. Powell a

moment. "Do either of your parents have an implant?"

"No."

Surprised she asked, "Have they ever discussed with you why they didn't want one?"

"No." He hesitated. "They've been together a long time and are very close. I suspect their lack of hearing has actually brought them closer than possibly a hearing couple. They share *everything*. If they both couldn't share this as well—" He shook his head.

"Thank you for telling me."

"You're welcome." He changed the subject. "We usually refer our patients to a psychologist. It will help you deal with the transition from non-hearing to hearing. I could arrange for you to meet with my father instead. He's a licensed psychologist and works exclusively with the deaf."

"Before or after the surgery?"

"Both."

Would his father give her reassurances about his son as a surgeon? Placing herself into a stranger's hands was a difficult decision to make. Why hadn't Dr. Turner said something sooner? "Yes. I think I would like that."

Graham forced himself to smile. "I'll arrange it at the same time we schedule your surgery."

Why had he been so open about a personal subject with a patient? He should have just kept it at "no." When she'd turned her attention on him, the intensity of her sea green eyes had weakened his professional need to keep his distance.

He had never allowed an instant attraction to a patient to affect the way he conducted business. But after being surrounded by the subtle scent of her perfume, he'd been driven to touch her. Her hair had been heavy and soft. Her skin like silk.

She was a patient. He could lose his license if he got involved with her. Unless…unless he waited until after the surgery and there were no further professional ties between them.

Carl turned on him as soon as the door closed behind Katrina. "What the hell do you think you're doing, Graham? I shouldn't have to remind you these people have lived through years of trauma and isolation because of their hearing loss. They don't need anyone pointing out their, for lack of a better word, defects. Not everyone is as well-adjusted to their condition as your parents."

Graham stiffened. "The whole point of the study is to document all the different causes of deafness to see if some kind of surgical procedure can be implemented to intervene. You could have been a little more persuasive with her."

"After she's been singled out as handicapped her entire life, I can certainly understand why she doesn't want to be used as a medical guinea pig to study an anomaly that has nothing to do with her hearing." Carl shook his head. "You wanted to study it to satisfy your curiosity. Not because it could cause her issues later."

That was sanctimonious crap. "You're just as interested in it as I am. She's probably the only person on the planet with that particular genetic abnormality along with the others. Who can say whether or not they're tied together unless they're studied? But we won't know now because she's refused to allow us a second look."

Carl released an impatient sigh. "You can't steamroll over people's feelings to get what you want. And you can't throw money at them, either. This was the first time you've ever shared anything personal with a patient since we've been partners. It was a surprise, but I think that might have been what kept her from canceling the surgery."

Shit! Surely not. "Why would she cancel the surgery? She wants to hear." She would benefit from the procedure in so many ways. Why wouldn't she get it?

"Did you not notice her expression? The reason she turned you down for the study is because you didn't attempt to develop a rapport with her before you dove right in. She was here to be reassured that she was making the right decision about the surgery. You didn't attempt to do that before pushing for her to have more scans and another exam. You're a stranger to her. Why should she trust you?"

Because he was going to help her hear. He hadn't had any trouble convincing people to allow him to make their lives better during the past ten years. What the hell was the problem now?

But Carl was the patient liaison most of the time, and he was the surgeon. He had learned early in his career that his strength lay in his skill, not his bedside manner. Their partnership had been beneficial to them both. So he needed to listen to Carl, or at least appear to.

"Okay. What do you expect me to do?"

"Stop coming across as an arrogant ass and start being a little more sensitive to our patients."

Graham laughed. He *was* single minded and arrogant at times. "Maybe after she can hear, Ms. Larson will change her mind and let us take a closer look at that sinus."

Carl shook his head. "I wouldn't bank on it. If she doesn't cancel the surgery we'll be lucky."

"She won't. I know how difficult it is to conduct business meetings when you can't follow along with a room full of people all talking at once. Unless she's provided with an interpreter at work, it would prove very difficult for her."

"That's what I'm talking about Graham. You sound as though you hope she does have difficulties so she'll be sure to have the surgery."

Damn it. That wasn't what he meant at all. "Of course I don't wish that on her. I was being realistic about her situation." He swallowed his annoyance. "My parents often find it difficult if they don't have an interpreter during meetings. They miss important information otherwise. I used to attend some of the opera house budget meetings myself for that reason." Enough was enough.

Carl's expression cleared. "I'm sorry. I misunderstood."

"If I could heal every deaf person on this planet, I'd do it, Carl. To live in isolation because of a handicap is unjust. And there are people out there who actually treat the hearing impaired and the blind as though it might be contagious. I won't even go into how their children are treated, regardless of their hearing status. So if I'm abrupt or less than sensitive, it's because I'm focused on doing whatever it takes to help these people. Because I'm unwilling to wear my heart on my sleeve to do it doesn't mean I'm unsympathetic." He wasn't allowing this to turn into a walk down memory lane. He had no desire to rehash his childhood experiences. He picked up the file and strode to the door.

"Wait, Graham." Carl's demeanor took a thoughtful turn. "What you said about their children."

Carl would snag on that one thing. "Yes?"

"Was it that way for you?"

"Of course it was. Imagine being the only hearing member of a family of three. It accelerated my learning curve, but it also isolated me as much as it did them."

"I'm sorry."

His partner's sincerity made him uncomfortable. Graham shrugged. "I've put it behind me and moved on."

Carl stared at him. "I don't think you have. I think you need to get out in the world, meet a woman, and make a real connection to someone."

"You mean I need to get laid." Graham smirked, amused.

Carl grinned. "That, too." His expression shifted to serious. "But more. I think you need to have a life outside of this office and our patients."

His mother had said the same thing.

"I recently broke it off with Janet. I'm not sure I'm ready to jump right back in with someone else." Or was he? It was hard to block out thoughts of Katrina Larson's blue-green eyes and perfect figure. Her scent was what had caught his attention. She'd smelled somehow...familiar. That familiarity was niggling at a memory that just wouldn't come. Where the hell had he smelled her perfume before?

Graham looked up from studying the tile floor. "Do

you think I need to try to smooth things over with Ms. Larson?"

"How would you propose to do that?"

If he mentioned visiting her at her residence, Carl would argue against it. And professionally it wouldn't be the smart thing to do. "What do you suggest?"

Carl remained silent a moment. His thin face locked in thought. "Your suggestion for her to meet your father was a good one. Maybe you should just let him to smooth things over. They left everything behind and immigrated here, didn't they?"

"Yes, they did. From Scotland. They're going back to visit in about a month."

"They'll have something in common with her. She left everything she was familiar with to come here for school. She has no family to support her decision one way or another. Will your father persuade her or let her decide?"

Good question. "He'll let her talk it through and then make up her own mind."

"That's what should happen anyway. An unhappy patient doesn't reflect well on our practice."

Carl had a point, but if she was able to hear, it would make things so much easier for her, and possibly for him. Even though he had the ability to communicate with her, he'd never dated a deaf woman. The relationship would be reminiscent of living with his parents, despite the different emotional dynamics. He'd have to think long and hard about it. He looked up to find Carl waiting for his reply and gave a brief nod. "I'll make the arrangements."

Chapter 11

Katrina ignored the headache pounding at her temples and tried to concentrate on her boss's lips. Disappointment and anger settled in her chest.

"You understand the reason behind this, Katrina?"

"I understand that I did all the work and now you're bringing in someone else to mess with my design because of my communication difficulties."

Emory remained silent a moment. "You're very good at design, Katrina and with one-on-one discussion with the customer, but in the boardroom today, when several people were expressing their opinions, you lost track of the conversation and became confused."

"I can bring in an interpreter next time who will help me keep everything together." The company should have been open to that from the beginning. And she should have asked for someone. She was so used to making do, to not asking for special concessions, it hadn't occurred to her.

"The customer wants music on the site to match the commercial he's asked us to create. How do you propose to add music?"

How would she? She'd worked months on this project. The client had raved about her design. But her handicap made it impossible for her to time the music to go along with the opening of each page.

Drew came to mind. Would he help her with something like this? "I have a friend who's a musician who might help me with the sound. I think I at least deserve a shot at it."

Emory nodded but looked doubtful. "Let me see what you can come up with and we'll go from there."

"I'll need a copy of the song used for the commercial as soon as it's available."

"I'll see that you get it," he said, turning down the hall toward his office.

She rushed to her small cubicle to recover from the nerve-racking morning. Why had she gone to her doctor's appointment on the same day she was scheduled to attend this meeting? She'd walked in already flustered, had demonstrated the capabilities of the website, then missed two comments because the men turned their heads to talk to one another. It had gone downhill from there. She lay her head on her desk and struggled to suppress the tears burning her eyes.

She swallowed against the knot in her throat and managed to quell the emotions, but not her disappointment with her boss. Emory could have helped her by explaining what she'd missed, but instead he stood back and watched her struggle. But why? To purposely point out she should be relegated to the back room, somewhere to work alone instead of meeting clients? Had he been testing her? If so she'd failed...miserably. So there would probably be no promotion and no bonus.

She'd spent years learning to lip read successfully, and more years to make sure her vocal tone was as close to normal as she could make it. But she'd never move up into any sort of managerial position because she couldn't stay on top of things due to her hearing. Reading body language and other signals only went so far.

She had to take people at face value, and that wasn't always enough. There was always more to people than what was on the surface.

The cochlear implant would only help to a certain extent. She needed to resign herself to the fact that she'd always be a drone and never the boss. Unless she ran the show.

Drew pulled into the parking lot outside of Katrina's apartment and switched off the ignition. His hair clung damply to his head from a quick shower.

It had been nearly a year since he'd spent a day in the ocean. He hadn't realized how much he missed it until he was submerged and swimming along the bottom. He'd taken underwater recording equipment and guided it to where he heard the most sound. He recorded fish, dolphins, whales, the movement of kelp beds, as much of the wildlife as he could, but also the distant sounds traveling underwater. He'd opened himself to the ultrasonic noise he was able to pick up, and he hoped he captured some of the sea songs that fell within Katrina's hearing range. He'd loaded it onto a flash drive for her and bought her a set of headphones, hoping she'd be able to hear some of what he'd recorded.

The project had given him even more pleasure because he was doing it for her. It had inspired a song for the band, too. Before racing over to Katrina's, he took a few moments to write down the bare bones so he wouldn't lose the tune.

Using the code she'd texted him earlier in the day, he entered the building, anticipation winging through him. He exited the elevator and strode down the long hall to Katrina's apartment.

Twenty feet from her door, he experienced a tightness around his rib cage and paused. It wasn't a muscle contraction but a sensation, as though outside emotion bombarded him with vibrations. He'd never experienced anything like it. Concern quickened his steps. He rang the buzzer and waited for Katrina to answer.

When she didn't open the door after a few minutes, his unease ramped up. He was reaching for the button again when the door opened. Though she smiled, tension tugged at her lips and her forehead was creased with the remnants of a frown.

"Hey," she said, her voice soft. "I didn't see the light flashing right away."

Her blue-green eyes were shadowed, tinted by emotion to the gray of a storm-tossed sea. Her smile was tight at the corners.

Drew took a step forward and she stepped back to allow him inside the apartment. He rested a hand on her shoulder. The words what's wrong sprang to his lips but seemed too pushy. How could he explain that he could feel her turmoil? As freaked out as he was about this new development, how would *she* feel? "How was your day?"

She blinked hard and swallowed. "A little trying, but it's over now. Or at least that part of it."

The sensation that had followed him from the hall and into the room increased. "Tell me what happened."

Indecision flitted across her features. "My business meeting didn't go well. I missed some things during a conversation, and I've probably blown the opportunity to oversee my own projects." Pain and disappointment shimmered around her.

"I'm sorry, Katrina."

She raised one shoulder in a shrug that was more eloquent than tears.

Drew stepped closer and slipped his arms around her. At first her spine remained stiff, then she relaxed into him and rested her head against his shoulder. Her arms looped around his waist and instantly he hardened while at the same time he longed to ease her hurt. He cupped the back of her head and stroked her hair. The emotional vibrations softened.

Was this connection forged because they came from similar species, or was it more? Had he already bonded to her in some way? The thought shook him. He'd just spent an entire afternoon doing something for a woman he'd only known twenty-four hours. Was that bonding, or a desire to do whatever it took to seduce her into his bed?

"What is it?" she asked, drawing back.

He searched her face. "Nothing. How did the doctor's appointment go?"

Her tension returned, and he regretted mentioning it.

"They're scheduling the surgery," she said, "but the surgeon who's supposed to do it—he was pushing me for more tests. It seems I have some physiological anomalies that are different than humans and he's curious. When I turned him down he wasn't happy."

"What kind of surgery are you having?"

"I'm having a cochlear implant."

A cochlear implant. Would she be able to hear him sing? And would his voice affect her the way it did human women? Damnit. Frustration stormed through him. Just when he thought he might have found what he was looking for....

But when she'd said she'd lived in silence for so long...the look on her face...

What would it be like to have to live in total silence always?

He'd go insane.

She'd done the right thing. The danger of humans finding out they had non-human species walking among them was always there. They saw difference as either a threat, something to pity, something to study, or something to destroy. He ran soothing hands up and down her back and was rewarded when she leaned closer in to him.

He raised her chin so she'd focus on his face. "What kind of differences?"

"It seems all the parts of my inner ear and my auditory nerve are all larger than is typical for humans. And I have an extra sinus in my forehead."

"But he still thinks you'll be able to hear if you have the surgery?"

"Yes. But it will probably damage my underwater hearing in that one ear. I can't go back to the sea anyway, but what if the surgery doesn't work and half of what I do have is gone forever?"

It was a tough decision. But being forced to live in a silent world while on land was no picnic. It affected every portion of her life. The flash drive he'd brought her was in his car. He'd wait to give it to her at the restaurant. Wait until she was steadier. "I can't make the decision for you. But I can listen while you talk it out."

"I have to go through with it. The meeting this afternoon proved it. How am I ever going to do anything more if I can't communicate with people?"

"What is it you want to do?"

"I'd like to have my own design firm someday."

Ambitious, but doable if she could hear. She had the talent. "This surgeon, he must have been really pushy if you got upset about it."

"He was. He even offered to pay for part of the surgery if I'd let him do more scans."

Not a good sign. If he discovered what she was, it could affect more than her alone. It might open the door to speculation about other species.

"Maybe you should cancel and look for someone else. If he suspects there's more going on than a genetic aberration—"

"I thought about changing doctors, but it might take months to go through the same process and get as close to surgery as I am. And the next doctor is going to see the same things on the scans."

A valid point. Drew's hands moved soothingly over her back. Her level of upset was escalating again. "Why don't I give my father a call and ask him about this? Although he's a fertility specialist, he does know other doctors. He might have some suggestions."

She smiled. "That's right, he's a fertility specialist. How appropriate."

His own smile was wry. "Yeah, I know. If you're going to have special skills in the art of seduction, you might as well learn about the benefits of it as well. That's what he says."

Katrina laughed.

Just that sound triggered an immediate hard-on. God, she had the most wonderful laugh.

She cupped his face with her palm and ran her thumb along his cheekbone. "Your father sounds like you. It would be wonderful if he could give me some insight into this."

And he needed his father to give him some insight into what he was experiencing with her. Though her distress had abated, he was still reading her feelings as clearly as an emotional blueprint. "We could swing by the house on our way to dinner," he suggested.

She hesitated. "They wouldn't mind?"

"Of course not. They'd be glad to meet you." And they'd read more into the fact that he'd brought a girl home with him than he intended. But he could deal with that part later.

"I'd like to meet them. I haven't met many others."

He tucked her hair behind her ear. "Get your purse and we'll go."

She stepped back and glanced down at her work clothes of dark slacks and a silk blouse. "I need to change."

"You look beautiful the way you are, Katrina."

"That was sweet. And you know it."

At his grin, she stood on tiptoe and brushed his lips with her own.

Instant need, his and hers, rolled over him in a staggering rush. He reached for her. With lips and tongue he greeted her as he'd wanted to before running into her emotional force field. The longer he kissed her, the lower her stress level dropped. He nuzzled her neck and she shivered.

He had to remind himself to draw back to speak to her. Her sea green eyes had gone dark, and she had a dazed look of desire on her face.

He smiled. "We could stay in tonight and worry about all this other stuff tomorrow."

"You are such a temptation," she sighed.

"Good."

She laughed.

To be wanted without the added boost of using his voice was amazing. "You are for me, too. But I'm trying to take things slow, as you asked me to, Katrina. Go get your purse and we'll leave before we both give in to the temptation."

Chapter 12

Katrina's studied Drew's long-fingered hands as he gripped the steering wheel. Talking in the car was one of the things she couldn't do. She couldn't follow a conversation spoken out of the side of his mouth, and he couldn't take his eyes off the road long enough to face her. What would they say to one another if they could?

She wanted him so much. The need was an incessant ache. It left her edgy and at sea about what to do. Every time they were together the feeling was stronger.

If they acted on it, they might bond, and if they didn't act on it…

She'd regret—wonder—for the rest of her life about what they might have had together.

And what would Drew's parents think when he showed up with a deaf half-breed? How would she feel if her only child bonded to someone with a handicap that might be hereditary?

They'd want better for their son.

Drew rested a hand on her bare thigh, his fingertips grazing the soft skin along the inside of her leg. Rivulets of sensation rushed up to intimate places in her body.

She laid a hand over his. She caught his glance in her direction. She should never have insisted on changing into a dress.

When he turned the car down a residential street, Katrina forced her attention to the houses they passed. Each was large and spacious, but none were ostentatious. It looked like any other upper-income neighborhood.

He swung into the wide curving driveway of a two-story house and pulled up in front of the two-car attached garage. The house had unusual roofline levels that gave the front dimension and set it apart from the rest of the homes they'd passed. White California lilac bloomed along the front of the house, and smaller plants budding in blue were on the cusp of doing the same.

"This is lovely, Drew."

"It's home, or was until I was eighteen and moved out to go to college. Despite our differences from humans, we try to blend in and do what's expected." He released his seatbelt, opened the door, and slid free of the vehicle to come around and open her door.

They did attempt to blend in. To hide. The nuns at the children's home had insisted they all conform, to bend to what was expected. Especially her. Katrina looked down at her feet, the raised edge of the scars slightly visible beneath the makeup.

Drew opening the door beside her jerked her back to the present. She released her seat belt, took his hand, and allowed him to assist her out of the car.

Nerves set to life a sudden flutter beneath her rib cage,

and when Drew directed her forward with a hand against her back, she stopped.

"What is it?"

"I'm a little anxious."

He ran a comforting hand down the back of her arm. "My parents don't bite. They'll be thrilled to meet you."

After her difficulties at work, she was well aware of her limitations. It was humiliating to have to ask for his help. It undermined her confidence and made her dependent in a way she struggled against every day. She bit her lip and turned to face him.

His patience only caused her to feel more insecure. Her gaze fell away and she toyed with the middle button of his shirt. "If I get confused during the conversation, I'd appreciate it if you'd help me catch up." Did her request make her seem weak to him?

With a finger beneath her chin, Drew lifted her face, his eyes tracing her features. "I'll make sure you don't get left behind, Katrina. While you were changing I called ahead and explained about your hearing loss."

"Thanks. That was a good idea." She mustered a smile, though uncertainty twisted her stomach into knots.

He urged her toward the front door, which opened before they reached it. She read the man's lips as he said, "I've been waiting for you to come in." He stepped outside to give Drew a hug and a slap on the back. When he turned to her, she immediately saw his resemblance to Drew. He had the same breadth of shoulder and height, the same unusual tricolored eyes, and dark hair. There was a difference in the shape of Drew's jaw and the fullness of his lips, but the two were strikingly handsome standing together.

Drew's father turned to study her, his smile laced with charm. "So this is Katrina."

Drew gave her a wink before making the introductions. "Yes, this is Katrina. She reads lips very well, but you have to face her when you speak so she won't miss what you're saying." Drew rested his hand against her back while smiling into her eyes. "Katrina this is Dr. Blake Saunders, my father."

Katrina forced a smile she hoped looked normal and offered her hand. "It's nice to meet you, Dr. Saunders."

He held her hand cupped in his own for a moment, and she felt the calm he projected. "Please call me Blake. We're thrilled Drew thought to bring you by."

Blake released her hand. "Come in and meet my wife, and we'll talk." He motioned them forward, leading the way into an open tiled foyer where a wide staircase swept up to the second floor.

Blake turned to the left and walked into an open living room-kitchen combination. A long, butter-colored sofa sat in the middle of the floor facing a fireplace, with a boldly patterned rug stretched beneath toward a tiled hearth. Two matching chairs finished out the grouping. Dark, highly polished tables with glass inserts sat within arm's reach.

The walls, a sage green, made the space restful. Niches in the walls on either side of the fireplace held elaborate abstract sculptures of carved wood. One was of an Orca and the other a humpback whale. There were several interesting, eclectic pieces of furniture Katrina was interested in looking at more closely, especially the chair and table created from suitcases.

In one of the leather chairs before the fireplace nestled a woman. She rose with a grace that drew Katrina's eye. The heavy bun of dark hair that perched atop her crown gave her petite frame height, without which the two men would have towered over her. Her skin had a golden hue and her features were more striking than beautiful, her eyes exotic, her lips sensual.

Knowing Blake Saunder's Siren history, Katrina had expected the Mer part of Drew's genetics to come from his mother, but Katrina sensed something else. His mother's background was possibly the complication he had been hesitant to talk about.

Katrina could sense other people's heritages and abilities, but this woman was something she had never encountered.

Drew positioned himself so she could see him speak. "Mom, this is Katrina. Katrina, my mother, Celeste."

"It's nice to meet you, Mrs. Saunders."

"We are glad to meet you, Katrina. Come sit down." She motioned toward the couch. "Would you like something to drink?"

"No, thank you."

Drew waited for her to settle, then joined her on the couch. He touched her arm. "Katrina and I will be going out to dinner before I have to go to the club."

"How long have you known one another?" Blake asked.

"We met about ten days ago, but we only started seeing each other a few of days ago," he answered.

Blake and Celeste exchanged a glance.

"You are both adults, but I hope you are taking things slowly," Blake said. Katrina read disquiet in his expression.

"We are being cautious, Dr. Blake," Katrina replied. "We both know the dangers of jumping into the deep end without thinking things through."

He nodded. "Good."

After a few minutes of small talk, Blake approached the subject they'd come to speak to him about. "How long have you been deaf, Katrina?"

"I'm not entirely. I can hear in an aquatic environment. But on land my hearing is limited to sound above or below human hearing levels. I can hear a dog whistle but not the human voice."

"Why not return to the sea where you would be more at home?"

Katrina paused a moment. For the first time in years, she was among people who understood her kind. "When I was a child of three, I was pushed feet first into a tub of scalding water and burned."

Drew shifted and laid a hand on her arm.

Celeste motioned with her hand. "Was it an accident?"

"No. It was an attempt to cure me of transforming. One of the women who worked in the children's home where I was raised thought I was possessed and hoped to banish the demon by burning it out of me."

Drew slipped an arm around her and hugged her against him. Katrina reached for his hand and gave it a squeeze. The warmth of his body, the protective strength of him, eased her tension. She looked up at him and read the distress in his eyes.

"It was many years ago." She shifted her attention back to his parents. "I was in the hospital several weeks. The burns healed too quickly, and the scar tissue couldn't be excised. The woman was arrested for assault and placed in a psychiatric hospital because they assumed she was hallucinating."

"And you?" Blake asked, compassion in his expression.

"I learned never to submerge in water for any length of time and to hide what I am."

"The aftereffects of the scars?" Celesta asked, glancing at Katrina's feet.

"My flukes cannot form completely."

Celeste looked toward Blake. He leaned forward to rest his elbows on his knees and clasped his hands before him. "There are doctors who specialize in treating our kind, Katrina. There may be something that can be done."

If given the option, would she turn to the sea to escape her current struggles? And go where?

"I have no family on land or in the sea. The Merman responsible for fathering me won't acknowledge me, and my biological mother abandoned me at birth. I have an easier time on land despite my hearing issues. I have to move forward."

"You could still have the opportunity to enjoy that part of yourself you've been forced to abandon," Celeste urged. "We may live on land most of the time, but we are first and always aquatic by nature."

"I can make arrangements for you to see Dr. Mason," Blake offered. "He's a close colleague. It wouldn't hurt to explore your options. He might be able to help you."

"I wouldn't want to live my life submerged, Dr. Saunders."

"Neither would I, but you could feel more whole again."

Katrina nodded. She understood what he meant. There was a freedom in transformation and in utilizing the part of herself she considered her true nature. "I'd be open to talking with him and seeing if something could be done after the cochlear surgery."

"What difficulty is it you want to discuss with me about that?"

"I wondered if you know the doctor who is scheduled to do my surgery. Dr. Graham Powel."

Celeste lifted her hand slightly. "I met him at a charity event at the opera. We sold tickets to raise money for surgeries like yours. He was charming—and very focused."

"He pressured me about allowing him to do more studies of my skull, and even said he would pay for part of my surgery if I'd agree to it."

Blake frowned.

"I'm concerned he might discover more than I want him to. But to start over with another doctor in this field…"

"He can't do any kind of treatment without your consent."

"He can if it's under the guise of necessary treatment during my surgery. I'm not saying that he would, only that he'd have an opportunity."

Celeste leaned forward. "If you're distrustful of his intent, you shouldn't allow him to operate, Katrina."

None of them could understand what it was like to live in total silence. To be treated with less respect because of a disability. To be regarded as though you were stupid because you couldn't hear. To be passed over for things because of it, as her boss had done this afternoon.

"Is there someone else you know who practices this particular specialty within our community I could go to?"

"I don't know of anyone, but I can put out feelers and possibly locate someone," Blake offered.

"I'd appreciate it. Thank you." She was finally beginning to relax. Changing the subject she motioned toward one of the objects of art. "I love that table made from a suitcase."

Celeste smiled and rose. "Let me show you how it works."

Katrina slipped free of the protective cocoon Drew had created for her. "Thank you," she mouthed before turning to follow his mother.

Drew looked back at his father.

Blake wasted no time. "Have you bonded with her, Drew?"

"I don't know. I can feel her emotions as though they're my own."

Blake's face tightened. "That's the first stage."

Apprehension lodged between his throat and lungs, making it difficult to breathe. How had it happened when they hadn't made love?

"Is she experiencing the same thing?"

"I don't know. She was very upset over a business meeting and the interview with the doctor. I was so focused on her—" He shook his head.

"She's beautiful."

Drew's eyes lingered on Katrina as she and his mother went from one art piece to another. They'd settled into an animated discussion.

His uncomfortable emotional tide subsided. She'd been concerned for him the night before. She hadn't done anything on purpose to trigger this. "She is beautiful. And when she's with me, I know what she's feeling about me isn't triggered by my voice." He smiled. "In fact, she disapproves of me using my gift during shows. That's how we met. She walked out during a performance, and I tried to follow her."

"So she can hear the subliminal things you do with your voice?"

"Some, but not all. They don't affect her the way they do humans."

"So earning her affections is going to require a little more work than usual."

His father's wry smile triggered his own. "You don't have to sound so pleased."

His father laughed. "I'm not, really. If you could use your special abilities you could help things along." He shook his head. "I'm concerned for your sake and hers. You'll need to learn to close down the link between you, otherwise it will become overwhelming. It's both a blessing and an intrusion to know what another person is feeling."

Drew rubbed his eyes with the heels of his palms. "How am I supposed to shut it down?"

"There's a door open between you. You have to mentally close it. It will take more than a few minutes for me to teach you. If you come by tomorrow, we'll work on it together."

"Okay." This wouldn't be the first time his father had helped him adjust to one of his gifts. What had it been like for Katrina in a human orphanage with no support system? He flinched from the thought.

"Can you feel her emotions right now?" Blake asked.

"No." Drew relaxed somewhat.

"So it's only when she's experiencing some strong emotion you can pick up on it."

"Yes." Not just pick up on it. Her earlier distress had rolled over him like a tsunami. Her anxiety over meeting his parents had been easy to read. But had that been more body language than emotion?

His father's features tensed. "You have to make up your mind, Drew. You can continue to pursue her and hope she learns to love you, or you can break it off now and walk away before you fully bond with her."

"And what would it be like if I fully bond?" he asked. He needed to know. Not that it would probably help.

"If she returns your feelings, you'll finally be complete. Like you've been missing a limb and suddenly recovered it. You'll be the happiest you've ever been. I'm not saying you won't disagree at times. Or have ups and downs like any other couple, but you'll be closer to her than you can imagine, certainly closer than you are even to us."

If she didn't reciprocate his feelings and bond with him, it would be the complete opposite. He wasn't going to force his father to say it.

How could this happen to him so quickly? He had made love to hundreds of women and never formed an emotional bond, and now he was attached to a Mermaid he hadn't even had sex with. Was it some kind of fateful payback for all the callous things he'd done over the years before he'd gained control of himself?

But, depending on Katrina's response to him, it could be a gift. If he wanted to try for it.

"Are you going to tell her you can feel her emotions?"

"I don't want to put that kind of pressure on her. She'd worry it was something she'd done that triggered it. And it isn't. She's the one who insisted we need to go slowly."

"Because of your mother's *Encantado* bloodline, things might have accelerated on their own."

And what would Katrina think about his mother's special gifts? All this paranormal baggage attached to his life clouded every issue. Humans had it so much easier.

"But despite the obvious complications, none of this would have happened if you didn't already have feelings for Katrina, Drew."

"I'm attracted to her, more strongly than any other female I've come into contact with. And I'm compelled to protect her."

"Because of her deafness?"

Was it because of her disability? He'd spent the entire afternoon taping sounds he hoped she could hear. Her hearing challenges had inspired it, but a desire to please her played a bigger part. "Not entirely."

Celeste and Katrina wandered back into the room with a

pitcher of drinks and glasses.

"I've convinced Katrina to stay for dinner if you agree, Drew."

His mother's lightly accented voice held a lilt Katrina would never hear if she didn't go through with the surgery.

"Sure. Dad and I can grill if you'd like."

"Of course I would," his mother replied.

Drew laughed. Her arrogant princess of the house routine was both a source of amusement and an irritation at times. He and his father had both played to it and spoiled her. He wondered if Katrina, with her ingrained independence, would take to a little spoiling, too.

Katrina enjoyed watching the dynamic between Drew and his parents, but was more fascinated by his parents' relationship. They clearly doted on their son and showered him with affection, but most of their concentration was focused on each other.

Their interaction was like a subtle, sensual dance. Celeste touched Blake's arm, he caressed her back, she brushed close and he reached out to hug her. She reached for the pepper and he was already handing it to her. They could no more refuse to touch one another than they could stop breathing. What was it like to be that in tune with another being? To read their thoughts and feelings so easily?

After a meal of grilled salmon garnished with homemade pineapple salsa, seasoned rice, and a salad, Katrina and Drew rose to say their goodbyes.

At the door Celeste embraced her and kissed her cheek.

"Come back soon, Katrina."

"Thank you, I will. It was a lovely meal."

Drew's father hugged her as well. "I'll get back to you with the information we spoke about as soon as I can."

She nodded. "Thank you."

Drew took her hand as they walked to the car. "I told you they'd like you."

"They're amazing. And the way they are with each other." She placed a hand over her heart.

He grinned.

"Do they read each other's thoughts?"

"No. It's more an emotional thing. How would you feel if someone could read you like that?"

How would she feel? She studied his features while she thought about it. "Growing up, we had so little privacy. I'm not sure how I'd feel. I think I'd be embarrassed for my every feeling to be examined."

"It isn't so much examined, but shared."

"Since I'm not fully Mer, and you're not fully Siren. It might not work that way for us." And what was she doing even talking about it, as though she'd accept something that close? She'd spent a lifetime alone inside her head. How would she deal having someone else privy to her feelings?

Drew reached for the ignition. "Would you like to go to the club with me tonight, or do you have to work?"

She'd had enough of her job for the day, especially after this afternoon. But not nearly enough of him. "I'd like to go with you."

Drew smiled. "Good."

Chapter 13

The way Drew drove the crowd to a fever pitch and then eased them back down was masterful, and almost painful for Katrina to watch. When he made music, he was in his element. His mind, body, and heart were totally engaged.

She wanted to feel what it was like to have his voice caress her. Without the cochlear implant, she would never be able to share that with him. If they were to become a couple she needed to experience what he was in every way she could.

A couple. Now she'd seen Drew's parents together and learned what bonding meant, she couldn't stop thinking about the possibilities.

Would making love with Drew be as powerful as what the women felt listening to him sing? Could any man live up to that hype?

But he wasn't a man. His heritage included one of the most seductive species on earth. Even if she hadn't been aware of that important difference, she'd have found him compelling, attractive, desirable.

The sweet smell of fruit juice, liquor, and perfume blended with sweat and human endorphins hanging in the air like incense. Above it all she caught Drew's scent, musky with heat, spicy with sex, with a touch of the sea. He didn't use the subtle smell to seduce. It was a part of his being Mer, Siren, and whatever preternatural cocktail his mother added to the mix.

After the group took a break and disappeared backstage, the bouncer, Clyde, approached her table. The man was huge, muscular, and smiled at her with a touch of flirtation. It probably worked for him with most women, but she had her mind so full of Drew she wasn't tempted. "Drew wants you to join him back stage."

Katrina nodded and rose.

He took her arm to guide her through the crowd to the side stairs. "Third door on the right."

"Thank you."

She climbed the stairs and walked down the hall. She paused at the door Clyde had indicated and tapped at it. It opened so quickly she gasped. Drew had a towel hung around his neck and was drinking from a bottle of water. His hair was glued to his nape with sweat, so wet he looked like he'd taken a shower. He was panting from exertion. "I wanted to check on you and see how you're doing."

"I'm fine." Unable to keep from touching him, she stepped forward and, taking the end of the towel wiped his face clear of sweat. Something more was going on. He was agitated, and the dark pupils of his eyes were dilated. "What is it?"

"The lights get hot," he explained.

"I can see that. But this is more than the lights."

He grasped her hands and held them. "Your scent is driving me crazy, Katrina."

Her pulse hammered when she saw the fierce, aching need in his face.

"I'm up there singing to all those women and surrounded—saturated—with your fragrance, and all I can think about is how much I want you."

She had been doing the same thing, only she could hide the repercussions of her desire a little more easily. His cheekbones suddenly sharpened, became more defined. A feverish rush of heat flared off of him, and every nerve in her body responded. She was wet and ready in an instant.

He shoved his hand into his pocket and withdrew a set of keys. "I need you to take these and drive home. I'll have one of the guys drop me by your apartment after the show to pick up the car."

What had she been thinking to allow her thoughts, her emotions such free rein? She'd obviously been putting out pheromones along with all the humans. "I'm sorry, Drew."

"Honey. Don't ever apologize for wanting me. After being desired for the pleasure I can give with my voice…to be wanted for just me? It's a gift."

Not if it tortured him so. The need to mate was so strong for them both, but Drew had the added demand of his Siren nature to deal with.

She could ease him. All they had to do was have sex. "How long is your break?" she asked.

His gray-blue eyes grew darker. "Not long enough."

The words *are you sure?* sprang to mind.

Drew grinned as though he'd read the thought. "Look at this place, Katrina."

The dressing room was drab, though clean. A couch, a few chairs, a mirror that stretched the length of the small room, a dressing table, and the castoffs of all the performers who'd occupied the space cluttered one corner.

Drew cradled her chin and pulled her gaze back to his face. "When we make love, I want to have plenty of time to explore every way we can fit together, and take our time about it."

She drew a trembling breath and her legs went weak. All the intimate areas of her body tingled and throbbed, and she could feel her face heating with a fierce blush.

"Take the keys. I'll be there in an hour or so to get the car."

"Okay." She could barely get the word out.

"Let Clyde walk you to the car."

"He doesn't have to. I can take care of myself."

"Let him walk you. I'd do it myself if it wasn't such a madhouse out there."

She was still too affected by the images he'd conjured of them making love to argue. "Okay."

"There's a surprise for you in the console between the seats. I was going to give it to you when I took you home. I hope it will entertain you until I get there."

"Okay. Thank you."

She stepped closer, the desire to kiss him nearly over-whelming. It might make things more difficult for him.

Drew caught her mouth with his in one sweet, searing kiss, then set her away.

Dizzy with need, she slipped from the room.

Drew dragged air into his lungs and fell into one of the chairs. The farther away she traveled, the easier it was for him to block her scent, her feelings. The seesaw of her emotions had made it very hard for him to concentrate on the performance. He'd never been so aroused in his life.

He had to talk to his father tomorrow and learn how he was supposed to close off the link between them. He shouldn't bring her back to the club until he could control it.

It would be easier on him if he stayed away from her until he had a handle on this. Stay away from her…he couldn't say forever. He didn't think he'd have the discipline to do that.

How could his emotions, his reasoning change so drastically after spending less than twenty-four hours with her?

A knock came at the door and he went to answer it.

Roma shoved past him into the room, bringing with her a cloud of Chanel No. 5 and woman. A skin-tight red dress clung to her generous curves and cupped her large breasts, its low cut neckline displaying a wealth of cleavage. She looked like pure sex. "We have to talk, Drew." Her bottom lip quivered. "You can't break things off with me and not give me a reason."

Fuck! He didn't need this. "I thought I made it clear, Roma. You aren't in love with me. I'm not in love with you. We were wasting our time with each other."

"We were good together, Drew," she whined.

"In bed, sure. But beyond sex, we have nothing in common. So I broke it off so we could move on."

She slid her arms around his neck and leaned into him, pressing her heavy breasts against his chest. "But I didn't want to move on. I'm in love with you."

Even the way she said the words sounded pouty and false. Drew untangled himself. "You were in love with the sex. And now you've heard about the recording contract, you want to cash in on our relationship."

Her mouth flew open in a sexy O she'd probably practiced in front of a mirror. "How can you think that?"

"So you have heard about the contract." He knew it.

"Of course I have. It's all everyone is talking about. But that isn't the reason I'm here." She pasted on a look of hurt. "I thought you cared about me."

Why had he gotten involved with her? Because she was superficial and he'd known there'd be no chance of them bonding. Sex with no strings, as always. Why had he continued to make the same mistakes over and over when all along he'd wanted more? "I do care about you, Roma, but I'm not in love with you. I'm looking for someone I can spend my life with, not just pass the time."

Her dark eyes grew glazed with crocodile tears. "Was passing the time with me so terrible?"

"No. We entertained each other. And we gave one another pleasure. But it's never been anything more than friends with benefits."

He could read the mercurial wave of her emotions as they crossed her face. Disappointment when he didn't fall to his knees begging for another chance. Then anger.

"And what if I say I'm pregnant?"

His heart skipped a beat. No way. He'd used protection *every* time. He checked in her scent. When a woman was pregnant, her normal essence changed, because the baby added something to it. Roma's scent was the same as it had always been. He'd known she was narcissistic and self-serving, but he'd never seen this manipulative side before. What little feeling he had for the woman died.

"I'll call my father and arrange for an appointment. He's one of the top fertility specialists in the country. He can do a test tomorrow. But I'll want a paternity test as soon as the baby's born."

Frustration and outrage warred on her face, and she planted both hands against his chest and shoved hard. Drew didn't even pretend to stumble back, but met her dark look with a hard one of his own. "We're not playing games anymore, Roma. It's over."

She stomped to the door. "You'll regret this. I don't know what you think you have in common with that girl. She can't even hear you sing."

Something to be grateful for. "Leave Katrina out of this, Roma."

"Why would you want her? She's deaf." She spoke as though being deaf meant she had a communicable disease.

Anger stormed through him, and he clenched his hands into fists. He dragged in several calming breaths and waited for the backwash of rage to roll off of him before he spoke. "Katrina's beautiful, smart, artistic, and we have things in common you would never understand."

"And you think you're in love with her?"

"Who I love or not is my business."

"I don't think you're capable of loving anyone. You're a cold bastard, Drew."

"You didn't think I was cold when I was between your thighs giving you what you wanted. Or when I was humming in your ear to help you get off. Should I make that appointment for you with my father?" he goaded her.

"Go to hell." She stormed out of the dressing room and nearly collided with Rand. The man raised a brow and one side of his mouth quirked. "Is there a problem?"

"You can go to hell, too." She stomped off, her hips twitching.

Rand grinned at Drew. "We could hear the two of you through the wall, dude. That is one conniving bitch."

Drew grudgingly answered. "Yeah, she is."

"She's not really pregnant?"

"No." Drew shook his head. "Just a ploy."

"Katrina's definitely a step up."

"Yeah, she is."

"Are you feeling better despite all the drama?" Rand asked.

"Yeah." Tormented by emotions and his own desires, he'd been more than abrupt with Simon before he disappeared into the empty dressing room to try and fight off the needs bombarding him. "Did you draw the short straw to come check on me?"

"Yeah."

Drew laughed. "Sorry, I was an asshole. I was sick. I took some aspirin and I think my temperature is coming down."

"Simon said you were burning up with fever. If you need to call it a night, we'll figure something out," Rand said, his expression sympathetic. "It might be better if you did. The rest of us don't want to catch whatever you're coming down with."

Whenever Rand did something nice, he always had an ulterior motive. Was he hoping to prove the band could do without their lead singer?

Drew had never missed a performance, and he wouldn't allow himself to do so now. He couldn't rag Rand about his behavior and then go to Katrina in the hopes of having sex with her. And if they did…

He'd always told himself he controlled his sexuality, not the other way around. He needed to man up now, and control it. "I spent all morning at the beach, and I think I got too much sun, sand, and surf. I appreciate the offer to cover for me, but I'll finish the gig. I'll need a ride afterwards to Katrina's to pick up my car, though."

Rand looked disappointed but nodded. "I can drop you."

"Thanks." The guys were fantastic musicians. Why not showcase their talents? Maybe that's what they needed to do anyway.

They wandered down the hall to the stage. He motioned to Simon and Tony to join them in the wings. "I'm still running a fever. How would you guys feel about taking the lead on a few songs and I'll back you up for a change."

"We haven't practiced anything like that Drew," Tony said.

"Sure we have. Every time you pick up your guitar,

you're practicing a solo performance in your head. It's time they learn how talented you guys are. Let's relax and jam for the rest of the evening and make music."

The surprise on Rand's face was worth the risk. Why hadn't it occurred to him to encourage this before? Because his Siren and *Encantado* backgrounds made him as narcissistic as Roma, and he liked being the front man. This connection to Katrina had opened his emotional eyes, not just to her, but to his fellow band members.

A wide smile broke across Simon's face. "Let's get started."

Chapter 14

Katrina forced herself to concentrate on her driving as she made her way home in Drew's car. She couldn't entirely block out the situation. And the repercussions they presented for Drew were worse than she'd imagined. He'd been struggling against the transformation, feverish, and in pain. She needed to learn how to control her emotions when around him. He picked up on her scent too easily.

The more she thought about it, the more distraught she became. What if all the preternatural crap proved such a deterrent he didn't want to see her again? Why couldn't they be like a normal man and woman, enjoy being attracted, get to know one another, and fall in love? Instead, they wanted to tear each other's clothes off, mate and hope for the best.

Katrina parked in front of her apartment and paused to look inside the console. The only thing in there were a cell phone charger and a box with her name written across the front in a bold, manly scribble.

She gathered her purse and the package and climbed out. In the elevator, she continued to study the box and could feel the shift of something inside as she tilted it.

Once inside her apartment, she tossed her purse into a chair, tore free the tape securing the lid and opened the box. Headphones and a small flash drive. Why would he purchase head phones for her? She couldn't hear.

Curious, she moved to her computer and plugged in the drive. She clicked on the video message first, and Drew popped on the screen. She paused it a moment to admire his masculine, strongly defined features.

Even on the computer screen he projected sensuality, his eyes looked so dark and intense. She pressed a hand to her midriff. He'd be here in a little more than an hour to pick up his car. Would he be okay? Would he tell her he didn't want to see her again because of what had happened at the club? If he did, what then?

She'd regret it for a long, long time. More than that. Tears welled up and she blinked to keep them from falling. Meetings between their kind were so rare. There were so few of them. But it was more than that. In those moments of torment at the club, she'd wanted to ease his pain. It hadn't been about her receiving pleasure from having sex. It had been about her need to soothe him.

They hadn't had sex. She couldn't have bonded with him yet. Otherwise, she'd be obsessed with him, wouldn't she? She was just obsessing because she was attracted to him.

She started the video and read his lips. "You'll need to put on your headphones and crank up the speakers. This is an experiment of sorts. I hope it works."

If he'd given her headphones, he was hoping she could hear something. She'd love it if she could reward his efforts.

She plugged in the headphones, positioned them on her head, and turned up the volume as high as it would go, then clicked on the audio file he'd saved on the drive. It began to play, and for several moments she heard nothing, then suddenly the high squeak and rumble of whale song came through the headphones. Not the sounds within the range of normal hearing but the tones beyond those frequencies. The song swooped and dived, devoid of a chorus and a bit disjointed, but so glorious.

Tears blurred her vision and she reached for a tissue. He'd given her a gift that reached far beyond kindness, beyond seduction. And there was more. She recognized each sound, each soft song sung by the sea.

An hour later, when the light over the door blinked, she closed the file and set aside the headphones. She opened the door and for a nanosecond they just gazed at each other.

"It worked," Drew said, amazement and satisfaction aglow in his expression.

"Yes." Katrina caught his hand and tugged him into the apartment. She slipped her arms around his neck and held him close. "Thank you, Drew."

He gave her a gentle squeeze in return.

She leaned back to look up at him and caught the faint scent of perfume on his shirt. And for a moment her heart plunged. But, no. If he'd been with another woman, she would know. There was no hint of that, so it had probably been just an overly affectionate fan. "Are you okay?"

"Yeah, I'm fine." He looked tired.

Had she put those lines of stress around his mouth? "How did the rest of the set go?"

"Good. We jammed for over an hour, and the audience loved it."

"I'm sorry I caused you pain. I'll try to be more aware of how my emotions affect my scent."

"No." He shook his head and guided her to the couch to sit down. "If you worry about how I'll react to you, it's going to put too much stress on us both. I want you to be able to relax with me and forget the Mer and Siren aspects of this. I want to be a regular man with you. I've never had normal, Katrina. I've never had a real relationship. All I've had is the physical side of things, never the emotional."

The way he looked at her set off a sizzling heat in places she tried to ignore. His scent rose, and she quickly shut down the feelings. "I've never had a normal relationship either. How can you, when you're hiding the biggest part of yourself from the person you're with? Between that and my hearing issues, there were just too many obstacles."

"I don't have an issue with your deafness, Katrina. In a way it's an advantage. If you were able to hear, I could have seduced you with my voice when we first met. It would have been as empty as all the other relationships I've had. We could have ended up bonding before we even knew each other. This way we're forced to discover each other a little at a time, like any normal couple. We just need to find a natural rhythm when were together."

He rose to his feet. "It's almost one. I'd better go."

She didn't want him to leave, but she couldn't ask him to stay. He'd had too hard a time at the club earlier. She sensed it had taken more out of him than he was allowing her to see. He paused at the door.

She couldn't thank him enough for the drive. "I love my gift. It's the most amazing thing anyone has ever given me. You'll have to tell me how you accomplished it."

"I will." He grasped her hands and bent his head to kiss each one. "I'm glad you liked it."

She couldn't just let him go. After what had happened at the club, what if he didn't come back. "Will you come to dinner tomorrow around six?"

His brows rose. "Sure. Are you a good cook?"

She smiled. "Lousy, but I won't poison you or anything."

Drew laughed. "We can always order out."

"It won't be necessary. I was only teasing. I can cook."

He seemed hesitant to kiss her. She tiptoed to slide her arms around his neck. "Normal girlfriends and boyfriends kiss each other goodnight." She kissed him softly, then rested her cheek against his. He relaxed and his arms tightened around her, pulling her in against him. Instantly his body warmed to hers.

Would he decide this was too much trouble, she was too much trouble? She inhaled his scent and held it. If they lost one another before they'd ever had a chance—The idea triggered an ache of loss that caught her by surprise. She was trembling when he released her. "I wish you could whisper in my ear like the audio file you made for me."

"Maybe one day, Katrina."

That day couldn't come quickly enough to suit her.

"Now, deep breaths, and picture the door closing between

you."

He and his father had been working on visualization exercises for nearly an hour. It was somewhat like meditation with a twist. The measured breathing and relaxation techniques had eased the turbulence of his thoughts and feelings.

"Have you and Katrina had sex yet?"

Drew's eyes flew open. He found his father had risen and was leaning back against the edge of his desk. He hadn't expected to answer questions about their relationship. He'd never kissed and told. Even though they hadn't made love, it felt disloyal. A breach of her privacy, and his own.

He focused on the slash of early morning sunlight cutting across his father's right shoulder. He'd interrupted his father's routine, but Blake had immediately set aside what he was doing to help him. Luckily it was Wednesday, his day to work at home.

Drew shook his head. "No, we haven't had sex. Night before last, I gave her a ride home, and when we kissed I started to transform—"

The surprise and alarm he read in his father's expression was not comforting.

"How far did the transformation go?"

"It affected my facial bones and caused enough of an expansion of my chest and diaphragm to make my shirt tight."

"You said something about last night?" Blake prodded.

"She went with me to the club for part of our performance. I was able to control the transformation, but I'd spent all morning and afternoon underwater, taping sounds for a project."

"Which made it more difficult to transform."

"I still had to fight it. I had to ask her to take my car and drive home so I could finish the gig." Sending Katrina away when he'd needed her so much had been more than difficult. Dealing with Roma had been an irritant he could have definitely done without. Between the two, no wonder he felt like flotsam washed up on the beach this morning.

"You have to concentrate, Drew. And practice. Imagine that part of your mind as a door you're shutting between you and Katrina. And then you lock it."

And what would happen if he wanted to unlock the door again? How was building a shield supposed to help him control his response to her scent?

He ran his hand over his jaw. "I've already bonded with her, haven't I?"

"Only you can tell. But I suspect you're close. Have you said anything to her about how you feel?"

"No. We're not that far along. We just met. I want to give her time to accept me without the added pressure of knowing I might be bonding with her." Last night when he'd picked up his car, he'd read how pleased she'd been by the audio file he created for her, and sensed her grief when she told him goodnight. If he could read her thoughts instead of her emotions, he'd be able to understand why she was experiencing sadness. As it was, he got the emotional feedback and not the rest. Which he found frustrating as hell.

"I never expected it to be this way," Drew said.

His father shot him a wry smile. "I understand. I felt

like I'd been hit by a truck. Every emotion you pick up on is exaggerated and overwhelming. Especially for males, who are less emotional to begin with."

He'd never felt so many emotions in his life. It had intensified his hungers. So he had to find a way to suppress them, too. Shit!

"She doesn't seem to key in on my emotions mentally, but through body language. But when I'm…struggling, she's caring and concerned. Do you think her hearing issues might enable her to block my feelings?"

"I don't think it's her hearing difficulties, but, based on what you've told me of her background, the strict upbringing, the lack of privacy, being tormented because she was Mer, she might have built shields at an early age to protect herself. It would have been a survival mechanism." Blake grimaced in sympathy. "Imagine all the things she must have had to endure being deaf in such a closed environment."

Anger sharp as shark's teeth whipped through Drew. How could anyone have shoved her feet into water hot enough to burn her? And the woman had believed Katrina was the monster.

He'd never had more reason to be grateful for his upbringing. He had been treated like the crown prince by his parents, and the wonder boy in high school and college because of his intelligence, musical abilities, and physical prowess. And now he was gaining success as a musician.

He ran a hand down his jaw and his beard rasped. He'd been up most of the night stewing over the situation. He was glad Katrina had built shields, but he also hoped she'd be willing to lower them and let him in.

"It would have been easier for you to learn to control your own shielding if you'd brought her here with you."

"She's at work and I couldn't ask her to take the day off. She's coming up on an expensive surgery. And from what I've learned about it on the web, most of it won't be covered by insurance. Have you been able to locate a surgeon who specializes in this type of treatment?"

"No. I still have a few calls out, but I don't believe there is anyone. But I've checked into Dr. Powell. He's won several awards, and is one of the top surgeons in his field."

"But that could mean he's very…curious." Drew frowned. "We can't ask her not to go through with the surgery, Dad. She's—" He swallowed. "She wants her own business some day. Wants to be able to control the projects she takes on. She lives in total silence. I don't know how she bears it."

Blake rested a hand on his shoulder. "And you want her to be able to hear your voice."

"Yes, but not to seduce her, or not completely. She wants to be able to hear me, too."

"I'm sure she does."

"I went to the dock yesterday, took the boat out, and swam for hours. I took an underwater mike with me so I could record the sounds, and then I made her an audio file. She said she could hear what I'd recorded. The joy she was feeling…" The simple act of talking about it swamped him with emotion.

Jesus, he *was* bonded to her. He slouched back into one of the chairs in front of the desk.

His father sat down in the chair next to him.

Drew leaned forward, rested his elbows on his knees and linked his fingers together. "It doesn't matter to you or mom that she's deaf, does it?"

"No. We want you to be happy, Drew. We want you to know the joy of what we have. But you're going to have to be patient and let things progress."

"I have to be able to block off some of this so I can stay longer than fifteen minutes in a room with her without turning."

"That would be helpful, too."

Drew gave a bark of wry amusement.

Blake's answering smile only lasted a moment as he shifted toward him. "Some of this is your mother's and my fault. We knew when we had you that you might have to face some challenges related to your special gifts. Two seductive species coming together in one child." He shook his head.

"Does Mom do anything different to block things out?"

"It's different for each of us, but it's a mental discipline. She may use a different image, but it's a muscle like any other."

"Once the door is closed, how do I open it again?"

"Opening it isn't a problem, Drew. It's keeping it closed that provides the challenge. It's become second nature for your mother and me to give one another privacy. It's intrusive to read everything another being is feeling, and exhausting to be the receiver, as you're finding out. It might be easier for you if you spent shorter periods of time with Katrina to give you time to adjust."

He'd been as solitary as Katrina. And now he wanted to spend every waking moment with her. How was he supposed to adjust to that?

"You need to sleep, son. When you're tired it's more difficult. Why don't you go upstairs and rest for a while?"

"I have to practice with the band at one." It was good this was his day off, too. Mondays, Wednesdays and Sundays, though they practiced, the evenings were their own.

"I'll wake you before I leave for my golf game."

He did need to sleep. His eyes felt scratchy and dry, like grains of sand coated the lids. But he needed to practice the techniques his father had taught him. They'd have to become like a muscle memory in order for him to get through this.

And if it was this bad now, how would he survive if Katrina didn't reciprocate his feelings?

Chapter 15

Katrina stared at the design on the computer screen. She loved her job. Loved setting her artistry loose to create something original. It was meticulous work, but once the project was done, she experienced a sense of accomplishment and satisfaction nothing else could touch.

At the moment all she could think about was Drew. He'd been subdued the night before, visibly tired, and it had been her fault. She'd behaved thoughtlessly.

In the days since they'd met, the damn preternatural side-effects had tormented him from the beginning. Why wasn't it doing the same to her? Was there something wrong with her?

Cheryl swung into her cubby and parked her rear on the counter next to Katrina. "Are you about finished? I'm starving."

"Yes." She saved her work and closed out the program. She needed a distraction and some advice. But how could she ask questions without revealing too many secrets? She slid open the bottom drawer of her desk and pulled out her purse.

They wandered down the street to a down town deli and ordered a Reuben sandwich and chips to share, and a drink for each of them. They found a table outside the restaurant, even though the day was a little crisp, and spent a short while people-watching while they ate.

"How are things with Howard?" Katrina asked. She crumpled her napkin and stuffed it into the empty bag their lunch came in.

Cheryl grinned. "He's great. We're great."

"Good. I'm glad." Katrina was relieved Drew's gift left no lingering affect to disrupt the normal development of their relationship.

"How are things going with Mr. Sexy Voice?"

"He's more than that, Cheryl."

Cheryl's smile dimmed. "So it's getting serious quick?"

"No. Yes. It's a little difficult to explain." Katrina remained silent for a moment. "I met his parents."

"Whoa! Really?" She leaned forward and propped her elbows on the table, her expression of surprise saying *already?*

Katrina smiled. "They're both really unique."

"How did you happen to meet them?"

"I told you about the weird vibe I got from the doctor who's going to do my surgery."

"Yeah." Cheryl raised a brow, concern in her expression.

"Drew took me to their house so I could talk to his father about the guy. He's a doctor, too."

"What did he say?"

"What I already knew. If I didn't trust the guy, I

shouldn't allow him to do the surgery. He's checking into other surgeons, but he won't find any. I've looked for a long time. I thought Dr. Turner was going to do my surgery. I like him, he seems very caring, and we've built a rapport. Somehow I must have missed that very important piece of information during our last meeting, or misunderstood." Tears suddenly threatened and she blinked rapidly to stave them off. "I should have taken you up on your offer to go with me to the appointments." Her anxiety level rose. "The surgery has been scheduled for a week from today."

"That's a good thing, isn't it? You can get it behind you. This other doctor, what about him creeps you out?"

"It was the way he looked at me, touched me, that made me uneasy."

"Was it an attraction thing?" Cheryl leaned forward, her demeanor protectively aggressive. "He didn't make a pass, did he?

"No. He couldn't do that with Dr. Turner watching. It was more subtle. There was something avid in his expression, and the way he tucked my hair behind my ear…" She shivered. "Then he was pushy about wanting to do more scans."

"Maybe he was attracted to you. Guys are guys. But he can't date you as long as you're his patient."

"I'm not interested in dating him—ever." Since she'd met Drew she hadn't any interest in any other man. But as controlled and controlling as Dr. Powell seemed during the consultation, she could only imagine how much more he might be in his personal life.

Cheryl rested her fingers on Katrina's arm in a soothing

gesture. "You're all worked up today. Did something happen between you and Drew?"

She'd never had a friend as close as Cheryl. Her friend shared everything with her, while Katrina told her only the information that wasn't affected by her being a Mermaid. She longed to have a friend she could trust with the supernatural stuff too. Could she trust Cheryl with all her secrets?

"We didn't have a fight. But trying to build a relationship with someone like me is more work than with a normal woman, as he's already discovering. I'm afraid he'll get tired of everything being such a struggle."

"If he does, he doesn't deserve you, Katrina."

"If I don't do everything I can to make it easier for him, I don't deserve him, either."

"If you're talking about sex, guys don't need easy. They need to earn the right to be with us. We're not just playthings or sperm depositories."

Katrina smiled at Cheryl's fierce expression. "Drew doesn't treat me like that." She'd break his neck if he did. "Besides, he wouldn't have taken me to see his father if he felt that way about me. He understands I'm not going to jump into bed with him right away."

"He has this strong sexual vibe. I was worried that you'd given in to it and he was being a dick."

Katrina laughed. "No, he's not being a dick. But physically we're so attracted to each other, the world could catch fire and we wouldn't even notice. It's almost too much to resist."

"But?" Cheryl encouraged.

"What if it burns itself out for one of us and not the other?"

Cheryl remained silent for a moment. "That's the question we all ask ourselves, Katrina. He seems like a nice guy. A little more elemental than I like in my men, but you have that kind of vibe too."

Katrina leaned forward. "What do you mean?"

"You have this…" Cheryl tilted her head. "It's hard to describe. You're like one of those Japanese geishas, all cool waters, grace, and control, with secret passions beneath the mask. And he's all in-your-face sensuality, sex, and fire. It kind of makes sense you're drawn to each other. They say opposites attract."

Katrina stared at her. Cheryl might act like the fashionista party girl, but she had depths of her own, and there was nothing wrong with her instincts about people. She'd proven it to Katrina more than once since they'd become friends.

Cheryl smiled. "You won't ever know if you suit each other unless you give it a shot. And what's that quote? ' *'Tis better to have loved and lost than never to have loved at all.*'"

"I'm not saying you should rush home, invite him over, and jump his bones for a night of wild monkey sex, but when you've finally made up your mind to trust him…" Cheryl shrugged.

Katrina sat silent a moment. "What does he sound like when he speaks?"

Cheryl frowned and looked away for a moment. She swallowed. "His voice is deep, but not *deep* deep, just manly deep, if you can imagine that. And when he sings it's a little raspy, and sends chills down your body."

Katrina ran a hand over her brow. She told herself she didn't feel jealous of the women who were able to enjoy his voice. He wasn't physically being unfaithful, and she had no right to feel he was, but the sharp twinge of hurt and frustration set her teeth on edge.

She was going to have to deal with this if they became a real couple. He was a Siren. It was in his nature to seduce. It was an unavoidable aspect of how he made his living. And it could be worse. He could have chosen to be a male stripper.

"So you're going to have the surgery even though you're not crazy about the guy who's doing it," Cheryl said, distracting her from the thoughts circling endlessly through her head.

"I guess so."

"There will be a nurse and an anesthesiologist in the operating room with him. So he can't do anything weird during the surgery. You can ask for the other doctor to be present when you have to go back."

"You're right." But the vise-like anxiety clamped around her chest all day remained. She'd been poised to receive a text from Drew canceling their dinner plans. Surely he wouldn't stand her up without texting her. She checked her phone, though she hadn't felt it vibrate and, seeing no new messages, stuck it back in her pocket.

"I've invited Drew to dinner tonight. What do you think I should fix?"

"Those divine Greek kabobs you make and the flat bread and salad."

Katrina laughed. "I'll make extra so I can bring you

some for lunch tomorrow."

Cheryl grinned. "Genius idea. Extra tzatziki sauce."

When they stood to get back to work, Katrina touched her arm. "Will you come to the hospital with me for the surgery?"

"Of course I will."

"Thanks, Cheryl." She wanted to ask Drew to come, too. What was it he'd said last night? They needed to find their rhythm. She was going to control her feelings and rein in her libido. Maybe then they'd be able to slip into the right rhythm.

Graham put the images of Katrina's skull up on the computer. He found her condition one of the most fascinating he'd ever seen. The extra sinus didn't seem attached to any part of the normal system that ran above the eyes and below. It was completely self-contained, positioned directly in alignment with her frontal lobe.

She'd said she rarely had headaches, and that she only occasionally experienced sinus issues.

Then what purpose could the damn thing serve? If only she'd allow him to take more scans before the surgery. Damn it!

He dragged her personal information from the file, which included a copy of her driver's license. The photo didn't do her justice. She was much more than the dismal picture could capture. He didn't know why he felt that way, why he was certain of it. He sensed there was *more* behind her wall of shy reserve.

There was something about the way she smelled which attracted him. How odd was it that her scent would capture his attention. Most women used perfume, and he enjoyed certain fragrances, but he'd never been able to pinpoint what scent Katrina wore. It smelled natural and light, barely there at times, then stronger at others. It was somehow familiar to him, but attempting to attach the scent to a specific memory had defeated him.

He'd ask her next time they met. Maybe once he knew what it was, he'd be able to put aside this nagging feeling of something he'd forgotten but needed to remember.

Restless, he got to his feet to pace. Why couldn't he get this woman out of his head? He wanted to spend time with her, to learn why she looked so wary whenever he got too close. What was it about him that put her on edge? He knew he came across as arrogant and pushy sometimes, but he could be charming too. He hadn't had the opportunity to be charming with her, but he would.

He needed to go home and put this out of his mind for a while. He tucked the pages back in the file, lingering for a moment on the home address Katrina had provided.

He couldn't go over to her apartment, but he could drive by and maybe catch a glimpse of her.

What was he thinking? He wasn't desperate for a woman, and he wasn't a stalker. He had to get this obsession under control.

Drew grasped the handles of the thermal bag his mother had insisted he take. Rehearsal had gone well, and he was free for the rest of the evening. After finding out he had dinner plans with Katrina, Celeste had called him to come by and pick up dessert, then pushed the wine on him.

He wasn't even sure Katrina drank wine. Last night at the club she'd had a soft drink, and the night before she'd barely touched her champagne.

He keyed in the security code, and walked through the lobby to the elevators. On the way up he practiced the breathing techniques his father had taught him and visualized closing the mental door to block Katrina's feelings.

After he got out of the elevator, a little more than half-way down the hall to her apartment, he slowed, expecting to feel the pressure against his chest as he had the night before. Nothing! She was either late getting home, or he had finally gotten a handle on this. He sighed with relief, allowed his shoulders to relax, and moved on to her door.

He pushed the doorbell, and after only a moment's wait it swung open.

"Hello." A quick smile lit her face.

He no longer felt her emotions, but he hardened immediately anyway. "Hey." He advanced into the room when she stepped back. "I brought dessert and wine." Though his hands were full, the need to kiss her swept over him. He handed her the dessert container instead.

"Thank you. The only thing I have that qualifies as dessert is rocky road ice cream. The only bottle of wine I have is one the girls at the office bought me for my birthday. We're having Greek kabobs, made with beef instead of the traditional lamb, orzo, flat bread, and salad."

A bar separated the kitchen from the living room. It was there she had laid out her pans, bowls and ingredients. She slipped the yoke of an apron around her neck, wrapped the ties around her slender waist, and then tied them in front, covering her leggings and a lightweight, thigh-length sweater.

"You really can cook." He flashed her a delighted smile.

"You might want to wait until it's done and you taste it before coming to that conclusion," she teased as she pushed up her sleeves.

He chuckled. It was a relief not to be bombarded by her emotions and fighting his own. For the first time in days he felt like himself. "Since we're having red meat, I can open the red and pour you a glass to sip while you cook."

"That sounds nice." She retrieved a corkscrew from a drawer and handed it to him, then set two wine glasses on the counter.

"Do you like cucumbers?" she asked. "I was going to add them to the salad."

"I haven't met a vegetable I didn't like," Drew answered. He fitted the corkscrew into place and popped free the cork.

"Me, either. But I thought most men were all about meat."

"I haven't met a steak I didn't like, either." He poured them both a glass of wine and set hers close at hand.

He pulled up one of the two bar stools. "Can I do something to help?"

She was busy slicing a cucumber on a chopping board and didn't realize he'd spoken. He took the opportunity to observe her.

This was the woman he would care for and desire for the rest of his life. Yes, there were preternatural forces at work, but he had chosen her that first night at the club, when he'd tried to stop her from leaving. He'd looked for her for days. As choices went, he couldn't have done better.

She sliced two tomatoes then, lifted the cutting board to slide the vegetables into a freshly torn lettuce and spinach blend. She grated carrots, dropped in some pitted Kalamata olives, tossed the salad with a spoon and fork, then added crumbled feta cheese. She expertly drizzled a cooked dressing over the top and stored the salad in the refrigerator.

When she moved to the meat marinating in a glass dish she looked up.

"Does being deaf really intensify your other senses?" he asked.

"I know I'm a little more sensitive to smells than some of my hearing friends. But I can't tell if it's because I'm deaf or my Mer qualities have something to do with it. If being deaf does cause the difference, it may be because without sound to distract me I concentrate more on scent, taste, and vision to maneuver through life."

That made sense. "Do you need any help?"

"No, thanks." She started slipping cubes of meat onto wooden skewers between cherry tomatoes, pearl onions, zucchini, and green peppers.

"You do realize you're fixing enough for an army."

"Yes. I promised Cheryl I'd bring her some for lunch tomorrow."

"She's a close friend?"

"Yes, closer than any other friend I've ever had. She's sensed some things about us both, but doesn't realize it goes more deeply than she understands. She says we're both elemental."

"Elemental?"

"Earth, Air, Fire, Water. It seems I'm more water and you're more fire."

"Well, she's got part of it right." There was certainly enough sexual fire between them.

"You seem more relaxed today."

As opposed to last night when he'd been exhausted from the throes of sexual deprivation and emotional overload? "I am. I hung out with my father for a while this morning, took a nap, and practiced with the band. And now I'm eating dinner with you. We could go for a walk on the beach afterward since it's my night off." Until he learned more about what they had in common, he chose the one thing he knew they shared.

"That sounds lovely." She placed the skewers on a rectangular cookie sheet, checked the oven, and slid the pan in. She poured orzo into a boiling pot of liquid, took out a lemon and began grating the peel with a file-like grater, releasing the tart scent.

"What's in the pot?" he asked.

"Chicken stock, onions, garlic, a few spices, and I'm going to sprinkle in the lemon peel while it cooks.

"You really do cook." There was an intimacy to sharing this process with her he'd never recognized before. He could envision them spending moments like this every night while they shared their day and unwound.

She laughed. "It's something I can excel at. But I can't grill. I don't have a deck or balcony to grill on."

"I do. Any time you want to grill, you can come over to my apartment and we'll do it together."

Her look settled on his face in a way that shot blood south and made his temperature rise. He shifted his focus to food and introduced a conversation about what they both liked to eat. Her favorite was chicken, while his was steak.

"We'd have both missed out on our favorites if we'd stayed offshore."

Katrina periodically checked the kabobs, drizzling the marinade over them while they cooked.

He was learning how to wait until her attention could be directed at him so they could communicate.

"Will you teach me how to sign?" he asked.

"What is it you want to learn to say?" She leaned back against the counter and sipped her wine.

"All the important things."

"So you can learn how to pick up deaf chicks like me?" Katrina laughed.

Drew cocked a brow. "Your place or mine?"

She shook her head.

"Believe it or not, I've never used any kind of line to pick up a lady." And more times than not he hadn't had to use his Siren wiles either.

She studied him for a moment. "I believe that. All you have to do is smile."

He did just that, and laughed when she blushed and then shifted her attention to the counter timer she'd set. She removed the kabobs from the stove and turned off the pasta.

"I didn't have time to fix fresh flat bread, but I bought some from a bakery close by. I'll get the tzatziki sauce and the salad while you pour us more wine."

She placed the bread, salad, and sauce on the table and removed her apron. Then they served themselves from the stove. Because he just had to touch her, Drew purposely brushed his hand against the small of her back while she spooned the rice-like pasta onto his plate. Though she never looked up, her scent rose to blend with the spices she'd used in the food and she shifted closer.

They sat at her small, round table. She asked about each member of his band.

"Simon is the old man of the group. He and I met in college. He'd been discharged from the Marines a couple of months before, and he'd joined up right after high school. He's probably the most musically talented person I've ever met. He can play multiple instruments, but he can really make an electric guitar sing. He's married and they're expecting their first child."

He chewed a small cube of the deliciously marinated meat. "Tony, our base player, is from a large Italian family. He was the first in his family to go to college. Most of his siblings and cousins have gone into vocational things. When he went into music, his parents were a little upset. They were looking forward to having a doctor or lawyer in the family. They're a little more accepting now he's signed a recording contract."

He paused for a moment, noticing the color and variety

of the table setting with mismatched colored bowls and plates. The artistic flare she brought to the food and the table triggered his smile.

"Rand is the only one of us who didn't go to college. He's come up hard. His father abandoned him and his mother when she was six months pregnant, and he's never come back into the picture. His mom raised him alone, but she's had some issues and been in and out of rehab."

"Is that why he has such an attitude?" she asked.

"Some of it. Sometimes I feel he's behaving the way people expect him to. He's a naturally gifted musician and songwriter, but he somehow always ends up going off track. Right now he's on the straight and narrow. If the three of us can keep him moving in the right direction, maybe we won't have to shit-can him. He'd be hard to replace." Drew was surprised how much regret he felt at the idea of losing Rand. He was a pain in the ass, a rabble-rouser, and an aggravation, but he could be funny when the mood struck him, and he was a demon on his drums.

Katrina's voice broke into his thoughts. "You can't be responsible for anyone but yourself. If he wants what the four of you have earned badly enough, he'll keep it together."

"I hope you're right."

She urged him on with, "And then there's you."

"Yeah." How much could he share with her?

"Where and when was your first performance as a musician?"

"High school. Three other guys and I threw together a band a month before an annual talent show. We were all closet musicians but had never played in public." He grimaced. "It was pretty ugly."

She laughed. "And when did you discover you could affect women with your voice?"

"That same night. My father had tried to warn me. I didn't realize what he meant until after the show. For days afterward girls followed me around the school like groupies." What he'd first thought was cool, ended up being—he shook his head—like being stalked.

"Isn't that what's happening again, Drew?" Her expression was so earnest.

He considered her words for a moment while he finished his last bite of beef and green pepper. He took a sip of wine to wash it down. "I don't know. But I couldn't hold the other guys back by refusing to sign the contract. There's a balance of talent between us that makes our music popular. It isn't all just about my voice."

Though he sensed she wanted to say more, instead she asked, "Would you like coffee with dessert?"

"I thought we might go for that walk first, then eat dessert later."

"Okay." She leaned back in her seat. "How powerful is your voice?"

He hesitated, reluctant to tell her.

She leaned forward and rested her elbows on the table. "I saw the way you worked the crowd at the club. How you built them to a fever pitch, then gave them what they craved, then eased them back down. How are you going to reproduce that digitally?"

Defensive because of her questions, he felt his anger

begin to build.

She continued. "Theoretically you could addict someone to that sexual high you create. When you sing, it's like you're having sex with every woman who hears you."

Why was she suddenly using this to push him away? He was tempted to drop the mental wall he'd built between them to get a better read on her, but the idea of being out of control again dissuaded him.

He had begun to bond with this woman. If she broke it off now and set him adrift…

Drew leaned forward and placed his hand over hers. "Don't do this, Katrina."

Chapter 16

Drew's his eyes had darkened with anger, and his masculine features were harsh with a scowl. Any human would have found him intimidating, but Katrina felt no fear. The pressure of his hand on hers wasn't heavy, and he wasn't trying to use any Mer abilities to calm her.

"I can't let my band down. I have to follow through with the contract."

"But you don't have to do your special magic on the recording."

He hesitated. "The recording company will expect a certain bang for their buck. They've seen what we do live."

"If you're using your special abilities to win over fans, it's cheating, Drew."

A muscle worked in his jaw. She could tell he knew what she was talking about. And the core of the issue for her was the fact that if they became involved, she couldn't bear the thought of him being unfaithful to her. Using his voice to seduce hundreds of women each night qualified. And if he had enflamed fans throwing themselves at him each night, he'd stray. Even bonding might not be strong enough to curb his need to seduce and possess. It was in his DNA.

But she couldn't push him away, either. To end things right now would be for the best. But she couldn't bring herself to do it. She'd been in a state of high anxiety all day, thinking he might not show up for dinner. Her heart had leapt at the sight of him. How would she feel if he walked away right now and they never met again?

How had things gotten so out of control so quickly?

She looked down at the table and brushed her fingertips over her forehead.

Drew cupped her chin and raised her face to his. His expression was serious, his gaze direct. "I haven't figured it out yet. But I'm trying to make some changes with the band, so we can focus more on the music and less on the women. It started out as a gimmick and now it's gotten out of control."

She hoped he was telling her the truth.

Katrina rose to clear the table and Drew did the same. He helped her put the food away while she made quick work of the dishes by way of the dishwasher.

She'd continue to urge Drew to quit using his Siren wiles on the women at the club. She wouldn't go back to the club to watch him perform until he did.

"I'll get a sweater. The breeze is always cool off the ocean." It was odd that living as a human she often felt chilled, but in the water as a Mermaid she rarely felt uncomfortable. She slipped into her bedroom to get the wrap and her small shoulder bag.

"My parents have an indoor pool at their house we

could use if you ever want to swim," Drew said as they left the apartment. "They put it in when I was young so we'd have privacy.

She didn't know if she was ready for him to see her transform. "I have difficulties in the water, especially in strong currents."

He frowned. "Who took you out into the ocean?"

He had shared so much about himself, she decided to be as candid. "I met a man when I first came here. He was Mer. Older. An artist. We had a relationship. He taught me about what it was to be Mer. I knew nothing about it since the only people I'd been around were humans. Those few who recognized there was something different about me encouraged me to ignore it or suppress it. But Mitchell took me out to sea. He had established ties with the Shoals and had passed the word I was looking for my father. Otherwise, I'd have probably never found him."

The pain of that time had finally faded, but only because her need to survive had pushed her to move on. But the scars were still there. "About a month after we returned, I caught the artist in bed with another woman, a human female, and we broke up."

What was wrong with her, that the men she chose couldn't remain faithful? They entered the elevator and she dared to look at Drew's face.

"I'm sorry, Katrina. He was a damn fool."

"Thanks. It was probably a good thing. We never bonded."

"Most who bond are faithful, Katrina. My father and mother have never strayed, and they've been together forty years."

"I'd like to think that could happen for us." The wistfulness in her expression offered him a ray of hope.

Drew nodded. They were both being so careful, one of the things he hadn't wanted. "I'd want that as well."

When she leaned into him, he grinned, and his arm tightened around her waist. It felt wonderful being close, the feel of his body against hers, his smell. She rested her head against his chest for a moment, then the elevator door opened. She straightened to walk through the lobby and out of the building.

They parked close to the Bahai Hotel and walked to the beach. At eight o'clock the light had a dim quality as the sun clung to the watery horizon. The breeze off the water was nippy, but wasn't as fierce as it could be. The scent of the sea, briny and fresh, was like an enticing perfume.

They walked down to the sand, kicked out of their shoes, and left them on one of the rocks used to shore up the sidewalk above. Drew caught her hand. Katrina was struck by the sheer normality of his actions. And for a moment she allowed herself to think of them as a couple, working toward more intimacies. She smiled.

He squeezed her hand to get her attention. "How often do you come down here?"

"Never." It was too much of a temptation.

"Why?"

"If you come with friends, they always pester you to swim. And in my case, if I came alone and went in, I might get into difficulties."

"Is the pull so strong?"

He would understand how seductive the water could be for their kind. "Sometimes."

He nodded. "I took out my father's boat yesterday and spent several hours underwater with a mike, recording sea sounds. That's how I made you the file."

"How did you keep from being seen?" She'd transformed so few times, her control to reverse it was tentative.

"I usually have better control of things than I've had the last couple of days when I'm around you."

"So, you've finally figured out how to control it around me?"

"Some. But I haven't figured out how not to want you every moment we're together."

Her mouth grew cotton dry at his expression. Just looking at him triggered a tingling heat between her legs and a surge in her heartbeat. She hoped the breeze carried away her scent so it wouldn't make things more difficult. "Me either. I thought you might not want to see me again after what happened last night."

"Whether I had a handle on this or not, I'd have been on your doorstep."

She slipped her arm through his. "We'd better keep walking before we get lost again."

She felt the movement of his chest when he laughed. The taut spiral of anxiety inside her unwound…and just as quickly began to build again. She was silent so much, because she lived in silence. The dusky light made it difficult to read his lips, though she continued to glance up at him.

Drew covered her hand on his arm and stopped. "Relax. I'm good. We don't have to talk. I'm content to just be here with you."

Touched by his understanding, Katrina blinked against the tears that threatened. She tilted her head against his shoulder, and when she pulled back he brushed the back of his fingers along her cheek, leaving behind a trail of heat.

Graham wove his Mercedes through traffic, following the car in front of him west toward the beach. He was giving into a compulsion that could ultimately get him into more trouble than he'd ever known. He'd parked outside of Katrina's apartment for an hour and sat in the car. Good thing the security pad outside the entrance had stopped him from entering.

He could not visit a patient at her apartment. He couldn't go out with one or have a relationship with one. He wasn't even sure it was what he wanted. He was compelled by something he couldn't understand to try to get closer to her. It went beyond his curiosity about her physical issues. It was that sense of familiarity that was driving him mad.

And now he was following the car she'd gotten into with a man. The way their hands clung, the way they reached for one another, it was plain they were a couple. Even if he wanted to establish some kind of relationship with her, he'd have to challenge the other man. The guy looked like he could hold his own in a fight, and that he probably knew how. Graham had never been in an actual fight in his life. Because of his work, he'd be worried about his hands the whole time he threw punches.

So what the hell was he doing here?

The car ahead turned down a side street toward one of the beachside hotels. They parked on one of the side streets. Graham pulled further up the street and found a spot. He twisted around in his seat, but couldn't see, then used his rear side view mirror to catch a glimpse of what they were doing. The man got out of the car and went around to open Katrina's door. The two clasped hands as they walked across the street. They weren't going into the hotel. They were headed down the public sidewalk to the beach. So they were going for a stroll.

The urge to follow her was strong. He wanted to talk to her, ask her things, but he couldn't formulate what it was he needed to say.

He wanted her to tell him why her smell triggered a shadow of a memory that hung beyond his grasp. Of course she couldn't, because she didn't know him. Knew nothing about him beyond his being the doctor who was going to do her surgery.

Dear God, he was going insane. He had to stop this. Now.

He twisted in his seat, looked behind him and pulled out.

He had to put Katrina Larson out of his mind and forget about this nonsense.

The night was clear, but there were few people on the beach. Katrina dragged her toes through the sand and felt the pulse of the water's movement as it ebbed and rolled back over the sand. She savored the sea's scent and Drew's. Her body seemed to absorb the sweet, moisture-laden air and her skin tingled and warmed.

Had she been able to hear the sea, she wouldn't have been able to fight the urge to immerse herself. She drew several deep breaths and pushed away the desire.

For an hour they strolled close enough to the water to feel the fine, misty spray kicked up and carried by the wind. Sharing it with Drew helped her keep things together. At one point, Drew tugged off the loose scrunchie holding her hair back, and the long strands whipped around in the breeze until she bundled them over one shoulder. It had been so long since she'd allowed herself a treat like this. She reveled in just being here, being with him.

On their way back to the car, Drew caught her about the waist, dragged her close, and folded his windbreaker around her. Katrina threw her head back to smile up at him as she waited for his kiss, a kiss she'd been primed for all evening. But it didn't come.

The light from the row of streetlights along the sidewalk above them outlined his profile but left his face in shadow. He caught her hand and held it out so the light captured it. A mother of pearl sheen gleamed from her palm. He turned it against his chest as two couples walked by and she averted her face.

When they had passed she asked, "Is it really noticeable?"

He nodded.

Why hadn't he told her? Because she couldn't have heard him if he'd tried. She bit back a groan of frustration.

They reached the rocks where they'd left their shoes and paused to put them on. The slip-on tennis shoes she'd worn no longer fit. She hadn't felt the partial transition of her feet as it happened because it had been so gradual, but they'd definitely spread and grown wider, her toes longer. They didn't look like flippers yet but were still strangely deformed.

Drew touched her shoulder. "Need a ride?"

She barely made out his words beneath the glow of the streetlight. "I can walk barefoot."

He scooped her up and strode up the sloped sidewalk leading to the parking lot.

"You should have told me," she murmured close to his ear.

"You were having such a good time, I didn't want to spoil it for you. And no one else saw you."

He sat her down next to the car and reached in his jeans pocket to retrieve the car keys. He pushed the button unlocking the doors and opened hers.

Katrina slid inside, and he hustled around the front of the car and got in. When the interior lights came on, she jerked in panic. "Someone will see, Drew."

"I have to look at you." His gray-blue eyes trailed over her features one by one.

Katrina was familiar with the exaggeration of her facial construction that took place when she changed. It wasn't as angular as Drew's, but was as though Mother Nature wanted each feature defined to be better observed under water. The mother of pearl glow of her transformed skin was both a reflective help in dark water and protection from the elements.

Drew's eyes darkened and he glanced away for a moment, as if to steady himself. "You look unbearably beautiful. Just looking at you—I have to fight my own change."

The ache of need that rose within her was like nothing she had ever felt before. "Turn out the light, Drew," she managed around a throat so clogged by emotion it was hard to speak.

He twisted the control plunging them into protective darkness. They reached for each other.

Chapter 17

Finesse was forgotten in his ferocious need to taste her, touch her. He sealed his mouth over hers, and her lips parted, inviting the thrust of his tongue. The kiss went on and on until both of them had to either come up for air or smother.

As soon as they separated, she worked at the buttons of his shirt and skimmed her hand inside to caress his chest. Her touch was such pure heaven he groaned.

With the console between them, he couldn't get close enough. He ran a questing hand up the inside of her thigh, along the slick fabric of her leggings, following the shape of her leg to the apex. Katrina grasped his wrist, not to restrain him, but to guide his touch further up, and she rocked against it.

He couldn't make love to her in the front seat of the car on a busy street. They had to return to her apartment. He eased his hand away and reached for the ignition.

How he got them back to her apartment he didn't know. Her feelings had crashed through his mental door and ripped it from its hinges. His brain was swamped by her needs and his own.

The two of them bailed out of the car as though it was about to explode and came together to loop their arms around each other.

It was Drew who keyed in the security code and opened the door. Another couple entered the elevator ahead of them, so Katrina tugged him toward the stairwell. Three flights was nothing when he was looking forward to getting naked and making love with Katrina. Her fingers laced with his as they climbed the stairs, pushed through the door leading onto her floor, and rushed out into the hallway.

Her hands were trembling when she tried to put her key into the lock. He took it from her and opened the door, urgency affecting his own coordination. She swung through and tossed her purse in a chair and shook free of her sweater.

He had to get a handle on closing the mental door between them or he'd not be any good for either of them If he so much as kissed her right now, he'd embarrass himself. He drew slow, deep breaths to try and calm down enough to close it.

Katrina was barely aware of anything but the heavy beat of her heart. With every step Drew took toward her, her body grew ever more ready for him. A heated wetness built between her legs, and they shook, so much she leaned back against the wall to steady herself. She had never felt such a bombardment of need, such passion.

Drew moved in close, aligning his body with hers, yet

leaving a wisp of space between them. The heat he projected flowed over her skin in a caressing wave. His strange tri-colored eyes settled on her face, aglow with a light that kicked her pulse into a gallop. The partial transformation he'd been fighting all evening rolled over him, bringing with it a wave of cinnamon and the sea. She inhaled it as she cupped his face and traced the bones with her fingertips.

A tingling anticipation raced over her skin. When he kissed her, she forgot about anything but the taste and feel of his lips on hers. She strained closer to him, sliding her arms around his neck and urging him closer. A soft hum vibrated beneath the kiss, and even though she heard no sound, the sensation made her shiver.

He braced an arm against the wall at the same time he pressed his lower body against her, letting her feel the pressure of his arousal against her stomach. She parted her legs, aching to take him in.

His lips left hers to find her cheek, her jaw, then the sensitive area beneath her ear. The height difference between them seemed problematic until he cupped the cheeks of her butt and lifted her. Her shoes dropped to the floor as she wrapped her legs around his waist. That promising bulge beneath his slacks prodded her in just the right intimate place. Unable to control her response, she rolled her hips against him and felt his answering pressure.

"Drew?" She shivered as anticipation washing through her system.

The aggressive masculinity of his features appeared both familiar and strange. His tri-toned irises had darkened, his pupils dilated. The open look of desire on his face triggered a clenching heat low in her belly. Had she ever seen that much need in a man's face?

The enormity of what they were doing struck her. Had he drawn away just now to give her time to realize she might bond with him if they made love? Or he might bond with her.

With the ache of emptiness he'd inspired begging to be filled, the reasons behind why she should let him pull away were hard to even comprehend. "Don't stop."

He said her name, and for the thousandth time she wished she could hear his voice. His lips claimed hers and the heat built between them once again, but there was tenderness there, too.

Of all the men she had dated, hearing and non-hearing alike, not one had taken such care with her. No other hearing man had ever tried to bridge the gap created by her congenital issues as Drew was doing. And now the cherishing tenderness she experienced from his touch, his kiss, set her heart to tumbling.

Before now, he'd been all about heat and sex. Something else had taken over. Something that left her trembling and hungry for more.

His hand splayed against her back, holding her in place while he carried her into the bedroom, lowered her to the bed, and lay down beside her. He gripped the hem of her sweater and dragged it up while Katrina shimmied out of it. He rested a hand between her breasts, which were still covered by a thin, lacy bra, and ran his eyes down the length of her torso. The filmy fabric cupping her flesh suddenly felt too tight and confining as her nipples peaked, but he seemed to know. He lowered the straps of her bra, releasing her breasts, and caught one nipple in his mouth, his tongue feathering it along the underside while he applied a gentle suction that sent a burst of sensation sizzling through her. She arched up in response and gripped his muscular shoulders.

She didn't realize she was holding her breath until he lifted his head and slowly lowered his mouth back to hers. His soft, deep kisses fed a need she hadn't even been aware of having. Her hands curled beneath the fabric of his shirt and ran up the long, lean length of his muscular back to hold him closer.

Drew responded by dragged the shirt over his head and tossing it aside. At the first touch of their bare skin coming together Katrina felt him gasp when she did.

The light swirls of dark hair on his chest became a tactile fascination for her as she ran her palms over it. While he unhooked her bra and tossed it aside, she leaned forward to gently nip the well-defined ridge of muscle between his neck and shoulder, then soothe it with her tongue.

Drew shuddered and ran his hands down the waistband of her leggings to cup her bottom and skimmed his hands up to drag down the stretchy fabric clinging to her body like a latex glove.

Katrina laughed as the leggings clung to her feet, though they both struggled to free them. Drew's answering grin had her reaching for him at the same moment he jerked one of her legs free.

"You're too far away and you have too many clothes

on," she smiled.

"I can take care of that."

"Let me." Her hand collided with his as she reached for his belt. He allowed her to take over, and contented himself with seeking out the sensitive areas between her neck and shoulder, and along her throat.

She shivered as chills worked down her body, even as she slipped free his belt and lowered his zipper. She ran a caressing hand over the taut muscularity of his abdomen to the waistband of his boxer briefs, teasing him, teasing herself. His muscles tightened, pulling in his stomach, urging her to slide her hand beneath.

She did, but only to peel the briefs down and free him. "Come between my thighs, Drew. I want to watch your face while I touch you."

He kicked free of his clothes and turned, bringing himself into position between her legs, but holding himself above her. His cheekbones looked sharp and angular, his jaw as well. His eyes appeared almost black, the pupils so large they came close to completely filling the iris.

She brushed her thumbs over his flat, masculine nipples. They contracted and beaded beneath her touch.

He swallowed and bent his head to kiss her, the pressure of his mouth harsh and wild on hers, so filled with passion she wondered if it was possible to orgasm from a kiss. The sweet ache of need tripped over into pain.

She caressed the sculpted width of his ribs, then brought her thumbs together and followed the narrow line that bisected his abdominal muscles to his navel, then lower. When she brushed his erection, Drew tore his mouth from hers to say her name.

She trailed the backs of her fingers down his lower abdomen to skim them through the thick patch of hair surrounding his sex.

Drew's features tightened, and his jaw muscles rippled. When she finally cupped his erection and her fingers closed around it, his eyes closed. She felt the vibration of his groan. The intimacy they were sharing, the control he gave her, only intensified her excitement. The heat and size of him did the rest.

"Come inside me, Drew."

Drew's arms shook as he lowered his hips and she guided him home. With one slow, steady thrust he seated himself to the hilt, then rocked against her.

The sensual bubble they'd been suspended in broke, and the need to reach completion overwhelmed them both. With each deep thrust, their tension spiraled higher and higher until the end came all too soon. She gasped as she climaxed and ran her hands down his back to hold him while the contractions swept through her.

Drew had never been so aroused in his life. The sweet grip of her hands, her body, threatened to throw him over the edge. When he could hold back no longer, he recaptured their rhythm, the frantic need to seek his own release taking over. Her response drove him on as they sought the same pleasure again, her scent rising to urge him on. She cried out as another orgasm swept through her, and her inner muscles tightening catapulted him into his own release. With a groan he offered himself up to it. To her.

The morning light pierced Drew's eyelids, red-gold, hazy and unbelievably bright. They lay next to each other like so much flotsam left behind by a receding tide, their limbs still entangled from their last bout of lovemaking. At some point during the night he'd turned out the lights and made sure the apartment's door was locked. At his return she had been warm and waiting for him. Now he remained still, eyes closed, absorbing how perfectly they fit together.

His heartbeat leapt into a jog as Katrina stroked his cheek, his jaw, the back of his neck, and smoothed his hair. He opened his eyes and looked into hers, probing their depths.

"Are you okay?" she asked, her gaze searching.

Was she asking if he'd bonded with her? And what could he tell her? He decided to take the question at face value. "I'm fantastic." He ran his palm down her hip, snuggling her close against his body.

"I have an appointment this morning with a psychologist. It's an introductory thing for when I get my implant."

The implant. Would it be a help or a hindrance to him, to them? "Have they scheduled the surgery?"

"It's next Wednesday."

So soon? The idea of her going under the knife scared the shit out of him. What if she had an adverse response to the anesthesia or some part of the procedure? Would his father have any ideas about what her Mer physiology might react to negatively? "I'd like to be there for the surgery."

Her brows rose. "Would you?"

"Of course." She belonged to him now. She just hadn't realized it yet. He smoothed back a strand of butter-streaked hair from her cheek.

She smiled. "Yes, I'd like you to be there."

"I have to meet the band early this morning. The club doesn't open until nine, and we usually use this time to practice. Would you like to meet for a meal after work, or you could come over to my apartment and we can throw on some steaks."

"Either sounds good. I'd like to see where you live."

"It's an apartment. And come to think of it, a wreck at the moment." He grimaced. He had music all over his living space. He'd have to spend some time sorting and organizing. Laundry that needed done...dishes. Now that he thought about it the list could go on and on.

She laughed. "I won't be there to see your apartment. I'll be there to see you."

"Good thing." He leaned forward and kissed her softly. "With you working days and me nights, we'll have to grab every free moment to see one another."

She brushed her fingertips over his forearm. "Is that truly what you want? It isn't just the sex talking?"

Surprised by her directness, he studied her expression. "It isn't just the sex. Although that *was* off-the-charts mind-blowing."

Blood rushed to his cock. It pushed against her stomach and she raised a brow.

"It's a guy thing. If you talk about it, then you think about it, and then it happens."

Katrina laughed. "I have an appointment at eight-thirty.

I don't have time."

"We could shower together and enjoy two things at once."

Her blush was answer enough. "I don't like the water too hot."

"Our chemistry is volcanic enough." He kissed her cheek, threw back the covers and went into the bathroom to turn on the shower. Once he had the water running, he peered around the bathroom door. She was still in bed, the sheet modestly tucked up over her breasts. Her hair hung across one shoulder in a wavy mass, streaked with every color of blonde from silver to burnt sugar. It was ironic. He was a member of two of the most seductive species on earth, and Katrina had seduced him more thoroughly with her touch, her scent, her laugh, her body, than he'd seduced any woman with his voice.

He strode to the bed and held out a gentlemanly hand. "Your shower awaits, milady."

She placed her hand in his and rose from the tangled sheets like Botticelli's Venus. He kept his focus on her face, though her breasts, so generously proportioned, dragged at his attention. The brush of her look as it ran up his naked body had an even more stimulating effect.

He guided her into the bathroom and shoved the shower curtain back, stepped over the edge of the tub and drew her in with him.

"It isn't just the sex, Katrina." He said again as the water washed over his shoulder and torso. He proceeded to show her.

Chapter 18

Katrina studied the dark brown brick two-story house that housed Dr. Joseph Powell's office. A modest sign hung next to one of the concrete supports jutting out beside the front steps, the block print announcing his name and the abbreviations for the two degrees he held. A Psy.D. and a Ph.D. in Clinical Psychology. She had studied his credentials and history online and knew he did both counseling and clinical work.

Would he be arrogant like his son? Based on his website photo, he looked nothing like him. Maybe that was a good omen.

She climbed the steps to a wide, wood plank front porch which was framed in with the same brick as the house. An antique front door with leaded glass beckoned. She peeked through the blinds, but the leaded glass panels in the door distorted the room beyond.

She turned the knob, pushed the door open, and stepped into a room with twelve-foot high ceilings and triple-layered crown molding. A Duncan Phyfe couch upholstered in a blue stripe was framed at both ends by cherry wood tables and brass lamps. Wingback chairs, divided by a cherry cabinet, faced the couch from the opposite wall, a fireplace sat at the end of the room closest to the furniture grouping, and at the other, behind a Queen Ann table she used as a desk, sat the receptionist.

Despite her presence, the room had the feel of a well-cared-for home rather than an office. Katrina couldn't picture Graham Powell growing up in such an environment. She envisioned him surrounded by expensively upholstered furniture in slick fabrics, with tables made of chrome and glass.

"May I help you?" the woman asked with a kind smile.

Katrina stepped forward. "I have an appointment with Dr. Powell at two o'clock."

"You must be Katrina. Dr. Powell will be with you in a few minutes. If you could fill out these forms for us, we'd appreciate it." The receptionist was very good at sign.

"Thank you." Katrina sat down on the couch and looked at the documents before quickly filling them out and returning them to the receptionist's desk.

With nothing better to do but worry herself into nervousness, she turned her thoughts to Drew and the shower. Heat flooded her face. She hadn't been bathed since she was three. After she'd healed from the accident, she refused to let anyone touch her while in the tub. The nuns had been happy to allow her to wash herself. She hadn't wanted anyone's hands on her, for any reason, for a long, long time. If she'd had any lingering phobia about that, Drew had certainly cured her of it. The way he bathed her with his hands, kissed her, made love to her as though he were both caring for her and seducing her at the same time… Her heart rate skyrocketed.

There was something inherently wrong about sitting in the psychologist's office and fantasizing about her lover in great detail. She needed to get her mind off Drew.

She turned her attention to the couch she sat on and ran a finger over the wooden edging that followed the outward arch of its sides. It was a beautiful piece. One she could appreciate, though it wasn't her style. But then she'd only been able to afford modern American yard sale or thrift shop. Her budget had never stretched any further.

A man appeared from down a wide hall leading from the back of the house. His sable brown hair and even features were arresting. His pale green eyes settled on her and he smiled. He signed hello.

Katrina returned the salutation.

"If you'll follow me, we'll go back to my office and talk."

She rose to her feet and walked toward him. His scent reached her, and she paused, surprise shuddering through her. Dr. Joseph Powell wasn't human.

At the same time she experienced the realization and was studying him, he was taking a second look at her as well.

"It's okay. We'll talk in my office." He spoke and signed at the same time.

Wariness crept in as she followed him down the hallway to a door on the right. He turned to face her, then stepped back to allow her to enter the room. He closed the door and motioned her to a seat.

"Your son is adopted?" Katrina asked as soon as he was settled in a chair behind the desk.

"Yes."

"He doesn't know." There was no way Graham Powell knew about his parents.

"About the adoption or me?"

"Either."

He hesitated. "No."

She couldn't decide if that was good or not. "You know why I'm here?"

"Yes. Graham asked me to be your counselor during your transition from deaf to hearing. In fact, he spoke to me about you earlier, after he had done the initial workup. He didn't mention your name, but I asked if he would refer you to me." He hesitated again. "I recognized some things from what he told me."

She didn't know how she felt about having her doctor discuss her with his father, even if they both were doctors. "Have you seen many people like me?"

"A few." He leaned forward to fold his arms atop the desk.

"Because they wanted a cochlear implant?"

"No. I ran across them by chance."

Katrina nodded. "Your son is a good doctor?"

"Yes. And very dedicated. Graham would cure deafness in every instance if he could."

"Because he's angry you're deaf, or because he truly wants people to hear?" His motivations behind what he did would either set her reservations to rest or convince her she needed to call the whole thing off.

He frowned. "Probably a little of both." He cocked his head. "I'm surprised you picked up on the anger."

"There was a hint of impatience in his expression when he told me both his parents were deaf and had rejected having an implant."

"He continues to urge us to get them. Neither his mother nor I are close enough to human to pass during the testing that's required. Our physiology is too different."

"It seems mine is different enough to pique his interest. He pushed me to have further testing."

"He would. He's extremely curious."

"He breached my confidentiality when he spoke to you about me." Would he do so again if he discovered something more?

"He was leading up to asking me to see you when he mentioned you. He's spent a great deal of time building his practice. He wouldn't do anything to damage his reputation or break his oath as a doctor."

But Graham Powell seemed more protective of *his* interests than his patients'. So much so it had turned her off him as soon as he examined her. "Why did you want to see me?"

"Because you're special, and I want to help you if I can."

She studied his expression. This was the preternatural being who'd raised her doctor, but seemed nothing like him. Was it a mirage or the truth? And what was he? She hadn't figured it out yet.

"How can you help me?"

"For one, I can ask all the questions a regular counselor

would ask and turn my evaluation in to Graham."

"I've already been through an evaluation. They wouldn't have scheduled the surgery if they thought I wasn't prepared for it."

He shifted things on his desk and picked up a sheet of paper before him. "You and I both know because you're special their evaluation might not cover everything. Why do you want the implant?"

"I want to be competitive in my job and able to deal with clients. I want to be able to open my own graphic design business one day, and I can't do it if I can't deal with the public. I'm tired of everything being such a constant struggle. And the most important, I want to be able to hear my boyfriend when he talks to me."

"Is he hearing?"

"Yes. He's a singer in a band." She wasn't going to share anything else about Drew. The Powell family already knew too much about her as it was.

Joseph frowned. "Are you really doing this for yourself or for him?"

"I was already deep into the process before I ever met Drew."

He nodded. For half an hour Joseph eased her into a conversation about her early life and the extensive speech training she'd received to be able to function in the hearing world. He spent several more minutes on the implant and what she hoped the outcome would be.

"You realize you won't ever hear like a normal hearing person."

"Yes. But I'll be able to follow a conversation and not

feel so isolated because I miss too much to catch up."

"*If* it works." He encircled the word with a finger as if to emphasize it.

She bit her lip. "I know it might not."

"You'll need to prepare yourself for that possibility. You've pinned a great many hopes on this device."

If the implant failed to work, never being able to hear Drew say *I love you* was going to be the greatest tragedy of her life. The only thing worse would be if he never said it at all. She swallowed against the tightness that banded her throat. "I know." She looked away. "I won't have any choice but to live with it if it doesn't."

"Whether it does or it doesn't, I'll be here for you to help you work through it. My wife and I will be leaving for about four weeks, the same time it will take you to recover from surgery. I'll be back in time to support you when you get your external transmitter."

"Okay."

Joseph rose and walked around his desk, signaling an end to their meeting. He reached for a business card and wrote a number on the back. "I've written my cell phone number on this. We'll be in Scotland, but any texts you send will be forwarded to the phone I'll be using there. If you have any problems at all, don't hesitate to contact me."

"Do you normally do this much for your patients?" Katrina asked.

"No. My other patients will be seeing someone else. In your case, I am best equipped deal with any special circumstances that arise."

"Okay."

"When is your surgery scheduled?"

"Next Wednesday." Just saying the date triggered jittery nerves in her stomach.

"Graham will be doing the surgery without knowing some very important facts. You don't really know what could happen. Should you experience any adverse effects, please do call me. I know someone who might be able to help."

Katrina looked back down at the again, then glanced back up. "Why are you going out of your way for me?"

"I don't know of any Mer who's had a cochlear implant. You'll be the first. If you can tolerate the surgery, and if it works, there may be others who'll want to try."

"Do you know how many more of us there are?"

His features settled into lines of sorrow. "Too few, Katrina. We're both members of dying races."

She inhaled in his scent, tasting it, and caught a more mammal-like. Selkie. Graham had mentioned his parents were both deaf. So they might both be Selkies.

Living in secrecy underwater, and on land, made it very difficult to perpetuate either of their species. It was made worse by the ridiculous snobbery that kept those of mixed descent from being accepted. Eventually the gene pool would shrink, driving those underwater onto land in search of a mate. It had already begun to happen. Soon their race would be diluted until they and their culture would lapse into the myth humans thought they were. Maybe that was the way it should be.

Which was an easy thing for her to think and believe. She'd been lucky enough to meet Drew. Now if only he could love her.

Graham pulled into his normal parking slot next to the house. This was insane. He'd never pursued a patient before. Legally he couldn't approach her, but he couldn't stay away. Knowing she was going to be here with his father, he'd been unable to resist the opportunity to see her.

Only he would know his hidden motive for seeking her out. This was, after all, his father's house, his office. He had every right to be here. The chance meeting wouldn't seem contrived. Though it was. He'd pump his father for information about her while inviting him and his mother to dinner at his apartment. A dinner to spend time with them before their trip wouldn't seem out of the ordinary. He'd kill two birds with one stone. He'd see Katrina and satisfy his parents' need for contact with their only son and his need to see them.

Since this fixation with Katrina had begun, he'd more than once started to call his father, even come by to see him, to be reassured he wasn't losing touch with reality. The need to tell his father about this seemed a double-edged scalpel. Graham was an established doctor, wealthy, confident, and he couldn't risk losing control. He saw his patients, he performed surgeries. One hint of a mental illness would end his career in a heartbeat.

The dreams he was experiencing were frightening and graphic. He'd climb his way out of them in a panic, choking and out of breath, but when he tried to remember what they were about, he couldn't seem to grasp it. He rubbed the heels of his hands over his eyes. They burned from lack of sleep.

He'd expected Katrina's appointment to last at least an hour, and his father was a stickler for starting and finishing his appointments on time.

He exited the car, took his time wandering up the sidewalk to the front door, and smiled with satisfaction as Katrina came out of the house.

He pasted on his most charming smile as he reached her. "Hello, Ms. Larson." He didn't bother signing since he'd noticed she spent more time reading lips than she did watching him sign.

She looked startled. "Hello, Dr. Powell."

"I've just stopped by to see my parents a moment. Everything okay?"

The tension in her expression relaxed and she smiled. "Yes, everything's fine."

"Good. Are you getting excited about the surgery?"

Uncertainty flickered across her face. "I'll be relieved once it's over."

"That's understandable. Once it's behind you, the implant will open up the world a little more for you."

"I'm sure it will."

He glanced up at the façade of the house to see if his father's receptionist was about to leave. "How did you and my father get along?" he asked.

"Oh, very well." A small smile peeked out at him. The first one she'd given him.

"I knew you would." His father was openly approachable and seemed to have a natural rapport with his patients.

Why wasn't he more like his father? Why was this back and forth with her such a struggle for him? He'd never experienced this awkwardness with a woman before. "He'll want you to continue to check in with him after the surgery so he can keep tabs on your progress. He takes a lot of interest in his patients."

"I won't mind doing that."

"Good." He offered his hand, and after a minute pause she clasped it. "I'll see you at the hospital next Wednesday. Don't forget your labs on Tuesday."

"I won't."

He continued to hold her hand for a moment longer. "Would you mind very much if I asked you a personal question?"

The wariness was back full force, and he growled an inward sigh.

"What is it?"

"What perfume do you wear? I noticed it the first time we met, and I've been trying to place it ever since."

Katrina's brows contracted. "I don't wear perfume." Her expression cleared. "But it may be a combination of my soap and shampoo." She mentioned a body wash and shampoo made by the same company.

"Thank you for telling me. I thought it might be a specific scent my mother might like. They're leaving for a trip soon, and I'm looking for a bon voyage gift for her."

"Oh." She smiled, and for once it wasn't a polite distancing expression, but one directed at him with some warmth. "That's nice. I'm sorry I can't be of more help."

He released her hand with some reluctance. "That's

okay. I'll think of something else to get her. See you soon."

"Goodbye, Dr. Powell."

He watched her walk down the sidewalk and around the house to the parking area.

Sherry, his father's receptionist, had her purse in hand and was ready to leave when he entered the house. "Hello, Dr. Powell. His last patient left only a moment ago."

"Good, I swung by on the spur of the moment. If you want to go, it'll be fine."

"Thank you."

He locked the door behind her and walked back to his father's office. He pushed the button next to the door that would trigger a flashing light over his father's office door, waited a moment, and pushed it open.

Joseph was behind his desk writing notes. Was he writing about his session with Katrina or another patient?

"Graham!" he rose to his feet. His hands flew as he signed. "You just missed Ms. Larson."

Graham signed back. "I passed her outside. How did it go?"

"Very well. She's a bright young lady. She should do well with the implant."

"I thought so too. Did you like her?" Graham asked.

"Yes. She's beautiful and articulate despite her hearing issue. Sherry said she could barely tell from her speaking voice that she was deaf."

"She's had a great deal of speech therapy and put in a lot of effort." He hesitated. "Did she seem familiar to you in any way?"

Joseph paused a moment, apparently giving it some

thought. "No, I've never met her."

"There's something about her that seems familiar to me. She doesn't wear perfume but..." This was stupid.

His father eyed him. "Some people have a natural essence. And perfume works with a woman's body chemistry to make the fragrance individual to the wearer. Perhaps it works the same with the soap she uses."

"Maybe. But I know I've smelled it before." It was right there on the edge of his memory elusive and taunting.

"What brings you by?" his father asked.

Graham dragged his thoughts back from the edge. "I wanted to invite you and Mother over for dinner tomorrow night. I haven't used my grill in a while, and I thought I'd put some salmon on and roast potatoes and asparagus."

"Your mom's favorite meal."

"I can throw on a steak for you."

Joseph shook his head. "No need, the fish will be fine. We'd love to come. What time would you like us?"

"Seven. Will that be early enough?"

"Perfect."

As he watched his father sign, Graham wondered if he ever got exhausted with the process of using his hands to communicate.

"We enjoyed our dinner and stay at the Grant. It was a lovely anniversary gift."

"Good. I'm glad. I knew Mother would enjoy the history and décor of the place."

"Yes, she did. She's very excited about the trip to Scotland. Sherry will be coming by to check on the house while we're gone.

"I can come by some, too."

"Thank you. Whenever it's convenient."

"You've never said how it was you managed to emigrate from Scotland. Was it more difficult because of your hearing issues?"

"Some, but we developed a network of friends in the deaf community, and I'd come to America for graduate school, as had your mother. After we finished our education, we applied for citizenship. Our professors at the college were our sponsors. You had already been born here and thus were already an American citizen."

"And you never went back." Why hadn't he thought to ask these questions before?

"No. We had no family there, and our jobs were time-consuming. So were you." Joseph grinned. "You were involved with so much each summer, and then you were in school."

"And now you've decided to go back."

"Yes. It's been nearly thirty-five years."

Graham tilted his head. "Don't you mean thirty-six?" He was thirty-five now, and had been born their first year in the U.S.

His father's expression was blank for a moment. "You're right."

Chapter 19

S weat ran down the side of his face. Drew wiped it away with the towel hanging around his neck. Since the night he'd opened the door to letting the other band members share the limelight, he'd been thinking of ways to switch things up and keep it going. But it would take a lot of work to make this equal sharing venture a success. They had to keep the quality of their music high. Make their sound as pure rock as they could.

If he was truly honest with himself, he had to admit he'd been ready to get off the merry-go-round of wild, screaming women for a while now. It was time for this change. They'd already signed a contract. They could still do some of the things they'd done to make the band popular with the ladies. But to be more than a flash in the pan, they had to be a real band and he had to be a real lead singer. In other words he had to turn his Siren off or at least tone it down.

He played a chord. "Let's take it from the bridge, guys."

"Why are you pushing us like this, man? Rand asked. "We've arrived. We've signed a contract. We're going to record our music and have cash rolling in." The drummer had shoved a sweatband around his head to keep the streaming sweat out of his eyes, but his muscular arms gleamed with it and his T-shirt clung damply.

Drew had wondered when one of the guys would ask. He'd been waiting for it to happen. It came as no surprise that Rand was the one to challenge him. It was in the man's nature to push back if he was pushed. Though all of their work demanded some stamina, Rand's demanded more physically, and Drew had been pushing him steadily for hours.

"Let's take five and talk for a few minutes," Drew suggested. He dragged his chair from behind the keyboard and set it close to Rand's drums so the drummer wouldn't have to move. Drew jumped off the stage and went around the bar to get four bottles of water.

Simon sauntered over with some folding chairs from the wings, flipped them open, and positioned them so he and Tony could sit down. They slouched into the chairs as though they were as grateful for the break as Rand.

Drew tossed a bottle to Rand and the drummer caught it, cracked it, and downed half of it. Drew handed one to Tony and Simon, then settled in his seat, twisted the cap off and took a slow drink while he wondered how to start the conversation. They had a winning ticket already, and he was about to rock the boat in a big way.

"The other night when I was running the fever, you guys were rockin' some good music. You really pulled together. We felt more like a band than we had in a while. I know when we first started, we made the decision for me to take the singing lead, but did you notice how many men wandered in during the second half of the show?"

"I noticed," Tony said. "The whole back row was filled with more couples than single women."

He could always count on Tony for support. Drew nodded. "Because of a gimmick, my gimmick, we've played to a single demographic, women, and ignored the other half of the audience. It's kept us in gigs and brought in enough money for us to support ourselves, so it's nothing to shrug off. But if we don't appeal to a wider audience—even though we've signed a contract with a record studios, they won't renew us if the sales aren't there."

He turned his attention to Rand. "So that's why I've been pushing, Rand. We need that wider audience, so we can keep the contracts coming. I don't want us to be a flash in the pan. I'd like to see us still rockin' in twenty years, like the Stones, Wings, or Aerosmith. They've lasted because they created a sound, but were able to transition in style enough to appeal to a changing audience."

"I think we can ride this first contract into more if we work hard enough," Simon said, shooting Drew a nod.

"And the gimmick you were talking about?" Rand asked.

How had Rand missed the way the women reacted to his voice? But then he was sitting behind the drums every night keeping a steady beat, and since men weren't affected—maybe he really had been oblivious to it.

Now that he'd opened this particular can of worms, where the hell was he supposed to go with it?

Simon leaned forward to rest his elbows on his knees

and laced his fingers. "Drew projects a sexual vibe with his voice, Rand. All the women love it. You've watched how they respond to him when he's singing."

Hopefully Simon only meant sexual vibe like Elvis, or other singers known for their sex appeal. But then how could any of the guys not be aware of something hinky? Had he really thought he was kidding anyone? Even Sam was wary of him these days.

Tony jumped into the silence. "And sex is a powerful thing. But we need to be able to trigger other emotions with our music to bring in the male audience."

Drew relaxed a little. "Each of you need your own solo moments during performances."

"But you're still the voice, Drew," Tony insisted. "None of us can do what you can, vibe or no vibe. Your voice is what sold the recording executives on the band."

So they were back to square one again. "But it's going to take some major backup music and songwriting to keep us in their sights, Tony. You and Rand are the ones who are strongest in that department."

Silence hung between them for a beat then two. "I've been working on some stuff," Rand volunteered, almost reluctantly. "I thought it might be too hard core for us, but if you guys are game…"

Simon's face broke out into a smile. "Nothing's off limits, Rand. Show us what you got."

Rand went to one of the drum cases offstage, returning with a thick stack of sheet music. "I'm not as good with lyrics as Tony or you Drew, so some of it doesn't have lyrics yet. And most of it needs more work."

He handed each of them a song. Drew studied the sheet music Rand had given him, scanning each line, with first caution, then excitement. He got up and went to the keyboard, spreading the sheets out across the music stand. He played through the introduction and on into the piece. Rand joined him at the keyboard, and they worked out changes he thought needed to be made as Drew fattened the chords to make the piece sound fuller.

Tony and Simon worked together on some partial lyrics that might work.

The practice turned into a brainstorming session. After an hour, Drew handed Rand the sheet music with all their notations to take home and clean up on the computer.

It was when they were stashing their instruments and turning off the electronics, Rand said, "Hey, Tony, want to go back to my place? While we're hot, we might as well try to finish this thing. I'd like a shot at helping with the lyrics."

"Sure."

The two left as the early shift of wait staff started trickling in to set up for the evening. Drew flipped off his keyboard and organized his workspace, then looked up as Simon approached him.

He didn't beat around the bush. "Something's changed for you."

"Yeah."

He smirked. "Does it have anything to do with a beautiful blonde?"

"Yeah, some." Drew looked down at the keyboard. Simon was as close a friend as he'd ever had. How had he ever hoped to hide what he was from him?

"The way you're encouraging the band to be a band, to work through ideas… Whatever influence she's having on you, it's working for you."

"So you're saying I've stopped being a controlling ass-hole, hogging the limelight?"

Simon grinned. "Yeah."

Drew laughed. He could always count on Simon to be completely honest. "I've been thinking about a change for a long time. Felt restless and dissatisfied, long before Roma and I broke up. Then I met Katrina. She can't hear what we play, can't hear me sing, but she recognized what was going on from the start. She said it was a cheating. That I needed to use the music instead of my vibe to make a living. Or words to that effect."

Simon's expression grew serious. "It's time we all started pulling our weight instead of letting you pull it for us. We can handle it."

"I'm counting on it. I'd like to move forward in the direction we're going."

"So what's it like to try to win a lady over without the extra mojo?" Simon asked.

Drew laughed and shook his head. "Tough. I'm on rocky ground most of the time. I don't know what the hell I'm doing."

"Join the club, pal. It took me six months to get Brianna to admit she loved me. I walked around terrified it would never happen, and that some other guy was going to catch her eye."

He was beginning to understand that concept himself. Until Katrina was bonded to him, she could turn to someone else and leave him yearning for her the rest of his life. He couldn't let that happen. "You've never said anything about my vibe before."

"You've never acknowledged it actually existed before, either. Are you going to tell us where it comes from? How you discovered you had it?"

Drew swallowed. "It's a genetic gift passed down from my Dad. And I discovered I had it in high school."

"And how often did you use it?" Simon pushed.

Drew ran a hand along his jaw. "After the first time? Never. I ended up with a group of stalkers. I didn't use it again until we got the band together and were really struggling. Afterward I got caught up in the hype, the money, and, yeah, the women. But for a while now…" He raked his fingers through his hair.

"It's been a burden, Simon." He'd never spoken so openly about this to anyone. "And now that I've found Katrina…"

"Yeah, I understand what you're getting at." Simon stuffed his hands in his pockets and looked away. "Brianna's never been crazy about the screaming meemies. That's what she calls the other women. She stopped coming to our shows because it made her feel…aroused."

For the first time, Drew understood what Katrina had tried to explain to him. How had Simon felt, knowing Drew had been making love to his wife with his voice? What did it say about the whole situation if Simon's wife couldn't come to a show, or Katrina couldn't drop in for the same reason?

"I'm sorry, Simon. When we get all this sorted out, maybe you can get Brianna to come back to hear the *new* us."

"I'd like that." Drew could hear his relief.

"Why didn't you ever say anything?"

"The same reason you decided to keep doing it. The money. Once Bree and I got married, I had responsibilities. And now with the baby coming…" He swallowed. "If things start going south, what will you do, Drew?"

"It isn't going to happen. We're going to work our fucking nuts off and get everything going full speed ahead. The other night, when you guys took over, it brought people in. The atmosphere had a different vibe, didn't it? And we still made money."

Simon expression cleared. "Yeah, we did."

"We're good without the gimmick."

"We need to be great, Drew." He heard Simon's stress.

"We'll get there. You have more talent in your little finger than the rest of us put together. Rand's on board, and Tony always is. We need to up our game, and maybe these new songs Rand's been working on will help us do that. We're not going down before we've had an opportunity to prove ourselves."

"Damn straight." Simon gripped his shoulder. "I'm going home to check on my lady. It's getting close, and I get nervous every time I leave her. She's started her maternity leave and is taking things easy."

"Good. Tell her I send my best, and if you need me, call. You know where I am."

Simon gripped his hand and they bumped shoulders in a man hug. "Later, man."

Drew nodded. "See you tonight."

He was halfway to his apartment before it sank in that he'd actually told the band about himself. Not everything, but one of the big pieces that made him what he was, who he was. And they had accepted it and moved on. No big deal.

He pulled into his parking slot at the apartment complex, turned off the car, and sat for a moment He felt lighter, as though he'd dropped a two-ton weight from his shoulders.

Now if they could just hit their stride as a band without his special mojo, as Simon had called it… And if they couldn't? What then? The guys had gotten used to making a living with their music. Those added responsibilities Simon was talking about boomeranged right back on Drew's shoulders as much as Simon's. If they couldn't make it, they'd turn it back on him. He'd only have himself to blame, too. He should have never started using his Siren gift.

Chapter 20

Katrina stood in the middle of Drew's living room and studied the space. What did it say about the man (for lack of a better word) she was so drawn to? The apartment décor was masculine, but by no means a bachelor pad. It looked more like the working space her own living room appeared to be most of the time. A golden-brown toned leather couch and two chairs were grouped around a large, square coffee table. Matching end tables stood on either side of the couch, each with a buffed nickel lamp with a knife-thin base and cream-colored rectangular shade.

Taking up an entire quarter of the room, its mahogany surface gleaming with care, stood a grand piano, its lid up. Next to it, on a long, clear acrylic desk, stacks of sheet music were organized alongside a computer with several things attached to it—speakers, microphone, a keyboard, and other components she didn't recognize.

Drew touched her arm. "That's where I do most of my composing. The computer has a synthesizer attached to it, but I like to hear the chords on the piano when I'm working."

She nodded and wandered over to check out the arrangement, then moved on to the entertainment center, which was pretty barren by comparison, just a television, a few movies, mostly action adventures, and a DVD player. Then she noticed what she'd been looking for, a Bose MP3 player with extra speakers.

"How many songs do you have saved?" she asked.

Drew shook his head. "I don't know. Hundreds at least."

How could he love her if she couldn't be a part of his world? Her throat nearly closed at the quick, sharp slash of grief that hit her. She had to find a way.

"Will you play something for me on your piano?"

He looked surprised first, then smiled. "Sure."

Drew took a seat on the piano bench then patted the place beside him. She perched on the edge to give him plenty of room, and placed a hand on the top of the piano, so when he played she could feel the vibration.

When he prepared to touch the keys she laid a hand over his. "Wait. Can we close the top?"

She rose and waited for him to lower the bar propping up the lid and close it. When he sat back on the bench, she pressed her face to the top of the piano and watched as he played the first chord. The vibration resonated through her cheek, her chest. She soon differentiated the low notes as having a slower, more drawn-out vibration, the higher pitches vibrated more quickly but with less strength.

She concentrated on Drew as he played, the intensity of his expression, the grace and strength of his hands. The music was like a heartbeat beneath her face and chest, rising and falling like the call of the sea. She could feel the emotion of the music though she couldn't hear a single note.

The hopeful look on his face as he reached the end of the song almost broke her heart.

"I know the song has flow and passion. But I can't hear the notes, Drew."

"It's okay."

Joseph Powell's warning earlier today ran through her mind. "I may never be able to hear anything you play or sing."

He rose and stepped around the bowed frame of the piano. "Or you might be able to hear some of it after your surgery."

"There's no guarantee."

"I know." His features settled into serious lines. His dark brows clenched. "I want more in my life than just the music, Katrina. That's all I've had to care about for a long time."

She stepped close to slip her arms around his trim waist and pressed against him. They were both so isolated without each other. Was that all it was, a relief from the loneliness? Or was she really in love with him? Had she known him long enough to be in love? The hope in his face a few moments ago and the pain she felt on his behalf came back to her, and she tightened her arms around him again.

Was she destined to disappoint him? Or could they work things out, even if the surgery wasn't successful?

She studied the large reproduction of Adolphe Bougue-reau's *Nymphs and Satyr* hanging inside the entrance to the living room. "Did your mother give you that reproduction?" she asked, seeking a change of subject. She drew back to look up at him.

"Yeah, she has a sense of the absurd where I'm concerned. She buys abstract art for herself, then buys something classical for me. She wanted me to put it in my bedroom."

His look of male outrage tipped Katrina into laughter. "It's beautiful. I can see some resemblance between you and the satyr."

He narrowed his eyes at her. "I promise I don't have hooves, pointy ears, or horns."

"I'm so glad. I can think of several things to say about pointy things right now, but I'll resist."

Drew threw back his head and laughed.

"Why don't you show me the rest of the apartment?" she suggested.

He led her into the galley-style kitchen. Stainless steel appliances and black countertops dominated the small space.

"I usually cook my own meals. I used to go over to my parents' house and mooch off of them. Now I spend time cooking to relax before I go into work."

"Is there anything I need to do to help prepare dinner?"

"No, thanks. I've got it all covered. Salad's in the fridge and potatoes are in the oven. I'll throw on the steaks in a few minutes. And I thought we'd enjoy a movie together before I have to go to the club."

"What did you pick for us to watch?"

"I haven't yet. I thought you could help me choose. I

have Netflix."

The bedroom down a short hall from the living room was decorated in navy and browns.

A large, abstract triptych full of varying shades and tones of blue and yellow hung over the bed. It looked like water glistening in the sun from beneath the waves. She moved toward it and studied it for a moment. "An original?" She turned to look over her shoulder at him as he stood at the door watching her.

"Painted by an acquaintance. An up-and-coming artist my mother introduced me to."

Katrina sighed. "It's excellent. Do you lie in bed at night and pretend you're there?"

"Yeah. Sometimes."

That he stayed at the door instead of joining her was very telling. She sauntered back to him. "You said the place was a wreck, but it isn't."

"I rushed home today and cleaned up." He quirked a brow.

"You didn't have to do that, but I appreciate the effort." Her eyes strayed back to his bedroom. "If I open your closet doors how much stuff is going to fall on me?"

"I wouldn't want to have to take you to the emergency room."

Katrina laughed. "Let's put the steaks on so we'll have time to watch that movie."

Drew had a knack with the grill. The steaks were soon done to perfection.

"How's the website you were working on coming along?" he asked after several moments of silence while they dressed their potatoes, their salads, and began to eat.

"I've finished it. All but adding music to the opening page. My company is creating a commercial for them, and they want the site to open with the same music. A sort of auditory subliminal message."

"How will you do that?"

She could ask him to help her, but suddenly it wasn't important anymore who put the music into the design. "Avery, my boss, will give the project to another designer to add the music."

"But it's your project. You worked months on it."

The indignation she read in his expression triggered a smile.

"It's the company's project. They can do whatever they want with it."

"I could help you, Katrina."

"I thought about asking you to but decided not to."

His expression held a hint of confusion, but also hurt. "Why?"

"Because you want *more* than music in your life and I want to discover what *more* means for us, not waste my personal time on business."

His expression cleared and a gleam of interest lit his. "I'd be happy to help you."

She had wanted it so much, but what was between them was more important. Her time would come professionally.

She leaned forward to grasp his hand. "The way you watch out for me without making me feel pitied is the most fantastic thing. And I love how you try to find ways to bridge the gap between our hearing and non-hearing worlds."

The strong planes of his face relaxed into a smile.

"I know how exhausting it is to be with me," she said. "It's always a struggle."

"But it doesn't have to be when it's you and me. I don't have to worry about what I am, or hide it with you. I like how you bring an artistic flare to everything you do, your cooking, your living space, your work. And I'm crazy about your laugh." He grasped her hand and gave it a gentle squeeze. "We already have more than genetics between us, Katrina."

And it terrified her. Because once they acknowledged it, they'd move beyond the point of no return. If he should decide somehow she wasn't enough, it would be more than devastating.

It would hollow her out and leave her emotionally maimed.

But there didn't seem to be anything she could do about it. She had to relax and allow herself to enjoy being with him. He could be the most important thing in her life. A small voice inside her said, *He already is.*

"Will you come to the club with me tonight?" Drew asked as the movie credits scrolled up the screen. "I'd like you to help me with something."

"What is it?"

The idea had struck him as he'd sought something to distract himself from Katrina's slender body pressing against him. Her ability to read body language and sense things could help them read the crowd at the club, and gauge their response to the new show format. Though this was only the second night he'd be singing without using his gift, he wanted to see what her response was to it as well.

He explained to her what he had in mind.

There was concern in her expression as well as curiosity. "Are you sure you want me to go?"

"Yes. I'm sure." He had a handle on his response to her. He hoped.

"I'll concentrate on the crowd then, but you'll have to write down the songs in the order you're doing them for me to tell when and how the crowd is responding."

He raised a brow in inquiry. "You don't mind doing this for me?"

"No, of course not."

"Good."

They left a few minutes later for the club.

Drew allowed Katrina to choose where she wanted sit, and made sure she was settled with a soft drink.

"If for some reason my being here starts to bother you, Drew, signal me, and I'll leave and go home."

"We're leaving together, Katrina." Had she been able to hear she'd probably have reacted to the flat demand in his tone. As it was, she raised a brow. Perhaps she didn't have to hear to pick up on his possessive vibe.

"Are you sure you'll be okay here by yourself? You could call Cheryl and Howard to come join you."

"I'll be fine. I won't be able to concentrate on the crowd if they're here talking to me."

He nodded. "Okay. If you decide you've had enough,

you can slip backstage to the dressing rooms and hang there until we're done."

"Okay."

Reluctantly he left her there, nursing her soft drink and studying the crowd as the bouncers opened the door to them.

He returned a few minutes later with the list to find she had offered the empty chairs at her table to a couple.

"New friends?"

"You want a packed room, and there's no sense in wasting the extra seats."

He dragged the remaining chair at the table close to her and sat down. He placed a notebook, open to the list, in front of her. "We'll be taking a break after this number." He drew a line beneath the title.

"Okay."

He was still reluctant to leave her, his protective instincts working overtime.

"I've been on my own a long time, Drew. I'll be fine."

He nodded and leaned over to brush her cheek with a kiss. He approached Clyde at the back of the room. "Can you keep an eye on my girl, Clyde? She's out there alone tonight."

"Sure. Is she really deaf?"

Had the man figured it out for himself, or had someone told him? "Yeah, she really is." He could practically read the man's thoughts, broadcasting something like "what the hell did she come to a club for if she couldn't hear the music?"

"I'll keep an eye on her."

He worked his way through the crowd, pausing to shake

hands with returning customers he recognized. Roma sat close to the stage on the right, and he purposely cut across the center of the room to avoid speaking to her.

Ten minutes later when they went onstage, he was still worrying about Katrina sitting alone in the crowd. He forced his uneasiness away and concentrated on their performance. They opened with their nightly introductions, then went straight into a heavy rock rendition of one of Rand's songs. Instead of the Siren tone, he used the natural gravel in his voice to express emotion and threw himself into the performance.

Katrina studied the audience during each song. After the first four or five, some of the women left, while others remained. The couple who'd joined her at the table were into the performance, and even got to their feet to dance to three out of five of the songs. Several other couples followed their example. When last she'd been here, the women had been so intent on Drew's voice, none of them had even thought to get up and move to the music. The atmosphere in the club was different. Where there had been a wild, greedy breathlessness she'd blamed on the sexual pheromones floating around the place, there was now a different sort of excitement in the air.

She took pains to write down the men's reactions as well as the women's. The more aggressive the beat, the better the men seemed to like it.

During one of the love songs, she noticed several women rubbing their arms. Cheryl had said something about

Drew's voice raising goose bumps on her skin, and she noted that, too.

That was then she realized Drew wasn't using his seductive Siren tones. Her heart skipped a beat. She scanned the crowd with eager eyes. There were at least two hundred people in the club on a Thursday night, and every eye was on the band.

After the seventh song, a man sat down in the empty chair beside her. When he laid a hand on her arm she started and jerked away from his touch. Recognition hit when she looked up, and she stared for a moment. Dressed in jeans and a knit pullover that hugged his powerful shoulders, Dr. Graham Powell looked nothing like he had in the examination room. He also looked younger than he had at the office.

He signed hello.

Katrina laid her pen aside to reply.

"What are you doing here?" he asked, while signing.

She'd have liked to ask him the same question. "My boyfriend is in the band. I'm here watching him perform and doing some research for him."

He glanced toward the stage. "Which band member is he?"

"The lead singer."

He studied Drew, his expression intent. When he looked at her again he said, "He's very good." He glanced at the paper in front of her. "What kind of research are you doing?"

Why was he so curious about this, her, everything? It made her uneasy. "I'm making notes as to which songs the audience seems to respond to the most."

His brows rose. "How do you know which song they're playing?"

"I have a list of them in the order they're playing them."

"I see." His attention dropped to the notebook she held as though he wanted to read what she had written.

"Do you think I'll be able to hear the music he plays, hear his voice when he sings?" she asked.

He frowned. "You'll be able to hear certain tones, but not everything."

She bit her lip. She'd suspected as much.

"The longer you have the implant, the more you'll be able to hear. Your brain has to learn to decode the sounds."

If her brain worked like a human's.

And if it didn't?

She couldn't allow herself to think about it. It would do her no good to dwell on the negative.

"How did you two meet?" Powell asked.

"I came to the club with a friend. Drew later recognized me at a restaurant, approached me, and asked me to come back to the club for another performance." She was beginning to feel like this was an interrogation instead of a friendly conversation.

"Even though you couldn't hear his music?"

"I can still feel the beat against my skin, my feet. And when I'm close enough to the stage I can read his lips and enjoy the words."

Powell leaned forward in his chair. "But you can't really have that much in common."

It was an unexpected backhanded slap at them as a

couple. And it suddenly occurred to her what irritated her about this man. He had no social skills. Or if he did, he chose not to use them. He'd been charming when they'd met in front of his father's house, but normally he was pushy. Too certain of himself. But weren't all doctors supposed to have a God complex?

"We have more in common than you think," she replied, "since we're both artists."

"How long have you been together?"

"A short while."

He looked away for a moment. "Are you sure you don't wear perfume?"

She was shocked at the question. "Yes. I use body wash, shampoo and deodorant but I don't use perfume. Scents become too strong when I put them on."

"Then my father was right. He says a woman's body chemistry reacts to anything that has a scent. Evidently yours really does."

Why was he harping on that? Had mentioned it when they'd last met. Shock sent her heart rate up and she sucked in a startled gasp. He was human, but he must be picking up on her Mer scent. She'd never known that was possible. When she looked up, he seemed to be studying her with an intensity that was out of proportion to their conversation. She sought something to say that would lead him onto neutral ground. "I enjoyed speaking to your father."

"Thank you. I thought you might be more comfortable with him. He is easily the most patient and understanding person I have ever known. And he's a very good psychologist."

"I think so, too." By nature Selkies were nonaggressive, patient, nurturing. And perfect adoptive parents.

He glanced toward the door and got to his feet. "My date is here."

Katrina sighed with relief.

He shook her hand briefly. "You'll do well on Wednesday. We both will."

She watched as he strode toward the door and greeted a tall, willowy blond with a kiss on the cheek.

Knowing he had a girlfriend relieved some of her anxiety. Even if he could smell her Mer scent. Why would he become so fixated on it? She needed to speak to Joseph Powell and see if he could provide some insight.

She turned back to the stage and found the band taking their first break. She'd missed at least two songs. The couple sitting at her table was eyeing her with curiosity. They had obviously seen her and Dr. Powell signing. She flashed them a smile and decided to take a seat someplace else, so she could watch the audience and avoid their stares.

After a quick bathroom break, Drew snagged a bottle of water and left the dressing room to check on Katrina. Halfway down the narrow backstage hall, Sam stopped him.

"What the hell's going on with you and the band, Drew?" He chewed the end of his unlit cigar like it was a teething ring, a fierce scowl carving creases into his brow and around his jowly mouth.

Drew had noticed the shift in the audience himself. Some of the women had stayed for the first set, then left when they no longer got the sexual charge from the performance. Others still remained but were quieter. But more couples seemed to be taking to the dance floor, which was a good change. "What do you mean, Sam?"

"You know what I'm talking about. I haven't had to instruct the bouncers to police the upstairs balcony all night."

"Is that a complement or a complaint?"

"Well it's lowered my liability, for damn sure. But I've gotten used to having the place packed to the rafters with screaming women. What's changed?"

"Maybe the new wore off and they aren't getting the same buzz from the music."

Sam stepped close, whipped the cigar from his mouth, and used it to point at Drew. "Then give them the same buzz. I told you to keep your secret, not to turn it off."

So he had realized there was something more than just the music involved. "We're working on appealing to a different demographic, Sam. Wouldn't you rather your club be filled with couples instead of only the women? Men usually drink more. So you'll sell more beer and booze."

"The cover charges at the door are what pay for your band. Those go down, and we may have to renegotiate your contract."

Drew studied Sam's wide, homely face for a moment and fought back the anger and outrage shooting his temperature up to the boiling point. "We've made you a fortune the last six months, Sam. It's been beneficial to us all. My suggestion is that you give it some time and see where this goes. None of us wants to fuck up a good thing.

We'll be leaving soon enough."

Sam's brows rose. "Leaving?"

"Yeah. If the first album does well, we may go on tour." Nothing had been said to that effect, but it didn't hurt to plant the seed and get the man off their backs.

Drew folded his arms. "Think what a boon for your business it will be. You gave us a break. If we leave on good terms, we might even swing by and play a set or two now and then. Put your name out there. We leave with some tension, you'll never see us again."

Sam's teeth clamped around the cigar as though he wanted to bite it in two. He spoke around it. "I'll be keeping my eye on things."

"That's your job." Good. He'd gotten through to him for now. "I'll be keeping my eye on the band's interests."

Sam glared at him before stomping off down the hallway to his office, followed by the sound of a door slamming.

Drew forced his hands to relax from their fisted grip and released the anger burning through him. Their music was a damn sight better than any other band the man had ever hired. If Drew had never started using his Siren capabilities, he could have avoided all of this. It was his fault the band was experiencing any kind of lull.

Simon and Rand stepped out of the shadows of the stage curtain. Rand was the first to speak his gruff tone laced with anger. "We're still playing to a pretty good crowd. What the fuck's he complaining about?"

"Change is hard, and it's like stepping into the unknown, Rand. Some people want to stick with what's safe,"

Simon said.

Rand glared down the hallway toward Sam's office. "Fuck him." He looked back at Drew. "You don't flinch when you play hardball, man. It's the thing I like best about you. We always know where we stand. When it comes to the band, you'd fight to the death for us."

He didn't know about the death. He'd certainly wanted to give Sam a good shaking, preferably by the scruff of the neck. "I have a little wiggle room to play with because of the contract. But we still need to stay on top of things every performance."

"We're on it, Drew," Simon nodded.

Rand nodded, and the three of them strode onto the stage where Tony waited.

Drew looked out into the audience, but the spotlights, programmed by one of the techs, were too bright for him to see Katrina. Had Sam not waylaid him, he'd have had time to check on her.

He tilted his head back and sampled the mingled scents of liquor, food, and the human smells that permeated the space…and faintly over to the left was Katrina's essence. He was tempted to lower the mental door between them so he could read her emotions, but decided against it. His control was tenuous at best, and once the door was down, it was *down*. If there were anything wrong, her scent would change, and he'd know. He relaxed and centered himself again so he could concentrate on the music.

An hour later, when the band played their last song the crowd had thinned, but the couples left clung together on the dance floor. The sexual vibe in the room had nothing to do with his Siren mojo.

Drew exchanged a grin with Simon. It felt good to have made music without the added stress of satisfying hundreds of women's libidos. They'd actually sparked an ember with couples instead of just the ladies.

Simon stepped close to the keyboard and covered the mike suspended in front of his mouth. "Why don't you go dance this last one with your lady while we keep playing?"

Drew's smile widened into a grin. "Thanks, Simon."

Could Katrina dance? She couldn't hear the beat, but she could follow his lead. Drew played out the rest of the measure, then left his keyboard. He leapt off the stage and followed her scent to a small table close to the bar. She looked up from what she was writing when he paused beside her. He extended his hand and she accepted it, then rose from her seat. She raised her brows in question as she looked toward the stage.

"I wanted to dance with you."

Her lips parted in surprise, then her expression blanked. "I don't know how, Drew."

"Follow my lead, and I'll take care of the rest."

He guided one arm around his neck, clasped her other hand in his, then held her close. She was self-conscious at first, her body tense, but gradually the slow, easy sway of their bodies moving together relaxed her and created a different kind of tension between them.

Katrina's gaze, dark and sultry in the dim light, promised more when they were alone.

He pressed his lips to her forehead, and she snuggled her head against his shoulder.

When the song ended, Drew tilted her head back with a finger beneath her chin. "I'll be right back and we'll go home." His kiss was brief but adamant.

His bandmates were grinning like fools when he took the stage to end the show. He was in for some harassment, he was certain of it.

He looked back at Katrina in time to see a large man approaching her, and frowned. The man signed something to her, then walked away. Drew tracked his progress all the way across the club and out the door.

Who the hell was that guy? He didn't recognize the jangling sweep of alarming emotion for a moment. Jealousy, green-eyed and fierce, poised like an eel ready to strike.

Jesus, he needed to get these Siren/Mer alpha possessive emotions under control. The guy had only signed goodnight or something. But he was moved to muscle his way in between her and every other male she came into contact with. Every molecule in his body roared *mine*.

Chapter 21

From the moment Drew left the club, Katrina recognized a new kind of tension in him.

"Do you want to talk about my observations tonight?" Katrina asked.

"Not right now. I need to decompress for a few minutes first."

"Okay." She had never seen him this closed off. What the hell had happened between their dancing and his joining her after they ended their set?

When they reached his car, he unlocked her door and opened it for her. Inside the dark car it was impossible for her to quiz him to find out what was bothering him.

He flipped on the overhead light and turned to her. "I'd like you to spend the night at my place."

That he asked instead of expecting it told her two things. He wasn't taking her for granted or he wasn't sure enough of her to make demands. "Okay. But I'll have to leave early to go back to my place and change for work."

"I can run you home in the morning."

"Okay."

He seemed to relax somewhat. Silence fell between them while he drove to the complex. Inside his apartment, Drew tossed his keys onto a long table inside the door. He fell back into the soft leather couch and kicked off his shoes. When he patted the cushion next to him Katrina sat down.

"Tonight—you didn't use your Siren…"

"No." His lips quirked. And Simon calls it my mojo."

Katrina's heart skipped a beat. Had the guitar player figured out Drew wasn't human?

"The guys know I do something with my voice when I sing. Sam the manager at The Next Best Thing, does, too." He brushed back the thick, dark brown hair from his forehead, setting to light the warmer golden tones in it. "Simon said Brianna, his wife, had stopped coming to the shows because of it."

She studied his expression and saw regret there.

"We decided to work our way into appealing to couples instead of only the women. We'll be doing a little more heavy rock and fewer ballads. We have some new material we'll be working hard to showcase."

If he wasn't doing all this for the right reasons, it would never last. "It isn't because of what I said?"

"No. The women were getting out of control. Had been out of control for a while. I can't take the chance of having hundreds of stalkers showing up at my door because they've become addicted."

At his acknowledgement that one of her fears was possible, everything in her seemed to pause for a moment. She dragged a breath in, though her throat felt tight. "I think you're making a wise decision." But if it didn't work, he and the band would lose the contract they'd signed. If it looked like that would happen, would Drew fold to the pressure?

She ran a caressing hand over his arm. "You can't take full responsibility for the success or failure of the band, Drew. You're a group. It isn't all about your voice, or Rand's drumming, or Tony's bass, or Simon's guitar playing skills. It's about the collective. If it was only about what you can do with your voice, the other guys wouldn't have a following of women waiting for them outside the club every night."

He didn't look like he believed it.

"I have proof." She riffled through her purse and withdrew the notebook she'd been scribbling notes in all night. "I missed two of the songs before your first break. The doctor who's going to do my surgery on Wednesday was there tonight, and stopped by my table to speak to me."

"Was that the guy who said something to you after our dance?"

"Yes. You saw him?"

"Yeah. I saw him signing something to you."

"His parents are both deaf, and he signs as though he is as well. He swung over to say goodnight."

Drew ran his fingers through his hair again, roughing up the thick strands.

She held out the notebook, and he took it from her but didn't read it.

"Will you teach me to sign?" he asked, his expression grave.

It was the second time he'd asked her. "Yes, I'll teach

you. What would you like to say right now?"

A wry smile quirked up the corners of his lips. "That sounds like a trick question."

His mood was so odd, Katrina decided to respond with humor. "Let's go to bed." She signed as she spoke.

His smile spread. "How do you say okay?"

"You can use the universal signal for okay. Or you can spell it out like this." She used the alphabet of the deaf to sign an O and a K.

He mimicked her actions.

She rose and took his hand. He set aside the notebook and allowed her to guide him to the bedroom.

He touched her shoulder to get her attention. "I need to take a shower."

She signed okay and turned in the direction of the bathroom. She adjusted the water while Drew shucked his T-shirt and jeans.

Genetics had preprogrammed him with a swimmer's build, leaving his shoulder and chest muscles powerful and well defined, and his stomach, thighs and buttocks lean and muscular. But the rest of him was all Drew. He studied her with eyes that had darkened to gray-blue. His short dark hair stood up in disheveled spikes. His beard shadowed the lower half of a jaw and lips were just made for sin. He looked so masculine standing before her, unselfconsciously naked, his penis erect. Her heart raced. Longing and wetness pooled between her thighs.

She undressed with as much efficiency and speed as he had, tossing her clothes on top of his on the floor.

The wicked smile he gave her was more like the Drew

she knew, and a niggling worry crossed her thoughts, then as quickly raced away when he caught her hand. They stepped into the shower, and he tugged her in with him.

"Let me take care of you like you did me this morning," she murmured.

His throat worked as he swallowed, and his erection grew even more impressive.

She reached for the bottle of shampoo, and said, "Turn around."

Drew turned his back to her, braced his hands on the shower wall, and tilted his head back. Katrina took her time working the shampoo into his hair, then moved on to the sandalwood body wash while he allowed the water to rinse the lather down his back. She used the soap to moisten her hands so she could message his neck and shoulders, his muscles tensing and relaxing beneath her touch.

She caressed his broad back and buttocks, then stepped in close to rub her breasts against his soapy skin, her hands splayed against his chest as she worked the lather over his pecs and stomach from behind. She felt the unsteady rise and fall of Drew's breathing, and was almost relieved when he turned to face her. His lips were hot and wild on hers, drawing her tongue into his mouth and sucking it at the same time his rampant erection pressed and throbbed between their stomachs. His fingers kneading her buttocks, he held her tight against him, his hips pumping against her.

Katrina had never experienced such raw sexuality before, never felt such a desperate need to mate. "Drew." Her voice could have been a shout or a whisper, the conscious modulation of her tone lost beneath the influx of emotion.

She turned to step out of the shower, but Drew caught her back against him. His hands cupped her breasts pulling her beneath the water. He took his time rinsing the soap from her skin with water-slick caresses.

He nipped her shoulder, then sucked the spot. At the electric feel of arousal, Katrina reached back and gripped the sides of his thighs, and his muscles bunched beneath her fingers. He slid his wide hand down to cup her, his long fingers finding the center of her need, tantalizing it with his touch.

Heedless of the soap and water, they staggered out of the shower and into the bedroom, Drew's arm holding her back against him. He dragged pillows down to mid-bed, and she reclined belly-down across them, raising her hips. When Drew kneed her legs apart, she thought she'd never felt anything so sexy in her life.

He rested his forearm on the bed in front of her, and lowered his body over hers. His skin brushed hers with every movement. He guided himself into her, just deep enough to breach the opening of her body, and held himself there while he dragged the waterlogged weight of her hair over her shoulder. He nuzzled the tender skin behind her ear, then nibbled her earlobe.

As tempting tingles traveled from her ear down her spine, Katrina rocked back to seat him completely inside her, and Drew thrust forward, giving her what she wanted. The penetrating heat of him pushing inside her body was enough. She climaxed, the sensation rolling over her so fiercely every nerve in her body seemed to clench and then explode with pleasure.

Then he was moving inside her, building the friction necessary to bring her back up again. A sound, muffled and intermittent, penetrated the void she lived in. She heard the unsteady pattern of breathing, felt the heavy beat of a heart racing in time with her own, the movement of Drew's muscles as he thrust into her body again and again.

She couldn't differentiate between what she was feeling and the sensations bombarding him. They were connected in a way she'd never known possible. Their joined emotions were sweeping her up, overtaking her, rolling over her. The dual pleasure built, peaked, and he climaxed. His, hers, crashed over her, the combination so powerful, so consuming, Katrina couldn't catch her breath, couldn't think.

When she came back to herself, she was trembling, every muscle turned to jelly. Drew dragged the pillows away so they could recline together, spooning on their sides. His arms wrapped around her, his semi-soft erection still inside her.

"Are you okay?"

She heard the words more… like a thought… or at least she believed so. The experience of having another person's voice, a masculine voice, inside her head was so new she couldn't fully comprehend what was happening. "I'm fine."

At Drew's stillness she turned to look over her shoulder at him.

"Katrina—" he searched her face with hope and hunger.

Her throat went suddenly dry as dust. She'd bonded to him.

Drew tried to tamp down his excitement. He spoke aloud, "Tell me you can hear me."

She shook her head. "It isn't like hearing. It's like I'm sensing your thoughts."

"Can you feel my emotions?" he asked.

She turned her face away and gripped the arm he'd looped around her body holding her. "Wait. You have to give me a moment."

Drew's lips rested against her shoulder in a soothing caress. "It's going to be okay." Whether she could or couldn't hear him, it made him feel better to say the words. He had freaked out when he'd first experienced this, so he fully understood what she was going through.

When her tremors had calmed, she said, "It isn't like hearing. I don't know what it is." She moved to face him and inhaled sharply as their bodies parted.

There was a sense of loss when he slipped free of her. They were no longer part of each other. "I've been feeling your emotions since our second night together."

Her eyes widened in surprise. "Are you sure?"

"Why do you think I was having such difficulty the night you came to the club with me?"

"You can't read my thoughts, just my emotions?" She searched his expression.

"Only your emotions."

She relaxed noticeably.

His father's counsel had helped him understand that she needed to have her space, her privacy. He did, too. But what was she sensing?

She turned her head presenting her profile to him. "I could hear your heartbeat, your lungs breathing while we were making love, feel your pleasure."

He smiled as her cheeks reddened. He tilted her face back to him. "We're bonding, Katrina."

The distress in her expression bordered on panic. "It's too soon. Too fast, Drew. I'm half human. I can't depend on my Mer genetics to do it all for me, any more than you can depend on your Siren to do it for you."

He smoothed back the tangled mat of hair from her shoulder. "The way we made love just now was…" He shook his head. There were no words to describe it. "I've never experienced this kind of pleasure with a human. Have you?"

"No. Not even with the Merman I was involved with."

Those words gave him some encouragement.

She attempted to run her fingers through her hair to straighten it, and grimaced when she hit a tangle that pulled. "Though we both come from two of the most seductive races on earth, preternatural bonding might not do it all, Drew."

He didn't have to ask what she was talking about. Love. Being loved, giving love. It was a human concept, but one every human harped on as the most important. Though he could pass as human, he had no human gene to suggest any answers. Was he even capable of love? Possibly. He felt other emotions as humans did. Anger, pain, satisfaction, and—the latest—jealousy. He was still grappling with that one.

"You saw how close my parents are. How they complete each other. Isn't that as close to love as anyone, human or otherwise, could hope to attain?" He found it difficult to understand what the difference might be.

"Have you ever asked them if they love one another?" She dragged the comforter over them as far as it would go.

"I've never needed to. Who's to say that love is only a human emotion? It's been spoken of since the dawn of humankind, and I'm certain, many other beings as well." Though he never got cold, was never self-conscious of his nudity, Katrina had suddenly become conscious of both.

Drew rose, went to the dresser, and got a blue T-shirt and a pair of sleep pants with a drawstring waist. He offered her the T-shirt, stepped into the sleep pants, and went into the bathroom. By the time he returned with a brush, she'd donned the shirt and slipped beneath the covers.

He motioned for her to turn around and smiled when she complied. He sat down on the bed and, dividing her hair into sections, brushed through the tangles they'd created with both the shower and their fierce lovemaking. Having him care for her seemed to soothe her.

When her hair hung sleek and soft across her shoulder, he set aside the brush, bent his head to rest his lips against her shoulder and felt her shiver of response.

"Thank you. I'd have had a time in the morning getting a brush through it." She wiggled down beneath the covers and turned on her side.

He slid in beside her and faced her. "Are you still sensing my feelings?"

She shook her head. "It stopped when we...came

apart."

She had so many human characteristics. Every time she spoke of something intimate she blushed. Mermaids weren't normally so modest. It was ironic he'd finally found what he'd been searching for, and she was more human than Mer. Or was she?

He spoke his thoughts aloud. "We've only known each other a couple of weeks. We need more time."

She nodded and raised a hand to caress his cheek and jaw. Her blue-green eyes looking into his held a look of tenderness. "We have time." She kissed him softly.

He turned to spoon with her, and in moments she was sound asleep, curved into his body almost as closely as they had been when they'd made love.

But what if he couldn't give her what she needed? This thing called love. He'd written songs about it for the band. He could imagine what it was like. But what the hell did it *feel* like? If he did feel it, would he recognize it?

Chapter 22

D rew stirred beside her in the bed. Katrina woke. She lifted her head from his shoulder so he could reach for his ringing cell phone, and he listened for a moment. His back muscles tensed, before he switched on the lamp on the nightstand.

With his head turned, she couldn't read what he was saying. When he hung up he was smiling, then as quickly frowned. He turned to face her. "Brianna's in labor and Simon's taken her to the hospital."

"That's good."

"He sounded terrified."

Katrina swallowed a laugh. "Poor fellow."

Watching Drew's expression, she sensed he didn't know whether to be excited or concerned for his friends. He tried to remain detached, but she knew from the way he talked about Simon that they were as close as she and Cheryl. Everyone needed people in their lives who cared about them.

"Think I should go to the hospital for a while just for moral support?" he asked.

"Will Brianna want you in the room while she's in labor?"

He grimaced "Probably not. I'll call every couple of hours to check on them."

"That sounds like a better idea."

He slid back under the covers, and she cuddled up against his back, her arm around his waist. "They'll be fine," she soothed. He relaxed again and soon drifted back to sleep.

Graham arrived early at the office. Unable to sleep, he'd thought through the situation one step at a time. He'd start with the basics and study all her test results again. Next, he pulled up the computerized chart, including all the blood work, and printed it out. After an hour's study of every test and scan, he had found nothing unusual in Katrina's results, other than the anomalies he'd been so interested in from the beginning.

Her blood work was as textbook perfect as any healthy young woman in her twenties he'd ever treated. Every reading was so balanced it was almost too perfect. Even her vision was twenty-twenty. Nothing stood out except the extra sinus in her forehead and the increased size of her inner ear.

Since they'd had a psychologist evaluate her, he'd requested and gotten a copy of her hospital records relating to the burns she'd suffered as a child. Her abuse by a mentally ill worker at the home she grew up in was well documented. Because she'd had no parents to bring litigation against the home, nothing had come of the situation. Fortunately Katrina had received the care she needed, and the woman responsible for her injuries had been hospitalized for several years.

He was scanning the documents again when one passage stood out to him. *The patient has healed from the injury with remarkable swiftness.* What the hell did that mean? It had taken her two months instead of three? If only he had access to the daily charts, he might be able to figure this out.

He went back to the scans he'd done of her skull and studied it again. The cavity above her other sinuses lay in alignment with her frontal lobe. He clicked on the internet and went to the website he'd saved about whales and dolphins and looked at the location of the fat-filled pockets in their skulls. It was in exactly the same position as Katrina's.

This was impossible. The direction he was going was insane. There was no way human and Cetacean DNA could mix. No way at all.

But it wouldn't hurt to do a DNA panel to see what it read like. He could submit a sample and say the patient had requested it. He'd have to get a form signed when Katrina came in to get her blood work done before surgery.

He'd get a look at the size of her facial maxillary nerve during surgery, too. He'd bet it, too, would be larger than normal, like her auditory nerve.

He'd already crossed a professional line by requesting her childhood medical charts. What was one more transgression?

He had to know…

Cheryl leaned back against the counter in Katrina's workstation while Katrina tried to concentrate on positioning the image just right on the advertisement. "I'm almost done. Just let me finish this."

Cheryl tapped her on the shoulder to get her attention. "There's a handsome hunk coming this way."

Katrina eased up to look over the wall of her cubicle and smiled as Drew sauntered up the aisle, looking from side to side inside the cube walls. As he passed, female heads popped up to follow his progress, and a few male heads as well. She'd seen the phenomenon in restaurants, and even on the street. He captured feminine attention so easily. When he garnered male interest, it was because most men viewed him as a territorial threat when the women they were with gave him a second look. His features were symmetrical and masculine, with a mouth that promised pleasure and eyes … God, she had it bad.

Julia Arnold, one of the female designers, stepped out of her cubicle into his path, and he paused. From a distance Katrina couldn't read what he said, but the disappointment on the woman's face when she turned and pointed toward them was clear.

The moment Drew's eyes settled on her, her body quickened.

Cheryl touched her arm. "If he could bottle whatever male pheromone he pumps, every man on the street would be in line to purchase it."

Katrina laughed. If she only knew. "It's a genetic thing.

His father has it, too."

"If I wasn't already crazy about Howard, we could have a very interesting catfight over him." Her eyes danced with mischief.

"I'd hate to have to maim my best friend," Katrina said.

Cheryl's eyes widened in exaggerated shock. "Whoa, you mean you'd do me harm over a man?"

"Only this one."

Cheryl laughed and bumped her hip with hers.

"Hey." Drew's one word greeting, combined with his smile, brought heat to Katrina's cheeks. His attention shifted to Cheryl for a moment and he said hello. "How 'bout I take you two lovely ladies out to lunch?"

"I don't want to horn in," Cheryl said.

Katrina laid a hand on her arm. "It's okay." She studied Drew's expression. "Brianna had the baby?"

"Yeah. A little girl. Simon's pumped. They're all three doing fine."

"Good." He'd come to tell her the news and celebrate in some small way. Katrina hugged him, and his arms tightened around her while he brushed her cheek with his lips.

"I know you ladies don't have a long lunch hour. We probably need to get a move on," Drew suggested.

They settled on the deli they frequented quite often. Drew found them a seat and went off to the counter to place their orders.

Cheryl's head turned at something going on a few tables over from them.

"What is it?"

"Some asshole harassing his girlfriend." She looked over again. "Ex girlfriend."

Katrina studied the body language of all the people around them. They projected discomfort, though no one moved to do anything about it. Katrina half rose and looked in the direction of the disturbance. The woman was studying her food as if it was the most important thing at the table, her head bowed. The way she cowered beneath the man's aggression spiked Katrina's anger. Why was everyone ignoring this?

Drew returned to the table and set the laden tray down. Mr. Walters, the owner of the deli, an overweight man of fifty, stepped from behind the counter. He always had a ready smile for every customer, and Katrina could read his anxiety as he approached the man and said something.

The guy's cheeks grew berry red with anger, and he whirled on the owner, lashing out with an open palm. He knocked the older man back on his heels.

Drew said something she didn't catch before he strode forward, stepping between the two men and meeting the bully's menacing look. Though Katrina couldn't read his words, she could see the aggression in both men's stances. Every muscle in her body tautened, although she knew if it came down to a physical confrontation, Drew could easily overpower the other man.

"What is he saying?" she asked Cheryl.

"He just said, 'you don't want to do this.' The guy isn't saying anything, but Drew's talking to him too quietly for me to hear."

A few seconds later, the man turned away and stormed

out of the deli. The tension surrounding them immediately dropped, and the customers and employees seemed to take a collective breath.

A police car screeched to a stop in front of the restaurant, and the cops piled out and approached the departing bully.

Drew returned to their table and sat down. He gave Katrina a somber smile, but the heat of anger continued to pour off of him. She rested her hand on his thigh in a soothing gesture. He grasped her hand and continued to hold it for several minutes.

"What did you say to him?" Cheryl asked as she emptied the tray of sandwiches and drinks onto the table.

"I just convinced him what an ass he was making of himself in front of everyone in the restaurant, and that the customers could testify to his assault on the older fellow. The cops were a few blocks away, and I mostly wanted to keep him distracted until they got here."

Drew kept his attention on his food, the excitement and joy of only moments before ruined by the ugly scene. Cheryl shot Katrina a questioning glance. She shook her head. What had he really done to drain the man's aggression and encourage him to give himself up to the cops?

With Cheryl at the table, no one could stay subdued for long. Her natural vibrancy and humor soon had Drew smiling. Her emotional radar was in good working order, too, because she finished her sandwich and picked up her drink to leave. "I have some work to do, and you two should have a minute or two to yourselves before Katrina has to go back to the salt mines. Thanks for lunch, Drew."

He smiled, "You're welcome."

Katrina mouthed, *thank you* to her and said, "I'll be back in a minute."

Cheryl threw up a hand in farewell and sauntered out of the restaurant, her red ponytail swinging.

Katrina slipped her arm through Drew's and cuddled close on their bench seat. "What is it?"

"Sometimes my true nature breaks free and it's hard to control."

She thought about it for a moment. "I know you were angry, but you weren't out of control."

"Have you ever wanted to just give in to it?"

He was making too much out of what had happened. "Only with you."

A real smile finally broke free. He bent his head to brush her fingers with his lips. "Thank God."

Chapter 23

On their way back to the office, Drew said, "Simon wants me and the boys to swing by the hospital and see the baby for a minute before we have to go to the club tonight. We're not practicing today because he's with Bree at the hospital, so I have some free time to go gift hunting. Any suggestions?"

"I'd go to Fashion Valley and look around. A mobile for the crib, or maybe a nightlight. They'll need one when they get up in the middle of the night to feed the baby."

"Sounds like a good idea. Would you like to go to the hospital with me?"

Katrina shook her head. "I think it might be better for me to meet Simon's wife after she's had time to recover. I'm a stranger, and it might be awkward for her."

"Okay."

They paused outside the Graphic Design office. Drew flashed her a devilish smile. "I won't embarrass you by hauling you into a torrid make out session here on the sidewalk in front of your office." He brushed her cheek with a kiss, but he took his time about it. Her cheeks pinkened adorably.

He flashed her a satisfied grin. "I'll be back at five to pick you up." He sauntered off to his car.

Katina finished the ad and moved on to another project. By five she was eager to leave and meet Drew.

"What did you buy?" she asked as soon as she got in the car.

"A nightlight. It projects stars on the ceiling and plays a selection of lullabies."

"That's perfect, Drew. They'll love it."

At her apartment they fixed a meal, cleaned up, and watched a movie together.

"Simon's the first to marry and to have a child. With signing the contract, and all the changes the band's going through, it's an end of an era for us," Drew commented on his way out the door.

"Nothing remains static," Katrina replied.

"No, it doesn't." He cocked his head. "Am I taking too much for granted if I come back here tonight after the show?"

"No, Drew. I'll give you a key so you can let yourself in. I may fall asleep before you get back."

His slow smile set every intimate area of her body a-tingle. His kiss almost finished it.

Drew wiped his face with a towel and chugged half a bottle of water. How had such a promising day ended up so fucked up? He slouched into one of the cheap plastic chairs in the dressing room while he caught his breath. Had the lights onstage been hotter than usual, or was it because he'd been burning up with anger. He hadn't even acknowledged the pain yet.

His words to Katrina as he left for the hospital had been prophetic. It was the end of an era. Possibly the end of the only long-term friendship he'd ever had. The scene at the hospital had been—

He swallowed more water to help ease the ache in his throat and leaned forward to rest his elbows on his knees. He'd worked through his anger onstage, and now the pain was catching up to him.

"You okay, Drew?" Tony asked as he sat down beside him.

"Yeah." What else could he say?

"Your performance tonight… you were on fire, man. It was all the rest of us could do to keep up."

And he hadn't used his Siren vibe a single time. Bitterness scalded his tongue. He raised his head and forced a smile. "Thanks, Tony."

"Has something happened?"

Almost as sensitive as Katrina, Tony often picked up on the undercurrents between people. It probably wasn't very hard to do so right now. Thank God Tony and Rand hadn't shown at the hospital until after he escaped.

Drew stared at the floor for a moment. "No, nothing's happened."

It gave him no satisfaction that Simon looked as miserable as he felt.

Tony rose and slipped into his well-worn leather jacket. Drew caught his signal to Rand. "We'll see you guys tomorrow."

"Goodnight." Drew roused himself, tossed the sweaty towel in the laundry basket in the corner, and reached for his jacket.

"I'm sorry, Drew." Simon's voice sounded gravely. "She's still hormonal from the baby. I probably shouldn't have invited anyone to the hospital."

Though it nearly choked him, out of respect for their twelve-year friendship, he said, "It's okay."

"No. It's not. Are we going to be able to get past this?"

Drew looked him full in the face for the first time since greeting him at the hospital. "Only if you can look me in the eye and tell me you don't believe I'd do anything to hurt your child." The words felt like broken glass in his throat.

Simon flinched but he met his gaze. "I know you wouldn't, Drew."

"I'd sooner slit my own throat, Simon."

"I know." Simon's Adam's apple bobbed as he swallowed.

Drew suddenly felt hollowed out. "I won't come around again. You can reassure Brianna she and the baby are safe from my...*vibe*."

"That isn't what I want, Drew."

"It's the best thing for your family. For all of us." He walked away from Simon. From the situation.

He sat in the car for ten minutes, reaching for the emotional distance that had been such a part of him until Katrina had ripped it away. The ability to feel her emotions had somehow kick-started his. If this was a side effect of bonding, he could do without it.

He ran a heavy hand over his face, jabbed the key in the ignition and started the car.

To question his need to be with Katrina would have been a waste of emotional energy. They were water folk, they spoke the same language, shared the same experiences, and understood things about each other without having to discuss them. He pointed his vehicle toward her apartment.

Drew let himself in to find Katrina sound asleep on the couch. He turned off the muted television and paused long enough to admire delicate curve of her cheek and the generous swell of her breasts. What drew him the most was that hint of innocence that lingered about her. After having slept with so many women, maybe he deserved the title of monster for pursuing her. She deserved better.

Aware of his sweat-stained T-shirt, he slipped into the bathroom, stripped and got in the shower. The soap and water rinsed away the grime, but did nothing to soothe him. He exited the shower, dried himself, then wrapped the towel around his hips.

Katrina sat on the foot of the bed waiting for him, her face a little swollen with sleep. After a small hesitation he joined her.

She grasped his hand. "Has something happened to the baby?" she asked, her expression anxious.

She was just too damn good at reading body language and facial expressions.

"No. The baby's fine. It's the adults who are all fucked up."

She didn't flinch from his language, just continued to look at him.

In the next second he found himself telling her about going in to drop off the gifts. "Simon put the baby in my arms. She was so tiny, all pink, with dark blue eyes and fine brown hair. She cried like a little bird so I swayed with her and sang the first few bars of *You Are So Beautiful*. Brianna came out of the bed yelling about how she didn't want me singing to her baby. That whatever I was doing with my music needed to stay at the clubs. She didn't want it around their child."

Drew looked up to find Katrina's expression as stricken as his must still be.

"At first I thought she was high on something. Then I realized she wasn't. She actually believed I'd harm the baby if I sang to her. I laid her into the bassinette and got the hell out of there."

"What did Simon say?" she asked her voice a whisper.

"He tried to cut her off and kept saying 'Bree—Bree, this is crazy.' He apologized later, but..." Drew shook his head. "It makes me feel sick just to think anyone could believe I'd harm a child. That I would hurt one with my voice."

"You're not built that way, Drew. I know you're not. You're so protective of me. I know you'd be the same with any child." Katrina moved to straddle his lap and hold him. He automatically put his arms around her. Her fingers stoked his damp hair, and after a while she felt the tension of his anger and pain ease. He fell back on the bed, taking her with him. She pushed up on her elbows to look down at him and study his face.

"I've let them in too far, Katrina. They're my closest

friends, but I can't really trust them with who I am. I thought I could, but I was wrong. I'll have to pull back again. Just keep things all business."

Tears trailed down her cheeks. "I so sorry, Drew." She wept the tears for him he couldn't shed himself.

"I am, too." Regret lay like a two-ton weight in his chest. He wasn't human, and it was time he accepted he'd never truly be one of them, no matter how close they became.

At least he had Katrina.

Chapter 24

Katrina clenched her trembling hands in her lap. The hospital gown felt foreign against her skin, the cotton fabric woven to withstand a thousand washings. The antiseptic smell of the preop room was the worst. It brought back memories of her childhood as sharp as broken glass.

Her mouth had grown so dry with nerves she couldn't swallow. She longed for something to drink, but wasn't allowed anything before surgery. The chances of anything going wrong during the operation were slim, and actually weren't what concerned her. The possible side effects of being a Mermaid had caused this sudden round of anxiety.

After she'd been burned, she healed too quickly for the doctors to prevent scarring. When they tried to remove the scar tissue, it had been agony and only made things worse. What if the same thing happened this time?

The nurse looped a tourniquet around her arm, found a vein, and with only a small pinch started her IV. She released the tourniquet.

The cold fluid running into her arm gave Katrina a chill,

and she tugged the sheet up over her shoulder.

"Need a blanket?" the nurse asked.

Katrina nodded.

"Do you have someone with you?" she asked.

"My boyfriend, Drew, is in the waiting room."

Her boyfriend. Drew had become so much more in the past week. They'd spent every free moment together. Made love at least twice a day, sometimes more. She was learning intimate emotional things about him. He was a fantastic lover. Just thinking of making love with him set her aflame. He could be funny, with a self-deprecating humor about his Siren side. She was awed by the focus and passion he poured into his music. He had a fierce temper, though he'd never directed it at her. The blow he had sustained from his best friend had left him hurting, though he continued to act like he was over it.

Last night she'd invited Cheryl and Howard to go with her to the club to watch the band perform. The changes they were making had drawn a lot of attention, and the crowd had been as large as it had been on Saturday, their busiest night.

Cheryl raved about their performance. She hadn't missed Drew's Siren vibe at all, or if she had, she hadn't said anything. She wanted to come to the hospital with her today, but she was working on a big project and Emory, their boss, had thrown a fit about having two of his best artists out at the same time.

"Would you like your boyfriend to come in with you until they take you into surgery?" the nurse asked.

Katrina smiled. "Yes, please."

"I'll send him back."

She left and pulled the curtain closed behind her.

Katrina looked up expectantly when the fabric was jerked back a second later, but it was Dr. Powell who stepped into the cubicle.

"Good morning, Katrina," he greeted her.

"Good morning."

He reached for the chart at the foot of her bed, glanced at it, and slid it back into place. "I can tell from here you're a little nervous about the procedure. There's nothing to worry about. We're going to take very good care of you."

Instead of comforting her, goose bumps covered on her shoulders and arms. Not from a creepy factor, but from something else. There was a hint of desperation in the way he looked at her.

Drew pulled back the curtain and entered. Katrina nearly sighed with relief. "Drew, this is Dr. Powell, my surgeon."

Drew shook the other man's hand briefly.

Katrina studied the two men together. Both were the same height, very masculine, and powerfully built. One was dark, the other light. One was fire, the other ice. They seemed to size each other up, like two sharks about to go after the same seal. What was that about? Dr. Powell was her surgeon, nothing else.

"I was just telling Katrina the surgery will take about three hours, possibly a little longer." Graham signed as he spoke. "You'll be in good hands. My team members are very well trained, and we've worked together for the last five years."

Drew came over to stand next to the bed and took her hand.

"Do you have any questions, Katrina?"

"No."

"Good. The nurse will be back in about fifteen minutes to bring you into the operating room."

Katrina cleared her throat. "Thank you, Dr. Powell."

He nodded to them both, and, pulling the curtain aside, left the cubicle.

Drew dragged the only chair in the room forward and sat down.

For a moment Katrina thought he might say something about Dr. Powell, since there had definitely been something there between them for a moment. Instead Drew said, "My father's going to stop by later, and wait for you to come out of surgery."

"Oh, that's nice of him."

He rubbed her hands to warm them. "And Cheryl said she'd be here when you wake up, too. She said she laid a guilt trip on your boss, and he's agreed someone from the office needs to be here to check on you."

Katrina laughed. "When Cheryl decides she wants something, she usually gets her way."

Though he was trying to put her at ease, she could tell he was worried. His face was tight, and his usually gray-blue eyes were the hue of a stormy sea.

She turned on her side and stretched out a hand to smooth his ruffled hair. "I'm going to be fine. You and I both know what amazing healing properties we water folk have.

He kissed the back of her hand. "I know."

"I'll be able to hear you, Drew."

"You already do."

Her cheeks heated. "But it only happens when we're making love. I want to hear what you say all the time."

"When you trust me enough, it will happen. Until then, I think we communicate in other ways just fine."

"Yeah we do." She bit her lip at his comment about trust. Though he'd tried to teach her how to open up to him and allow their connection to expand, it hadn't happened yet. But apparently it couldn't be forced. "When we're in a group situation with your friends and mine, I won't miss so much."

"I know."

They'd been over and over this.

The nurse slipped behind the curtain and tugged it open. She signed, "Time to go, Katrina."

Drew came closer to the bed. The intensity of his look brought a quiver to the pit of her stomach. "I'll be waiting for you." He cupped her chin and lowered his lips to hers.

Katrina forced herself not to reach for him. If she did, she might change her mind about the surgery. "I'll see you in a little while."

Drew walked with Katrina to the operating room door, gave her one last kiss, and stood back to allow the nurse and an orderly to roll her through.

The nurse paused to say, "There's a waiting room for family down the hall there." She pointed to the left.

"Thanks."

She pushed through the door and disappeared.

Drew stood very still for a moment, reaching for calm. Worried didn't begin to cover how he felt. He'd never known such an overwhelming emotion. He wanted to lower the door between him and Katrina, but needed to be sure he was in control of his feelings before he did.

He wandered down the hall to the room the nurse had pointed out. There were two other people sitting on the gray cushioned seats, one woman reading a magazine, and the other watching the television mounted on the wall in the corner. He'd go crazy sitting in the small room with strangers for four hours, but he didn't dare leave in case something happened.

He jerked his cell phone out of his pocket and ran his thumb over the screen to unlock it. He started to call Simon, but changed his mind and hit Tony's number instead. Tony and Simon both had keys to his place.

"Tony. Katrina's in surgery, and I have a three- or four-hour wait until she comes out. Could you swing by my apartment and pick up my small keyboard and some music paper? I need to have something to do until she comes out."

"Sure. I'll be there ASAP."

"Thanks, man." He gave him the waiting room location.

"I'll find it. See you in half an hour."

Drew forced himself to go into the room and sit down.

The night before, he and Katrina had discussed what she needed done should something unexpected happen during the surgery. The conversation had been surreal.

Although he'd acted as though everything was going to be fine, and was fairly sure he'd succeeded, it had scared the shit out of him.

It wasn't going to happen. She was strong. Stronger than humans. She was Mer, which meant she healed ten times faster than they did. She was going to be fine. He was going to take her home tomorrow to his apartment and look after her until she recovered.

Unable to sit still, he went down the hall to the first office area he found and borrowed a pen and some copy paper. He tried to block off the occasional announcement from the PA system and work on the tune to the song he'd written after recording Katrina's underwater music.

When Tony appeared, he heaved a sigh of relief.

"Hope I got everything you needed. I brought earphones in case you want to play without disturbing anyone." He glanced around at the small group, now grown to three besides Drew.

Drew took the two-foot long keyboard, the headphones, and narrow stack of the music paper and angled his chin toward the corner he'd taken over.

Tony took a seat. "Think you'll be able to concentrate on writing while you're waiting for news?"

"I'm doing okay."

Tony raised a brow. "Yeah, you look it. You're a little green around the gills, buddy."

"She's going to be fine."

Tony nodded.

"Katrina doesn't have any parents or family. She has Cheryl, her best friend, and a few people she works with. So if anything major happens, Cheryl and I will need to take care of things."

Tony had a stricken, deer-in-the-headlights look. "Wow. Since I have like a thousand family members, it's hard for me to wrap my head around that."

"Me, too. The risks are low, but they're there."

Tony laid a hand on his shoulder. "Concentrate on the low risk part, and forget the other. She's young and healthy. She'll be fine."

Drew nodded. "I'm going to work to pass the time." And keep from going crazy.

"You're really wild about her," Tony said, sounding amazed.

Drew remained silent.

"As long as I've known you, you've never gotten really involved. It's always been about the sex, or just hanging out, or having someone to take to parties. But this is something real."

Drew had promised himself to keep his distance. He answered grudgingly. "Yeah. So?"

Tony smiled, then the smile stretched into a grin so big it threatened to split his face in two. He laughed. "I can't wait to tell Rand."

Drew narrowed his eyes, though he knew he hadn't entirely kept his wry amusement from showing. "Bastard."

Tony punched his arm. "I'm happy for you, man. No one should be allowed to avoid the clutches of the right woman."

Drew laughed aloud and shook his head.

"Do you think you and Simon might stow the shit and

make up anytime soon?" Tony asked with a little more cheek than normal.

Drew looked down at the empty sheet music. "We're okay."

"Yeah, sure. We're going to be working together for years, Drew. Think you'll be able to keep this distant, business-as-usual thing going for that long?"

Did he have any choice?

Tony leaned forward. "Did you know his old lady had been harping at him to get a day job and give up the band?"

Simon hadn't said a word. Music was his dream. How could Brianna ask him to give it up? That would be like asking him to cut off his hand. "He won't ever do that."

"If she keeps pushing, something will give."

It already had. She'd succeeded in forcing him to defect. Drew's jaw pulsed with anger. "I'll try to talk to him about it."

"Good."

Tony stayed a few more minutes, then left for a date. Though Simon's situation played in the background of his thoughts, Drew poured his concentration into the song. It was the first piece of music he wanted Katrina to hear after she got her implant.

He refused to believe she might never hear his music.

Chapter 25

Graham stood back from the operating table and studied Katrina's classically beautiful features, now relaxed in sleep. He'd sent off her DNA, but it would take weeks to get back. He ran the topography of her skull through his mind while Dr. Marianne Cline, the anesthesiologist, inserted a tube into her throat to help her breathe during the procedure. Dr. Cline, and Beth, his surgical nurse, rolled Katrina onto her side, checked her pressure and heart rate, and then Dr. Cline shot him a thumbs-up. "She's ready."

He had to think of her as the patient. At least until everything was over. This distraction that happened every time he was near enough to smell her was a handicap.

It clouded his mind with…what memory was he reaching for? It was driving him insane. He had been losing sleep, very unusual for him. When he did sleep, he was tormented by a dream of water closing over his head. He'd wake up choking, though nothing was in his throat.

Noticing Beth waiting for him, he stepped up to the surgical table. First he checked the area behind Katrina's ear. The nurse had shaved a small patch of her hair away and bathed the skin with Betadine to ensure the field was sterile. Using a marker, he drew in the incision path.

The moment he handed off the marker to his nurse and accepted the scalpel from her, he shut out all thoughts extraneous to this implant procedure. Cutting down through the temporalis muscle, he placed a template beneath to make a pocket for the implant, then marked the area where he would drill and contour the bone. He slowly drilled away a space in the mastoid bone to create an area for the electrode to coil and enter the cochlea. Checking his measurements carefully, he shaved away a shallow depression to allow the implant to sit behind the ear.

The drill had been feeding a saline solution into the site keep bone dust from contaminating the field, and he vacuumed it out with a small tube as needed. When the bone he was working on suddenly changed color, he blinked and lifted the drill away. Did the lights brighten just now? He glanced up at the surgical light above them. It looked fine, no flickering, no sudden flash. He waited a moment to allow his vision to return to normal.

"Is there a problem, Doctor?" his surgical nurse Beth asked.

"No." He went back to the area he was working on. Once again the surface shone like the inside of a shell. He suctioned the fluid away, and as the bone dried the sheen disappeared. He'd never seen anything like it. Was there a contaminant in the saline solution? Some kind of oil, possibly?

Jesus Christ! The idea shot his heart rate into the stratosphere. If that were the issue, Katrina could develop a dangerous infection. *Not, by God, on his watch.*

"Beth, step closer. I need you to observe and see whether it's the lighting or something is wrong with the solution running from the drill." He lowered the drill and continued to finish the small channel where the tiny electrode would travel from the implant to the hole in the mastoid and to the cochlea. A mother of pearl sheen swept across the small space, then subsided when he lifted the drill and suctioned the liquid away.

"It has to be the lighting," Beth said with a small frown. "I filled the reservoir myself. Checked the dates on the bottles, looked at the fluid, it was clear, and besides, it's a closed system to prevent contamination.

But there was clearly something wrong. All he had left to do was to drill the tiny holes where he would anchor the implant to prevent it from moving. To stop now and request another machine would open the patient to more risk of infection.

"Okay, I'm going to finish this. We'll put the patient on a round of antibiotics, and when we're done, draw a sample of the saline solution from the machine and send it to the lab. If there is a contaminant, we need to know what the hell it is so we'll know what we're dealing with."

"Yes, Doctor." Beth sounded subdued, wary.

He drilled the anchor holes, fitted the implant into the space, and sutured it in place. Using a special tool, he fed the electrodes' tiny wires into the cochlea, then sealed the hole he'd drilled through the bone with a tiny piece of muscle. The electrode curled around the pocket he'd created in the mastoid perfectly.

Though his fingers continued to work, his thoughts raced to the repercussions for Katrina should a contaminant be present. He clamped down on the distracting concerns. He'd done his best work. She was going to be fine, and she'd be blessed with the gift of hearing.

He took his time suturing the layers of muscle and tissue back together, one at a time. Though the scar would be hidden in the curvature at the back of her ear, there was no reason for it to be noticeable, even to her.

"That's a beautiful job, Doctor. If you ever give up otology, you could do plastic surgery," Beth said.

Was she praising his work in hopes he wouldn't fire her if something went wrong with the patient? He didn't give a damn whether it was her fault or not. If this patient went south, she'd be gone.

The angrier he felt, the colder his demeanor. He didn't reply, but stepped away from the table. "I'll be checking on her in recovery. Instruct the nurses to page me as soon as she's awake."

The nurse's expression had flattened out and grown more wary. "Yes, Doctor."

"Put a rush on that lab work," Graham ordered.

"Yes, sir."

He shoved through the doors into the scrub area, ripped off his surgical gear, and let fly the rage he'd been suppressing. "Fuck-fuck-fuck!" Then he took several deep breaths to bleed off some of the anger. Goddammit! The muscles in his arms twitched and he ground his teeth. He wanted to pound something. Instead he moved to the scrub sink to wash his hands. He allowed the water to stream over his skin, especially the insides of his wrists, until he was back in control.

He'd keep a close eye on her, and if there was any sign of infection, he'd admit her and start her immediately on an IV antibiotic. Katrina was going to be fine.

Katrina fought her way up from the drugs, only for nausea to drag her back down like an anchor. She curled in on herself and clamped her eyes shut to block out the spinning white and blue room.

When someone laid a hand on her shoulder she signed stop, then spelled sick.

If she concentrated, she could use her Mer abilities to end the nausea and the dull ache running from the crown of her head to the base of her neck, but to do so would cause an uproar if anyone observed her.

She sensed movement around her. If she opened her eyes, she'd throw up. In fact … "I'm going to throw up."

A plastic basin was placed in her hands. She heaved, but there was nothing in her stomach to come up. Sickness wreaked havoc on her system and caused the side of her head to pound like someone was beating her skull in with a hammer.

Drew scanned the nearly empty waiting room. It had been nearly an hour since a nurse had come to report on a patient's status and take the person waiting back to recovery. Katrina's surgery had already taken four hours and counting. He rubbed at his neck muscles, which were tight as guitar strings. A headache pounded behind his eyes, and his stomach bubbled around his worry like a bad bowl of chili.

When his father appeared at the door he felt some of the tension drain off. Maybe the nurses would tell him something.

He stood to greet him…and staggered beneath a wave of vertigo so strong he had to brace a hand against the wall to keep from falling.

His father rushed forward and gripped his arm, his expression tense with concern. "What is it?"

"Katrina," Drew managed, though the room continued to spin and his stomach pitched.

"You have to push it away, Drew. Block it off so we can do something to help her."

Drew dragged air into his lungs and mentally reinforced the door between them. When he opened his eyes the room remained stationary, but his stomach still struggled with the aftereffects.

His father eyed him with a frown. "Better?"

"Yeah."

"Come with me."

Drew grabbed his keyboard and sheet music and followed Blake as he stalked down the hall to a door with the word recovery printed across it in bold letters. He slid a keycard through the lock on the side of the wall, and when it clicked, jerked the door open. They entered a long, wide corridor with a nurse's station on one side and curtained alcoves on the other.

Katrina's scent guided them to the second one on the right, her distress adding a metallic undertone to her normal essence.

Drew's heart rate skyrocketed. Was she bleeding?

Blake shoved the curtain aside and strode into the narrow room. He ignored the nurse who stood next to the gurney and went directly to Katrina.

"Hey, you're not—" Recognition struck. "Oh, Dr. Andrews."

"Hello, Celica. Have you called Dr. Powell to let him know Ms. Larson is having some post-operative difficulties?"

"Yes, sir. I paged him, but he's been called to the ER for a consult and hasn't called back yet."

"A standard post-operative medication like Promethazine will alleviate her distress. Why don't you go order it up and call him to confirm? I'll stay here with Katrina until you come back."

"Thank you, sir." The young nurse glanced in Drew's direction.

"This is Drew, my son, and Katrina's boyfriend. She signed a release permitting him to be here. It should be on her paperwork."

"Yes, sir."

As soon as the woman left the room, Blake motioned Drew forward.

He tossed the keyboard and music onto the only chair in the room. "She's experiencing vertigo, pain and nausea. Is that normal?" He took position on the opposite side of the bed.

Katrina's face was pasty white, her skin translucent, and she was holding one hand protectively over the ear covered by a dressing.

"For most humans, this doesn't happen at all. The surgery accessed her inner ear, of course, but since she's Mer there's such a delicate balance there, the effects are exaggerated. I can't help her, Drew. Humans are easy. Without an emotional connection to her, I won't be able to help her, but you can. Concentrate on controlling the vertigo and her stomach will settle, then go after the pain." He glanced up. "You remember how to do this?"

"Yes, of course." Drew's heart drummed in his ears. He'd only used this gift once before on a human during an emergency. It was expressly forbidden because of the dangerous repercussions if done wrong. The concern he read in his father's expression twisted his anxiety level higher. If his father was this worried, he had to do something to help her.

In order to connect with her, he had to open the door between them. He visualized cracking it open, but her pain and nausea slammed open the barrier with the force of a battering ram. If he hadn't been holding onto the railing of the bed, he'd have fallen. The whole side of his head beat like a drum, the room spun like a whirlpool, and nausea threatened to overwhelm him. He gripped the bed railing and rested his forehead there. If he couldn't get himself under control he couldn't help Katrina.

"Put the physical discomforts you're experiencing behind a wall, Drew. Or shove them in a box. They're not real for you."

They sure as hell felt real. First the pain had to cease if he even wanted to think. Gasping, still struggling, Drew shoved his hand beneath Katrina's hair and cupped the back of her neck. He closed his eyes.

Don't rush it, he reminded himself. It had to be a gentle suggestion, not a shove. But the pain was an octopus—not the shy, innocuous creatures he knew them to be, but the bloodthirsty myth of old. It clung to them, its tentacles wrapped around his head and Katrina's, the suction cups digging into their flesh, burrowing into their skulls. The pain was paralyzing in its intensity.

Fear for her sent a spike of adrenaline through him and numbed his hurt, finally allowing him to function. One at a time he tugged the creature's arms off her head and wound them around his hand. As he pulled each one from her, the squirming limbs dropped away from his head and face and hung limp in his grasp. He pushed his hand down into the clear acrylic box in his mind and released his grip. The octopus uncoiled, shooting ink into the water, and he slammed the lid down before it could escape.

When the pain ceased, the vertigo rose up full force, making his stomach tumble. He held the image of a tilt-a-whirl at a carnival in his mind and projected it to her.

He and Katrina were sitting close together in a red, plastic-covered seat. They both clutched the round, wheel-like handle that controlled their spin, but it kept slipping from their grasp, and the seat whirled sickeningly while the machine's deck heaved. Despite them being water creatures, and accustomed to the fluid movement of the sea, nausea rolled over him, as it did her.

He visualized gripping the wheel, allowing it to slide through his hands while the gradual pressure of his grip slowed its spinning. Finally it slowed to a crawl, then stopped. Their seat swayed back and forth, slower and slower, until it settled into stillness. After a few moments, the nausea eased.

When Drew opened his eyes, his father was smoothing Katrina's hair back from the cuplike dressing covering her ear, then pulled the plastic basin she'd vomited into away and set it aside. "Better?" he asked as he focused on her face.

"Yes." Her fingers curled over his arm, and he patted her hand.

"It's only a temporary fix until you can heal yourself," Blake said.

"I understand."

She eased onto her back and, seeing Drew, groaned and covered the side of her face with her hand. "I don't want you to see me like this."

Drew grasped her hand and tugged it away gently. "Too late."

Though she had only this moment wakened from surgery, she looked exhausted, her normal bright blue-green eyes dulled to a grayish hue. Lines bracketed her mouth, a residue of the pain.

The nurse returned with two syringes and placed them on the table next to the bed. "Good call, Dr. Andrews. Dr. Powell had already written orders in her chart, but hadn't thought she'd need the meds until later."

Blake stepped aside to allow the nurse access. She took Katrina's pulse and blood pressure and frowned at the reading. "From one to ten, how bad is your pain, Katrina?"

She seemed reluctant to say. "It's an eight," she croaked.

Drew shook his head. It had been a twenty at least. Any human would have been screaming. Her Mer physiology had obviously multiplied the aftereffects of the surgery.

"I'm going to give you some medication in your IV. It will help with the pain and nausea." Celica plunged first one syringe, then the other, into the IV, emptying the medication into the line. She disposed of the syringes in a medical waste container, then laid a hand on Katrina's blanket-covered foot. "They'll be taking you upstairs, Katrina. Dr. Powell wants you to stay the night for observation. He'll release you in the morning once your nausea and pain are under control."

Blake caught Drew's eye. With Katrina's attention directed at the nurse she didn't see him say, "It's a good idea for her to stay, Drew."

The nurse left, and Katrina's hand curled around the forearm he'd rested on the metal bed railing. "How did you do that?"

He stroked her cheek. Remembering her response to his Siren singing ability, he was reluctant to tell her everything. It would probably scare her, and possibly make her wary of allowing him access to her emotions. "I made a mental suggestion to help you deal with the pain and discomfort. It wears off after a few minutes, so you still needed the shots."

She nodded, and her eyelids drooped as the double dose of medication hit her system. "Thank you for helping me," and she drifted back to sleep.

God, he hated seeing her in pain. Drew raked his fingers through his hair, his attention snagging on his father's expression of disapproval.

"You haven't shared everything with her." The accusation hung between them.

"I don't need to. She's already picked up on most of it."

"You can't hide this from her, Drew."

"I'm not hiding anything."

"If she finds out later, she'll wonder if you've held back because you're attempting to manipulate her."

Outraged, his grip tightened on the bars surrounding the gurney. "I'd never do that. *Never.*"

His father's brows rose. "You just did."

Chapter 26

Drew stretched his legs out and propped them on the bottom rail of Katrina's hospital bed. Once they'd moved her to a room, she crashed. She slept peacefully, but he was watchful of her every move.

His father's accusation about manipulating Katrina was unfair. He'd done what he needed to do to help her. That was all. After his experience in high school with the stalking groupies, he'd been careful how he used his Siren gifts. He'd used a mind-to-mind push just once during an emergency when he'd been in his teens. That one time had been under his father's instruction. The only other time was to deal with the bully in the restaurant. Blake had insisted Drew never use the skill again unless it was a dire emergency.

And though Drew had teased Sam a little about his addiction to cigars, he'd never had any intention of taking the man's vice away. To plant a permanent suggestion like that in a human's fragile mind would affect them for the rest of their lives. He wondered if it had helped or hindered the man in the restaurant.

The affects of such a mind meld between preternatural

water folk only worked short term. It seemed their brains were wired differently, and more resistant to a mental attack. Hundreds of year of evolution protected them from each other.

Occasionally he glanced up at the muted television in the corner, but his attention always returned to Katrina. After her violent reaction earlier, he was grateful she was no longer in pain, but as long as she slept, she wouldn't be able to heal herself. In order to leave the hospital, she needed to start the process to ensure she didn't go back into that pit of vertigo she'd experienced earlier.

He rose, leaned against the bars along the side of the bed, and gave her a gentle shake. He started to speak to her and realized it wouldn't help. He bent his head to kiss her instead.

Her lashes fluttered, and she brushed a hand over her face that would have hit him had he not pulled back. He grinned. When her eyes opened, his grin stretched into a smile. "Hello, Sleeping Beauty. How are you feeling?"

She blinked at him for a moment. "What?"

He repeated his question.

She paused, he assumed to take inventory. "Better."

He sighed with relief. Her eyes were swollen from sleep, the left one more than the right, and the swelling had spread to her temple and jaw on that side. He frowned. "Are you in any pain?"

"Only a dull headache on this side of my head." She cupped the bandage over her left ear. "How long have I been asleep?"

"About an hour. The medication hit you hard."

She nodded. "It will wear off soon." Apprehension knitted her brows. "Has the doctor been in?"

As though on cue, the door opened and Graham Powell strode into the room.

Drew frowned at his lack of warning. His father always tapped on the door before entering. But then, his patients weren't deaf.

He nodded to Drew then approached the bed, his eyes fastened on Katrina. He signed as he spoke. "How are you feeling?"

"Better."

"Good." He reached for the chart at the end of the bed, looked it over, then replaced it. "I'm going to check your incision."

She nodded. He raised the head of the bed so she was sitting up. Some of the color leached from her skin, and she cupped a hand against her stomach.

"Still nauseous?" he asked.

She swallowed. "It's settling again."

Drew gripped the hospital bed railing. Jesus, she needed to be able to heal, but the room was like Grand Central Station, with nurses coming in and out every few minutes, and now the doctor. Drew studied the man. He had lines of stress around his mouth, but his eyes were sharp as he studied Katrina. He eased the dressing from her ear secured by a strap around her head and peeled it away. A small amount of blood dotted the gauze inside the plastic cup. He studied the back of her ear, secured the bandage back, removed an otoscope from his pocket, and looked into her ear. Then he backed away a bit so she could see him sign to her, all business.

"It looks good. There's very little bleeding and fluid. The nurse will change the gauze and put a more permanent bandage in place. You'll need to leave it on for a few days. The dizziness and nausea you're experiencing are normal, but each person is different. Some it affects minimally, while others' experience is more severe. Your inner ear has been traumatized, and it will take a few days for it to heal, like the rest of your incisions. The swelling around your eye, temple and jaw is normal. That soft tissue has been traumatized as well. Once the swelling has receded, you'll feel much better.

"The surgery went very well," he continued. "You didn't have any excess bleeding, and there were no…" he paused minutely, "…surprises. If your nausea and pain are under control by morning, I expect to release you to go home then. Since it was so severe right after surgery, I want to keep you overnight to make sure you're on the road to recovery."

Katrina nodded then closed her eyes as the vertigo momentarily returned.

"Keep your bed elevated a little, and don't sleep on that ear. But I don't suppose I have to tell you that. We'll send you home with some pain and anti-nausea medication, but I expect things to calm down fairly quickly, and you'll be back to normal in a few weeks."

"Thank you." Katrina signed.

"I'll be back this evening after dinner to check on you."

She nodded. "Thank you, Dr. Powell."

"You're welcome. I expect you to do as well as my other patients." He smiled for the first time. "That's an order."

"I'll do my best."

He nodded to Drew again and left the room.

Drew wondered about the small hesitation before Powell said the word surprises. Had something unusual happened during the surgery? And what about the man made Katrina so wary? She had watched him intently the whole time he was in the room.

Powell seemed like any other doctor. He'd behaved in a professional manner. Would it have been different had Drew not been in the room?

Drew turned to Katrina. "Would you like something to drink?"

"I need a bathroom first," she said.

He lowered the bed railing. "Would you like me to carry you, or do you want to try to walk?"

"I'll walk."

She gripped his hand and eased to a standing position. "I'll try a little healing while I'm in the bathroom."

He signed okay, then looped an arm around her waist to hold her steady.

Katrina discovered reaching the bathroom was a major challenge. And though the room no longer spun, it still seemed to rock, and her stomach continued to feel queasy.

As soon as Drew closed the door behind her, she dealt with using the bathroom and moved to the sink to wash her hands. Using the toothbrush provided in the hospital patient kit, she brushed her teeth. She really needed water to spark her healing ability, preferably salt water, but she'd use whatever she had access to. She rinsed the sink out, pulled up the lever for the plug, ran lukewarm water into the basin, and removed the dressing covering her ear. She held her hair back in one hand, dragged in a full breath, and submerged her face in the warm water. After a brief moment, tingling warmth trailed along the side of her face and encircled her eye. She longed to submerge the ear itself, but was wary of showing too much improvement too quickly.

She concentrated on directing the healing toward the symptoms plaguing her the most, the vertigo and nausea. After two five-minute submersions, she felt significantly better.

She emptied the sink, dried her face with several paper towels, and checked her appearance in the mirror. The swelling was down, her dizziness had subsided, and with it the nausea. She removed the scrunchie securing her hair and finger-combed it before pulling it over to the side away from the incision. From the front, her ear appeared a little red and the swelling behind it pushed it out from her head farther than the other. Had she been able to submerge it, the swelling there would have disappeared, too. She replaced the dressing and moved to open the door.

Cheryl was perched on the edge of the bed, but bobbed up. "Are you okay? You've been in there a while." She rushed to Katrina's side and caught her arm to help her back to the bed.

"I was bathing my face and primping a little. I felt rather icky from—everything. I'm moving a little slower than usual."

"I totally understand. A girl's got to look her best, no matter what the circumstances. Drew said you'd had some dizziness and other issues right after surgery. I was going to your apartment to check on you when I got his text telling me you were spending the night here."

Katrina looked over at him as she slid back on the bed, and Cheryl spread the blanket up over her.

He signed "Okay?" She nodded.

"I'm fine, Cheryl. I had a stronger reaction to things than normal. They're being safe."

"Good." She wiggled back to the foot of the bed. "You look a little like those pale, languid beauties you see on old calendars from the thirties. Like Carole Lombard or Loretta Young."

"And how do you know about them?" Katrina asked.

"I'm doing a website for a customer who wants that sort of look, so I've been researching photographic techniques from that era. I'm really getting into it.

"Everyone at the office went together and got you some flowers." She pointed to the planter of small, live cactus artfully arranged in a clay pot.

"It's beautiful, and fortunately will be hard for me to kill. Please thank them for me."

Cheryl stayed half an hour and then rushed back to work when they brought Katrina's lunch of Jell-O, broth, and a soft drink. Katrina encouraged Drew to go get something to eat and go home for a while.

"You don't have to babysit me. I feel much better."

He sat next to her on the bed. "You're getting some color back in your cheeks." He caressed one with the pad of his thumb. "And you're much prettier than any thirties era movie star."

"And you're handsomer than Clark Gable." She gave one of his earlobes a gentle tug. "Your ears aren't nearly as big, either."

Drew laughed and she smiled, a sudden tenderness for him rising in her. He had been remarkable today. Patient, supportive, everything she could hope for in a mate. She cupped his cheek. "One day soon I'll be able to hear you laugh. I've wanted that so much."

His expression shifted to serious "Your laugh makes me hard every time I hear it."

She slipped her arms around his neck and tugged him close. "Everything about you makes me wet," she whispered in his ear.

When he drew back, his eyes had darkened and his cheeks were red.

"Vixen," he accused.

"Siren," she shot back. He laughed again and kissed her.

"I'll be back in a couple of hours."

She gave him a short list of things she needed from home, which he promised to pick up.

"You're really okay?" he asked, as he gathered his keyboard and sheet music.

"Yes, I'm fine. I'll work on getting even better later tonight after the hospital calms down."

"Sounds like a plan."

After he was gone, Katrina eyed the tray on the hospital table with distaste. She should have told him to bring her something to eat. But the fluids wouldn't do her any harm, so she nibbled at the Jell-O, sipped the broth, and drank the soft drink. The afternoon passed slowly.

She hadn't realized how much she'd grown accustomed to having Drew there to fill her silence. Even when they weren't speaking, his presence gave her a feeling of solidarity. She was no longer alone. He had filled a giant hole in her life.

Every night since they'd made love the first time he came home to her, eager to be together again. Was that bonding, or was it love? Or were the two things the same?

She could only be sure of her own feelings. She loved him. She'd always love him.

Graham closed his laptop and stifled a yawn. Not since his residency had he worked on so little sleep. He relished those days now. It would have been a relief to be working instead of revisiting the same dream about drowning over and over every night.

Sooner or later whatever he was going through would affect his work. It already had, actually. He was seeing things that weren't there. There hadn't been any contaminant in the drill solution, and he was no longer certain he'd actually seen the strange sheen on Katrina Larson's exposed bone during the surgery.

Beth had thought it was the lighting. For lack of any evidence to the contrary, he had to agree with her. In fact, he wanted to agree with her, because it kept him from fully facing this crisis. Or whatever the hell he was going through.

There could be physical causes. He could have a brain tumor, though he wasn't having headaches, dizzy spells, or blurred vision. But those symptoms might not manifest till late in the illness. He'd never know if there was a ticking time bomb in his head without further tests. But he couldn't have the tests if he didn't go to someone and tell them what was going on. And once he started that ball rolling...

Fear of being exposed was worse than what he was going through. Doctors and nurses talked. It would only take a whisper, and he could lose his practice, his reputation. Everything. Even if there was nothing wrong.

He didn't want to acknowledge the other possibility, because since that fear reared its ugly head, it made him quake inside. He could have a mental illness. If he did, his father would recognize it, and would help him. He'd be discreet. But once again, his life would be over. No one would allow him to perform surgery if he was mentally unstable.

Graham shoved his fingers through his hair and cradled his head in his hands. He didn't want to go back to the hospital and see Katrina Larson. As long as he didn't face her, he didn't have to think about his stalker-ish behavior. He'd pursued a woman because of how she smelled. How insane was that?

Pretty strange.

He could call Carl and ask him to cover for him. But it was his responsibility to check on her. He always did what was expected of him. He sighed and forced himself to his feet.

Once he was back from rounds, he was going to take

something to help him sleep so he could get a good night's rest. He did not have a brain tumor or a mental illness. He was stressed. That's all.

He was going to be fine.

Chapter 27

Katrina toyed with the food on her plate and waited for Drew to finish talking on his cell phone. His body language projected a listening tension, his face mobile with excitement. Her curiosity was piqued.

Drew ended the call and turned to face her. "That was our manager. We'll be going into the recording studio within a month."

"That's wonderful." At his frown, she asked, "Isn't it?"

"I don't know. I'm concerned we're still not ready. And now with Simon distracted because of the baby…" He shook his head.

Katrina laid her hand on his arm. "I know how hard you work, Drew. If anyone is ready to go into a studio, it's you."

He covered her hand. "I understand why Simon was afraid for Brianna. When you were in pain this morning, I felt damn helpless. I'd rather it was me hurting than have to watch you go through it."

Katrina pushed aside the tray and gripped the hand he laid on her knee. "I wouldn't want you to take my place, Drew. You locked away my pain until the nurse could give me medication for it. That was enough."

His frown intensified. "You know I'd never try to influence you through our connection, don't you?"

Katrina studied him for a moment. "You can't influence me if I'm not open to it, Drew."

The worry in his expression cleared, and he smiled. "No. I can't."

She patted the bed next to her. "But you have other powers of persuasion."

Drew laughed. "You know all my secrets."

Though it was a difficult fit, he stretched out beside her in the narrow bed. Katrina smoothed back the dark hair at his temple. "I told you about Mitchell, my ex."

Drew nodded.

"He tried to educate me about all the water folk we might meet when we went in search of my father. And one of the first he warned me about was Sirens. He didn't want me to be seduced away from him by some handsome devil like you. So I know about your gifts. I know how far you can go with the connection between us, but not about how it works with humans."

"Humans have no shields and I could permanently damage their minds. I've only done something similar twice before."

"When the man was bullying Mr. Walters, and…?"

"When I was in high school. My father and I were coming home from a trip and came upon an automobile accident. Being a doctor, he stopped. There were several severe injuries, but one of the worst was a young girl. She didn't have her seatbelt on, and had hit the back of the seat.

She had a head injury that was bleeding badly, broken ribs, a collapsed lung, and was disoriented. She was gasping for air and panicked. She fought my father when he tried to help her, so I calmed her while Dad worked on her until the paramedics arrived."

"Did she live?"

"Yeah, she did."

"Good."

"It sounds like this Mitchell guy helped you out quite a bit."

Being with Drew had given her a different perspective on her relationship with the Merman. "He took me in and kept me off the streets. And he encouraged me to finish high school."

"And in return he got to sleep with a nubile young woman and be your first lover."

She got a bit giddy when she saw the harshness of his features and the glow in his eyes. Was it jealousy she saw? Her heart raced with excitement and uncertainty.

"I was eighteen. And we only slept together for six months. He pushed me out of the nest when I probably needed to be out on my own anyway. I might not have gone to college otherwise."

"Are you going to look him up and thank him for that?"

She couldn't help but laugh. "No. He's probably bonded with some human female and has several children by now. It's been years and years since we meant anything to each other. Why would I want to rehash it, when what I have now is so much more?"

That seemed to mollify him though his brows remained

knotted in a frown.

"Are you jealous, Drew?" she asked. "If that's what it is, you don't have to be. I'm closer to you than I've ever been to anyone. I don't want anyone else."

He swung off the bed. "I'll be back in a few minutes. I'm going to go down to the cafeteria and get us both a drink."

Katrina sighed. "Take your time. I'm good and the doctor will be here any minute."

He paused by the door as though he wanted to say something, then turned aside and left the room.

Before she'd met Drew, she'd been afraid of opening herself to her emotions or her natural abilities. And at times he seemed to be the same. But whether he knew it or not, he was teaching her to be unafraid. Something else to love him for.

She was still smiling when Dr. Powell entered the room. Stress bracketed his mouth, and there was a strained look about his eyes. Beard stubble darkened his jaw.

He signed hello, then asked, "How are you feeling this evening?"

"Much better." Shocked at the change in him since this morning, she studied him. This was more than stress.

He moved around the side of the bed and tilted her face up so he could study the swelling. "You look much better. How are the pain and nausea?"

"Almost gone."

He used his stethoscope and listened to her breathing, then folded the instrument in his hand. "Your lungs are clear. Any dizziness?"

"A little." It came and went indiscriminately.

"That will lessen over the next couple of weeks." He went over the improvements in her condition since this morning. No fever, no more severe pain, blood pressure and heart rate normal. "If things continue as they are, I'll release you in the morning."

She'd be glad to go home. It seemed she'd been stuck in this room for a week. At least she'd been able to give up the hospital gown for sleep pants and a T-shirt.

"Are you okay?" she asked, taking in his bloodshot eyes.

"Yes. I'm fine. It's been a busy day. I'll get a good night's sleep and be ready to take on the world tomorrow."

"I'm sorry you had to make another trip this evening because of me." He looked really ragged out. His hand even shook as he set the stethoscope down next to her dinner tray.

"No trouble. That's what doctors do."

"Have your parents left for their trip?"

"No, not for a few more days."

"Maybe you should think about taking time off and going with them."

His mouth quirked. "This trip is supposed to be a second honeymoon. I wouldn't want to horn in." He lapsed into silence a moment, his gaze distant, as though something internal had caught his attention. Then he snapped back and focused on her again. "A trip somewhere doesn't sound bad. I'll give it some thought."

Each time she saw him, he seemed more human to her. The clinical scientist had experienced some kind of personality shift. Had it happened because he'd become more familiar with her after seeing her outside the office, or was something else at work here? Whatever it was, it disturbed her.

"Get some rest, and I'll see you in the morning." He lifted a hand in farewell and left.

"Have a good evening," she called after him.

After a moment's thought, Katrina slipped from the bed and went to the small locker-like closet in the corner where her clothing and purse were stored. She retrieved her cell phone and searched through her contacts until she found Dr. Joseph Powell's number. But when she reached to press her finger on the contact, she hesitated.

What was she planning to text him? That his son looked tired and like he hadn't slept in days? That his distant, clinical personality had suddenly shifted and he'd become more approachable?

His guard was down. His guard. That's what it was. He seemed vulnerable, where before he'd been impervious. It was as though something catastrophic had cracked his hard shell and left him open. But what could have caused it, and what could she tell his father?

What if all her analysis of his body language, his facial expression, using her Mer instincts, proved wrong? After a few more moments of debate, doubt set in, and she set aside her phone on the bedside table. She'd wait until morning and see if Graham Powell was better when he returned to discharge her. If he wasn't, she'd make the call.

A wave of dizziness struck her, followed by a wave of nausea. It was time for another short healing session. She longed to immerse herself into a tub of sea salt-laced water so she'd feel more herself and be rid of all the side effects from the surgery.

She went into the bathroom and closed the door.

Graham reached the west entrance of the hospital before he realized he'd left his stethoscope behind.

Exhaustion beat down on him. To hell with it. One of the nurses would find it and put it aside for him. He stepped outside into the early evening breeze, but paused. It had been a gift from his parents for his graduation from med school, and had a special engraving on it from them. If someone picked it up and took it home, he'd never see it again.

God damn it! He turned back and reentered the hospital.

Five minutes later, he entered Katrina Larson's hospital room to find it empty. He frowned until he noticed the closed bathroom door. He'd be gone before she ever knew he'd come into the room.

A wonderful scent overpowered the normal antiseptic smell that permeated every patient room. The fragrance was the same one he'd noticed the day he met Katrina. The same one that wove its way through his brain and tugged at that elusive memory he reached for in his dreams. She'd said she didn't wear perfume. Had she lied?

He followed it to the bathroom door, where it was even stronger. He savored it. Why did it call to him? What memory was trying to break free each time he smelled it? It was driving him crazy. It was like feeling sure he had something important to do and not being able to remember what it was.

He rested his hand on the bathroom doorknob.

What if she were sitting on the commode, or giving herself a basin bath in the sink? She'd be understandably upset if he invaded her privacy. But he could say he thought he'd heard her fall.

The fragrance tantalized him with the possibility of imminent understanding. If he could just remember where he first smelled it, he'd have the answers. He knew he would.

He twisted the knob and swung the door open halfway. Katrina leaned over the sink, her slender back bowed. She wasn't washing her face or rinsing it. She was holding her face in the water. Why would she do that?

His attention settled on her hand, which rested on the edge of the porcelain sink. The skin appeared whiter, and a faint sheen of blue and pink rippled across it. Exactly as the colors had spread across the bone this morning during surgery.

Oh, God, he was seeing things again. He stepped back to close the door.

Katrina straightened and put a towel to her face. The reflection in the mirror was hers, but her features looked more distinct, exaggerated, and her skin was alive with the mother of pearl glow.

Graham froze, every muscle in his body going taut with shock. This couldn't be a hallucination. Surely it couldn't. He reached for his cell phone and armed it to take a picture.

When it flashed, her eyes flew open. Water clung to her

lashes, her eyes widened in shock, and she gasped, whirling around to face him.

The face from his nightmares stared at him. Graham stumbled back, but she lunged forward and latched onto his wrist.

"Dr. Powell."

The strength in her slender fingers numbed his hand and the stethoscope fell to the floor.

"Please listen to me," she said.

Though he backed away, she advanced with him, still gripping his arm.

"Let me explain," her tone rang urgent in his ears.

He outweighed her by at least a hundred pounds, and yet he couldn't dislodge her grip, though he twisted his arm until it hurt. Fear narrowed his vision and shook him, hard.

"You have to calm down."

He couldn't catch his breath. His heart pounded in his chest, his ears. He felt the humiliating urge to urinate but controlled it. The door behind him opened, and he twisted around, hoping for help.

Her grip loosened. Graham heaved against it and broke free.

Drew, Katrina's boyfriend walked into the room. Graham barreled past him, out into the hall and broke into a run. They wouldn't follow him and attack him out here. There'd be too many people to act as witnesses. As he reached the nurses station, he slowed his steps and looked over his shoulder. The hallway stretched empty behind him.

"What the hell happened?" Drew demanded.

Katrina's scent saturated the air, clouding his mind with thoughts of sex, even as her open distress had him instinctively gathering her close to comfort them both. She trembled against him.

"He saw me partially transformed. He'd come and gone, but he came back for the stethoscope he left on the tray. He opened the bathroom door." Her hands gripped his shirt and she burrowed her face into his chest. "He took my picture, Drew."

Chapter 28

On Thursday morning, Dr. Carl Turner came to the hospital and discharged Katrina. Drew hadn't expected Graham Powell to show after Katrina had outed herself to him. Through no fault of her own. What kind of asshole opens the door on a woman in the bathroom?

It would take the bastard a day to process the confrontation. Another to go over all the medical information he had on her.

He'd be back to ask questions, and when he showed, Drew meant to be there to protect Katrina. Though security at her apartment building was better than his, it was smarter for her to stay at his place. Powell would have access to her home address through her files.

"I've got everything set up for you at my apartment. I even brought over your computer," he said once they were in the car.

Katrina's eyes widened in surprise. "You've moved me into your place?"

"Well, not completely. Mine is a little bigger, and I want you with me, Katrina. "You've just had surgery." He hesitated to upset her, but it was a concern. "And we don't know what Powell's going to do."

The tension in her face relaxed somewhat. She rested her hand against his chest. "I'm sorry I messed up. If he puts that picture out on the net—"

"He can't do that, Katrina. He's a medical professional, and sworn to protect your privacy. If he does, we'll say it's a hoax. Or that it was facial swelling due to your surgery. It will go away or end up being a big speculative curiosity."

"Why did he take the picture?"

"Because he couldn't be sure what he was seeing was real. That's my idea." The guy had been scared fuckless. Maybe he'd be too afraid to confront either of them and all this would go away. But Drew didn't think so.

Katrina's cell buzzed like an angry bumblebee, and she slipped her hand into her pocket to retrieve it. "The Powells are still looking for him, but haven't found him yet. Graham called in sick at work. He hasn't come to their house, either. Joseph has cancelled his appointments today and is out looking for him."

Graham Powell had gone completely off the grid. Did he think they'd come after him?

Maybe so. God only knew what he thought Katrina was. Or maybe he believed he'd been seeing things. Something the photo would dispel pretty quickly.

"He'll come out of hiding sooner or later. He'll go to his parents before anyone else. They're close, and no matter what he tells them, they'll try to fix this for him…and for us. They have as much to lose as we do." He rested his palm against the side of her face and his thumb traced the curve beneath her cheekbone. "It's going to be okay, Katrina."

With a nod, she sighed and leaned back against the seat. Every time he soothed her fears it worked for a while, then suddenly her anxiety would skyrocket, and she'd be back on pins and needles. She'd been shaken last night, in as much of a panic as Powell had been when he tore out of the room. Had he done something to her besides take the picture?

Drew reached for the key and started the car.

At his apartment, it took only minutes for Katrina to settle in. Drew fixed some lunch and then urged her to take a nap.

"I'd prefer a bath, then a nap," she said.

"Sure."

"Do you have any sea salt?"

"The kind you sprinkle on your food?"

"That will do."

He retrieved the sea salt from the pantry and handed it to her.

"Thank you." She slipped her arms around him and pressed close. "Don't come into the bathroom, okay? I don't know if I'm ready for you to see me like…that."

What was so horrible about her Mermaid shape that she was afraid for him to see? Her feet were red, the skin covered in scar tissue. Especially her toes. He'd seen them often enough without the makeup. How bad could the scarring be when her fluke formed? Not as bad as she imagined. The vulnerable expression in her eyes when she looked up at him hit him in the chest like a punch. "Okay, honey."

To get his mind off of what she might not want him to see, he wandered into the living room and spread out the sheet music he'd been working with on the piano stand. He played the chorus he'd completed, fattening the chords so the sound would be richer. And toyed with the lyrics he'd brainstormed so far.

It had to be right. It was going to be the first song Katrina heard him play when her implant was turned on. Graham Powell wasn't getting between them and that moment. In fact, he wasn't going to hurt either of them. He had more to lose than either he or Katrina.

Katrina was grateful for Drew's understanding as she curled up in the bathtub and lay beneath the water for long minutes at a time. She kept revisiting the look on Graham Powell's face when she'd turned to confront him. He'd been horrified at her appearance. She'd seen that look on the faces of the women who cared for her in the children's home. It had hurt every time. It had hurt last night. It hurt right now.

She wasn't a monster. She was a mammal, like him. She'd give birth on dry land, like any human female. She'd breast feed her babies like other humans. She had to surface to breathe, though she could hold her breath far longer than was humanly possible.

The big differences were she could hear distant sounds undetectable to humans and could navigate through dark water with her built-in sonar, and the high-pitched sounds she could make. As long as she had access to water, she could heal her body of most injuries.

But for all her human qualities, she wasn't human. Though she lived like one, ate like one, worked like one, had human DNA blended in her body, she was an imposter. She had tried to convince herself she was human so she could forget about being a Mermaid. The people at the children's home had insisted she conform, and she had.

There were days when she didn't think about it even once. She avoided going near the beach so she wouldn't long for something she couldn't have. But she couldn't do it anymore.

Because having one person know what she was presented a danger to so many others. Drew had only hinted at what he was, and it had caused chaos in his band.

She had to make her peace with who and what she was and accept it, embrace it. She had to make Graham Powell accept it. Make him believe she was the last of a dying race. Beg him to keep her secret. Because if she didn't, what few were left would be hunted.

Drew was right. Humans didn't want to understand anyone or anything different from them. They wanted to study, cage, or destroy it. They felt threatened or uncomfortable with any being who didn't follow the norm, even other humans. Or they looked upon them with pity. Or with horror.

They wouldn't pity her. They'd look at her as a sideshow freak to be dissected and studied. A member of a long-dead species they'd want to learn about. They'd start looking at her friends, the people she worked with, even Drew, and wonder if they were different, too. No wonder water folk avoided each other. If one were discovered, it would automatically lead to the exposure of another and another.

She couldn't live with being responsible for that. She loved Drew. Loved his generosity to her, the comfort, the joy he brought her in bed and out. A hundred other things. She wouldn't allow him to be hurt by her carelessness. It was careless to have tried to heal herself in the bathroom of a busy hospital. Why hadn't she waited? She would regret it for the rest of her life.

She'd have a greater chance of convincing Graham Powell that Drew knew nothing about her be-ing…different…if he didn't have an angry, protective Siren breathing down his neck.

Katrina pushed the bathtub drain lever with the edge of her fluke, and studied the misshapen fin. The spines creating its shape had formed, but the membranes filling the spaces between were either too thin or ragged and ridged Because of her burn scars, the tissue wouldn't stretch. She had been rejected by Mer society as much for the deformity as her human blood. Her mobility issues made her a burden to the nomadic Shoals that moved often to hide from human detection.

She'd be a burden to Drew and his family if Graham Powell outed her and triggered a witch hunt. She had to do whatever was necessary to prevent it.

She closed her eyes and waited for the water to drain. Once the tub was dry, the transition back to full human form took only a few minutes. She stepped out of the tub, wrapped her hair in a towel, dried herself, and then slipped on the robe Drew left hanging on the back of the door. With no blow drier, she towel-dried, brushed, and fluffed her hair the best she could.

She paused to retrieve her cell phone from her purse and texted Joseph Powell. "Will you send me Graham's number so I can contact him directly?"

The answer came immediately as though he were waiting by the phone. "Do you think that's a good idea?"

"If I can convince him I'm the only remaining Mermaid, maybe he'll forget any of this ever happened."

"No. He won't. He's too curious. Too driven. Give him time to contact me first."

Joseph's words took the responsibility from her hands temporarily, and her anxiety eased, but it did nothing to relieve her guilt. "Let me know if you change your mind."

His reply was short. "OK."

She set the phone on the nightstand.

When she went into the living room, Drew was at the piano drawing in the notes to a song on a piece of sheet music. She slipped in next to him on the piano bench and purposely flashed a long length of bare thigh. "Are you ready for a nap, or should I go to bed without you?" she asked.

Drew slanted a look in her direction, spied her thigh and the bare shoulder she'd allowed the robe slip down and reveal. He set aside the pencil he was using, his attention focused on the curve of her breast, then her face.

"You just had surgery, Katrina."

"I'm good. I'll need you to remove the stitches after our...um...nap."

His brows lifted in surprise. "You shouldn't have healed yourself so quickly."

"We both know I can't go back to Powell and Turner, Drew. Now their part of the process is over, it's best I don't. The next step is to see an audiologist. I'll find one."

He slipped an arm around her, pulling her in against him. She rested her head on his shoulder. His lips brushed her forehead.

His body was solid, strong, his arms protective. She needed to forget everything but him.

Would she be strong enough to give him up if she had to? The thought nearly drove her to her knees. There had to be a way to protect him.

She grasped his hand and drew him to his feet.

He pulled her back to him and placed a kiss on the curve where her arm began and gave it a little nip. She shivered in response.

They held each other as they made their way into the bedroom.

Drew's heart pounded as Katrina slipped free of his robe and tossed it on the foot of the bed. She stood at a three-quarter angle, and Drew hungrily ran his eyes over the perfect curve of her breasts, their nipples upturned, then the hollow dip of her waist, its concave curve defining her slenderness. She turned to slide beneath the covers, and his attention fastened on the lush roundness of her ass. He thought of how he mounted her from behind and delved deep into the moist warmth until he hadn't known where her body ended and his own began. He'd never felt so close to another being in his life. Every time they made love their connection strengthened.

Once he lay beside her, Katrina rested a hand on his hip. Her thumb ran back and forth against his pelvic bone, then she slid her fingers down his outer thigh, then back up the inside. Drew parted his legs, giving her access, and she gently cupped his balls and rolled them in her hand in a caress.

"Do you know how special you are to me?" she asked.

Drew searched her face and found a blend of tenderness and passion he'd never received from any other woman. His voice sounded husky when he said, "I know."

Did she know what she was to him? *His mate, his everything.* Then why couldn't he tell her?

She kissed him, and her tongue slow danced with his, feeding their building passion, prodding it to a peak before her hand ever encircled his erection.

She knew exactly how to touch him to increase his need. But he did her as well. He bent his head to kiss the tender peak of one breast and draw the nipple into his mouth. Her touch stilled as she became distracted by the caress. Her fingers curled along the back of his neck when he moved to suckle the other.

When he raised his head, she hooked her leg over his hip and opened herself to him, until the head of his penis brushed along her moist slit. He rolled, taking her beneath him, and with a slow push, they came together. It was like finding a lost piece of himself every time it happened.

They made slow, luxurious love, stretching out the connection between them for as long as it could last. He waited for the preternatural door to fall, and when it did, his control was wrenched away, swept along by the tide of their shared pleasure, the drive for more. Afterward they lay tangled together, the moist heat of their skin clinging as if they had melded together physically as completely as their mental connection.

Katrina continued to run her fingers up and down his back in a caress as soothing as it was erotic.

He raised his head and noticed the clock on the nightstand. "I don't want to go, but I have to. I don't have to tell you to stay in and not to open the door to anyone but me."

"No, you don't have to tell me."

Reluctantly he pulled away and got up. Katrina curled up and watched while he dressed.

"Like the show?" he asked when he caught her eyes on him.

She stretched and gave him a languid smile. "I never get tired of it."

He groaned. "I'm not kissing you goodbye. I'll just end back up in bed with you again." He was only half teasing.

She laughed.

He signed, "See you later."

She signed, "Okay."

As Drew's broad back disappeared breakdown the hall into images/the living room she signed, "I love you." She hoped he knew.

An hour later she had just finished putting on jeans and a sweater when her cell phone flashed on the bedside table. She grabbed it. Graham Powell's name and number showed on the screen. Though she'd half expected it to happen, her heart still leapt into her throat and her legs weakened with dread. She sank down on the bed and pushed the button to read the message.

"You have to help me. You have to tell me what you are."

The tone of the message stunned her. He was asking for her help. But why would he expect her to give him information that could destroy her?

As she debated what to do another text came through.

"You have been in my dreams for days. Every night I drown."

Katrina's hand clutched her sweater just over her heart. In a different context, the message would have been a romantic overture, but having seen Graham's bloodshot eyes and stress-lined face, she knew he was stating a truth.

His parents, both Selkies, had left their seaside home to adopt him. But how had they found him? What catastrophe had parted him from his biological parents? And did water folk have something to do with it?

Only two people knew.

She texted him back. "I'm not answering your questions over the phone. Give me a time and a place and I'll meet you."

Chapter 29

Katrina studied Dr. Powell's modern two-story house. It stood not far from Drew's parents on a quiet cul-de-sac. Lights shone through the large front windows and illuminated a living room with a fireplace.

Would his parents come? She'd both texted and emailed them, hoping they would join her for this meeting at Graham's home. Surely his emotional and mental health were more important than the secrets they'd kept from him.

She turned off her car, but didn't get out. Her phone lay on the console, its dark face accusing. She should never have come without telling Drew. But he would never have agreed for her to come at all.

He'd be in the midst of his show by now and wouldn't see the text until they went on break. She picked up the phone and typed in an explanation of where she was and why she'd felt compelled to come.

Feeling better now she'd messaged him, she shoved open her car door and got out. Halfway to the front door she sensed movement to her left and turned to see Graham Powell coming out of the shrubbery, something gripped in his hand. She froze at the sight of the pistol, the barrel black and threatening. Though she could heal with great effort, she was as vulnerable to bullets, knives, and other weapons as any human.

"You don't need that, Dr. Powell."

She couldn't see his lips move well enough to read his reply, but she understood his movement with the gun. She preceded him up the walkway and steps to the front door. Knowing were the weapon was pointed, her back tensed against the threat. Beneath the porch light she read his lips. "Go on in."

She turned the doorknob and entered a wide foyer. There were stairs leading up were on the left, and further to the left was a darkened room. On the right lay the large living room she'd seen from outside.

Graham motioned to the right with the gun, and she walked into the room and slowly turned to face him.

He looked far worse than the last time she'd seen him. He had the unkempt appearance of someone under extreme pressure. He'd obviously slept in his clothes, they hung in wrinkled folds down his frame, and his blond hair stuck up in spikes.

"Are you okay?" Katrina asked.

His green eyes flared. "No, I'm not. You damn near broke my wrist."

She glanced past the gun to his hand holding it. Dark purple bruises marked his skin. "I didn't mean to. You were upset, and I just wanted to keep you with me long enough to calm you."

"Upset?" He threw back his head and laughed. "You

were my worst nightmare."

Katrina flinched. "I'm sorry. I didn't realize I was holding onto you so tightly."

Graham strode toward her, the gun leading the way. Katrina backed toward the fireplace.

He stopped and his bloodshot eyes swept over her face. "What are you?"

She'd held the secret close for so long, the words refused to come.

"Whatever kind of monster you are, I'm sure a bullet will end you just like it will most things."

Her mouth went dry and her eyes were riveted on the weapon. "Yes, a bullet will end me. Is that why you've asked me to come here?"

"No. I want to know why you smell like a memory. Why your face, as it was last night, has starred in every one of my dreams since we met."

"I don't know. We never met before I came to your office. I'd remember if we had."

"How would you remember?"

"I have a photographic memory."

"Will you live as long as or longer than a human?"

"I am human, Dr. Powell." She wasn't lying. She was as much human as Mermaid.

He shook his head. "No, you're not."

"My mother was a young woman living somewhere near Juno, Alaska."

"And your father?"

"I don't know him." It wasn't a lie. Though they'd met that one time, he had made it clear he wanted nothing to do with her.

"Why don't your blood tests show anything out of the ordinary?"

"Why shouldn't they? I'm human."

He thrust the gun forward, his face reddening. "Quit saying that. You're not. You're something else."

Katrina raised a hand as though to ward off the shot, a yelp escaping her. A bullet would travel right through her hand and into her body; there would be no stopping it. Her heartbeat hammered in her throat, cutting her air supply by half. "What difference does it make what I am? I'm not going to hurt you. I never meant to frighten you. Why do you want to do both to me?"

"Because I have to know. And you're going to tell me."

He was never going to stop until he'd heard the words. His father was right. He was obsessed and driven by the demons haunting his dreams.

"Whatever it is you see in your dreams, it no longer exists. I'm the last."

"I don't believe you."

"If I say we were all deaf, are you going to start hunting down every deaf person on the planet and demanding to scan of their skull in hopes of finding another like mine? Are you going to ask your parents if you can scan them? In all the hundreds of scans you've seen over the years and in medical school, have you ever seen another like mine?"

"No. But that doesn't mean there aren't others."

"There aren't. I'm alone. And I'm just trying to live the only life open to me, Dr. Powell."

"Your boyfriend, the singer, does he know?"

"No."

Disbelief flashed across his features. "He had to have seen you as I did."

"Maybe he's able to accept me, to love me despite my being deaf and a little different."

If he allowed her to sit, he'd have to sit as well. Just talking like two civilized people might ease his manic anxiety. She made a move toward one of the wide over-stuffed chairs.

"No. Don't sit down. We're going out back."

Her hope died. "I won't be able to read your lips out-side."

"We'll see. I have lights on out there."

With the gun, he waved her through the dining area at the end of the living room. She passed a table with an inlaid top that looked like a tortoise shell.

They went through a wide doorway leading into the kitchen, and Katrina noted marble counter tops and appliances worthy of a chef. Everything was spotless. The house was a showplace decorated by a designer, but empty. No scattered papers lay on the kitchen table. No dirty dishes in the sink.

Did he live as isolated an existence as she always had? Until Drew. Tears burned her eyes. Why had she come? Why had she risked losing her life? If she'd just stayed home, all this might have gone away.

She came to a set of French doors leading out onto a wide patio and a pool. Light bloomed from beneath the water, reflecting off the glass-topped tables set around it, their pale blue umbrellas capturing the glow and holding it.

Her stomach twisted and she stopped.

He'd guessed something about her from the scans, and from her transformation. Graham stuck the barrel of the gun against her spine and reached around her to open the door. He prodded her outside.

Katrina rushed forward, trying to put distance between them, but Graham grabbed her shoulder and put the gun against the small of her back again. He guided her around the side of the pool to the deep end.

She stopped five feet from the edge and turned to partially face him. Every time she moved, she expected to feel the gun discharge and a bullet rip through her body. The air stank of chlorine. The smell settled in the back of her throat. The underwater lights in the pool reflected off Graham's face, creating dark shadows around his features, making it harder for her to read his lips. Her heart beat so hard it drummed against her wrists and throat. "I'm not getting into the water, Dr. Powell."

"I need you to do this."

Katrina turned. "You're a doctor. You promised to care for me. You took an oath to do no harm." She cupped the dressing over her ear.

She read the indecision in his face, smelled his fear, felt his torment. Pity rose in her.

If his parents had blocked his memories as she thought, he would keep fighting until he recovered them or went insane trying. Keeping her hands raised, she turned to face him. "Tell me about your dreams."

He shuddered and the gun shook in his hand. "I'm in the water, and I'm choking because water is going into my mouth. I can't breathe. There's a face that rises up in front of me." His gaze, intent and fearful, fastened on her with horror. "It looks like a mask, but it isn't. She grabs me, and I'm screaming, and water goes into my throat." His eyes went distant, but panic and fear still rolled off of him in waves.

Katrina gripped the top of the pistol, pushed it aside, and held it there, fearful he might pull the trigger by accident. She trembled as badly as he, his suffering affecting her more each minute. Why weren't his parents here? Why had they done this?

"I want to help you, Dr. Powell." She swallowed and blinked to clear her vision as tears welled, then rolled down her cheeks. She had come here knowing she might have to sacrifice everything to protect Drew and his family. To protect others like her. But she hadn't realized what she might have to do so to save this man.

Graham Powell was slowly drowning in his pain.

"You have to put the gun down, Dr. Powell. You have to trust me as much as I'm going to trust you."

"Your skin shimmers when it's wet," he observed. He reached out and touched her cheek.

The salt in her tears was causing the change. Her throat felt so dry and clogged with emotion it was hard to speak. "I'm not a monster. You don't have to be afraid of me. I won't hurt you."

He released the pistol, and the weight pulled heavy in her hand. With a backhand toss, Katrina threw it into the pool. She backed toward the edge of the water. He shuffled forward, following her. Her fingers trembled as she unzipped her pants and stepped out of them. She pulled the useless dressing from around her head and dropped it on the concrete.

She turned her palms up and he grasped them.

She'd wanted so much to have a normal life. To wake every morning in Drew's arms. To have his children. To share his family.

Though Drew had tried to teach her to lower the door between them outside of an intimate physical situation, she'd never been able to do so.

She wanted to do it now, more than anything else. She needed Drew to know how much she loved him. She closed her eyes and thought of him, and tried to capture how she felt when they were together.

She stepped back over the edge of the pool and plunged in.

Drew followed the rest of the band backstage for their first break. Things were going well. The club was packed with couples, and everyone seemed to be either jamming to their music or dancing to it.

Simon, Rand, and Tony filed into the dressing room ahead of him. He was surprised to hear a female voice greet them. He paused at the door as he spied Brianna sitting on the couch. The baby lay in a strange-looking carrier at her feet. He debated on whether or not to step in and get his cell phone, then decided to slip down the hall to an empty dressing room and just wait until she left.

"Drew." At the sound of her voice he paused with his

hand on the doorknob. With a sigh turned to face her. She'd semi-tamed her wild head of reddish-brown curls by pulling most into a scrunchie at the nape of her neck. Some of the baby weight still rested in her hips, but the black knit pants and loose top she wore looked attractive.

They'd never been close. There had always been the best friend's-wife thing hanging between them and he'd accepted long ago they were never going to be buddies. He'd been carefully friendly and shown her respect because of Simon. But he didn't have to take her shit and he wasn't going to.

"Why don't you come in and see the baby?" she asked.

What game was she playing? The last time they'd seen each other she'd been screaming at him to stay away. Some of the pain he'd experienced then echoed through him. "I don't think that would be a good idea."

She walked toward him, each step purposeful. She stopped directly in front of him. "I want to apologize, if you'll let me. I know what a bitch, more than a bitch, I was that night." Her bottom lip quivered and she swallowed. "I know I hurt you." She made a placating gesture with her hand. "I was afraid, Drew."

"Yeah, I could see that." He studied the industrial tile on the floor, seeking patience. "You don't have to be afraid of me. Simon's my closest friend. All I've ever wanted for him was happiness. That includes you and the baby, so I'm down with that."

"But it also includes having you in his life Drew." Her voice trembled with emotion. "I've been in a panic since I got pregnant, worrying about money, about the women trolling the bar, looking for a thrill. They hang around outside waiting for all of you, hoping an autograph will lead to more. You get them primed for it, Drew."

He understood what she was saying, but what Tony had mentioned to him at the hospital played into it, too. He had nothing to lose no matter what he said to her. The damage had already been done. "Things have changed for us all now, Brianna. But the one constant that hasn't changed is that Simon loves you. He's never lost sight of his feelings for or his commitment to you. And he's just as in love with and committed to the baby. We've worked hard for nearly ten years to achieve success. Simon's music is as essential to him as air and food. If you convince him to give up his dream, he'll be eaten alive by regret and he'll grow to hate you for it."

He looked away from her tear-streaked face. "There's always going to be women around drawn to the success and the hype of the music scene. Simon and I direct them Tony and Rand's way these days. It's up to you to decide to trust him or not. To decide whether you love him enough to set aside your..." he started to say insecurities and settled for "...reservations and look out for his happiness as much as he tries to look out for yours."

It took several moments for her to regain her composure. Though Drew was tempted to comfort her, he kept his distance.

She wiped her face with a tissue from her pocket. "I know you're saying all this because of how much you care about Simon. Which makes what I said to you even worse." She looked so forlorn he started to touch her, but balled his hand at his side instead.

"Will you ever be able to forgive me?" she asked.

"For Simon?"

"Yeah." She nodded, hope filling her eyes.

He couldn't expect Simon to remain suspended between him and Brianna. She was his wife. Simon owed her his first loyalty. Now that Katrina had come into his life, he understood that. But obviously Simon had been talking to her, and convinced her he meant neither her nor the baby harm. "Okay."

Relief flooded her features. "Would you like to see the baby before you go back on stage?"

He hesitated. It was going to take him a while to truly get beyond what had been said. "Sure."

He followed her back to the dressing room. Tony was making a fool of himself, cooing at the baby and rocking side to side in slow motion. "Your turn, Uncle Drew," he announced, and Drew had no choice but to lift his arms and cradle the baby when Tony transferred her tiny bulk to him.

He looked down into her dark blue eyes and smiled when she yawned and stretched. She studied him with wide-spaced eyes similar in shape to Brianna's but he saw Simon there too in the curve of her chin. He glanced up to find Tony and Rand grinning at him. Simon looped an arm around Brianna's waist and pressed a kiss to her temple. She turned to curl into him.

"What's her name?" Drew asked.

"We settled on Simone," Brianna said.

"I know it's a little—" Simon began.

"Perfect. It's perfect," Drew cut him off and smiled.

"Hello, Simone."

Back onstage Drew had just introduced the seventh song in the show when a wave of emotion rolled over him like a tsunami. It was a blend of tenderness and passion, but more. It was followed by a burst of grief so strong his eyes burned and his throat ached.

He stopped playing mid-note and grabbed for his cell phone, but his pocket was empty. The phone was in the dressing room in his jacket.

He crossed the stage at a lope until Simon brought him up short when he snagged his arm. "What's wrong?"

"Something's wrong with Katrina. I have to go."

Simon looked at his empty hands in confusion.

Drew jerked away. He didn't have time to explain. He leaped behind the stage and tore down the hall to the dressing room. Brianna was gone. He ripped the cell phone free of his jacket pocket hit the command, bringing up her text.

"Fuck!"

The water covered Graham's head, and he closed his eyes against it.

Relief flowed through him. This torture would end. He would learn what it was he saw in his nightmares and why it haunted him.

Though the pool was heated, the water around him

grew steadily warmer. He opened his eyes to find Katrina's calm blue-green eyes looking into his. They appeared larger, her chin more pointed, her widow's peak more defined. Her sweater floated around her, as did her hair. Her skin glowed as though veins of mother of pearl ran beneath its surface. A powerful current forced water up around them, but held them suspended three feet below the surface.

Graham glanced down at the lower half of her body. Blue-green scales covered her legs. Her feet had elongated, the bones turned to spines and a delicate membrane created a web-like fluke. Her tail would have been as beautiful as the rest of her but for the two jagged scars running up from the base, and the ridged areas of damaged tissue that created the fin.

Her body swayed back and forth, and water swirled upward in an eddy.

Graham jerked at the memory of a dark, powerful fin brushing against him in the darkness, the speed at which it moved terrifying.

The creature had a predatory grace, the way it darted through the water, back and forth, kicking up a wake that caused water to splash him in the face. Darkness closed in around him, penetrated by a dull yellow light that bathed the metal ceiling above him in a sickly glow. He clung to a cushion floating on the surface of the water. The air tasted metallic and smelled like oil, and his teeth chattered with cold and fear.

He watched the flutter of a fin weaving back and forth, getting closer and closer as his terror mounted. A face so white it glowed shone from beneath the water. It surfaced in front of him, water running in rivulets down its brow and cheeks. He screamed in terror, lost his grip on the cushion, and flipped over backwards. Instinct kicked in, and he flailed his arms and legs. His lungs seized, begging for oxygen. He was forced back up into the pocket of air by a hand beneath his butt. He gasped and coughed as oily water surged down his throat.

Katrina fought against Graham's grip on her hands. He was frozen in some kind of fugue memory state, his features blank. At any moment he would breathe in pool water and drown.

She ripped one hand loose and kicked as hard as she could to lift him to the surface.

He fought her, too trapped between the real world and the dream to realize the danger. She wrapped an arm around his chest and had no choice but to use her strength to subdue him.

They broke the surface. Graham's chest heaved as he yelled and fought against her. Suddenly he went still and turned to look toward the shallow end of the pool. Joseph Powell stood poised to leap into the water. Beside him Drew's father, Blake, gripped his arm.

Relieved tears blurred Katrina's vision as she swam toward them. "They can help you. Please let them help you," Katrina said. She towed him to the pool steps at the shallow end. The two men stepped into the water and half-dragged, half-helped Graham out of the pool.

He turned eyes dark with relief on her. His body shook

as though palsied. "I remember. They saved me."

Katrina nodded.

Blake touched her shoulder to get her attention. "Are you all right, Katrina?" The open concern on his face ripped away what little control she had over her tears. A well of grief opened up inside her. She had done the right thing, but at what cost?

"I'm sorry. He was in such pain."

"It's going to be all right."

She knew it was an empty promise. She couldn't take back Graham's memories of her transformation. "You can't wipe his memory again. It would destroy him. He doesn't know about anyone else. Only me."

Tears made it impossible for her to see his reply. She pushed away from the steps and swam to the deep end of the pool, where she settled at the bottom and curled there against the farthest wall, under the diving board.

Something dark hit the water, and with the sleek speed of a dolphin jetted toward her. Drew's feelings, both angry and worried, reached her before he did.

In his full Siren form, his chest, shoulders, and abdomen were bulked with muscle, and the scales of his tail shimmered an unusual purplish green. More trailed up his arms from his elbows to his shoulders, creating a kind of armor. The defined angles and planes of his face lent him the aggressive masculinity distinctive to his species. He had the bearing of a warrior, both sexy and regal.

"Don't get carried away." His words resounded in her head. "My mother's the only royalty in the family."

His dry, deprecating wit brought out a weak smile.

"I'm serious. She's a princess in her Pod."

Katrina's lips parted in surprise, allowing air bubbles to escape.

Drew grasped her hand and tugged her from the bottom to the surface, where she gasped in the air she needed. "Drowning yourself isn't a solution." He pushed her back against the side of the pool and pressed his body full against her.

She shuddered at the erotic feel of him aligning his tail to hers as she curved her arms around him.

The pale blue of his eyes expanded and began to glow. He rested his forehead against hers. "You're not going to run and hide, either. We're standing our ground, Katrina."

"If it were just the two of us, I'd agree, but there are so many others."

"My father says there's a way."

"They can't tamper with his mind again, Drew."

"No. But if he exposes you, he'll be exposing the only parents he remembers. If he loves them at all, he won't want to hurt them."

"Where were they? I texted and emailed them several times."

"They were out looking for him. Their cell phone was dead. They finally swung by here to see if he'd returned. They found the lights on, the doors open, and the two of you in the pool."

"You called your father?"

"Yes." He drew back and shot her a narrow-eyed look. He spoke aloud for the first time, as though his thoughts weren't enough to express his emotion. "I was half an hour away and couldn't get to you in time, Katrina. Do you know what hell I went through, knowing you were in trouble, and

I couldn't reach you?"

The same hell she'd experienced when she decided to take the plunge with Graham Powell and risk losing Drew. She rested her cheek against his shoulder, overwhelmed and grieving over the pain she'd caused them both.

His words flowed into her mind, comforting, joyful. "You could never lose me, Katrina. We're bonded mates. All the doors are down between us."

She looked at him. "Is that how you knew to come?"

"Yes."

She spoke aloud. "I wanted you to know how much I loved you. Just in case."

He tilted her face up to his. "I felt it from half a city away." His lips claimed hers, and his arms locked around her, almost to the point of pain.

"I'm not going to say the words until you can hear me say them," he said and eased back away from her.

"Does that mean—?" His feelings washed over her, cutting off her words and making her dizzy.

He urged her toward the other end of the pool. A woman stood waiting for them, towels folded over her arm. Katrina's anxiety rose again. "Who is she?"

"It's okay. She's Dr. Powell's mother. She's been waiting there to thank you."

Katrina brushed against Drew, deriving comfort from his nearness, feeling his love and care. Finally she allowed herself to experience the joy of it.

His ran a caressing hand ran down over her hip. His thought was a muttered growl. "And the next time we transform together, we're definitely making love."

Epilogue

Graham stood at the back of the enormous ferry and watched through the heavy glass window while the port of Troon disappeared behind them. He hadn't ridden on a ferry or any other boat since he was three. The vessel was huge, and more modern than he'd expected, with well-cushioned seats, lots of floor space, three restaurants, and a gift shop.

His father stood next to him and signed. "I can give you an approximate location between here and Ireland where the ship went down."

"Okay. That will be good enough."

In the three weeks since his meltdown, he'd pieced together everything he could remember of his past. As every memory he'd lost had resurfaced, he felt more settled, more together than he had since meeting Katrina Larson. Or perhaps ever.

"We never meant to steal your past from you, Graham," his father signed.

"It wasn't you who were responsible for that, Dad." He spoke and signed at the same time.

"But we stole your parents' identities so we could keep you."

"And uprooted your entire life to create one that would work for me." Graham laid a hand briefly on his father's arm before continuing to sign. "No two people could have ever loved a child more than you have loved me. I know how lucky I am."

He did. He could have floundered in an orphanage somewhere and missed out on the life they'd given him. Ever since they landed in Scotland, they'd been on a hunt for any remaining family he might have. They discovered none. A grandmother who had died twenty years ago had been the last. Would he have fared any better being raised by her, and then being left orphaned again? Probably not.

"They've given me permission to throw flowers over the starboard side when we reach the spot, so we'd better go down."

Joseph nodded. Graham and he moved to the stairwell where a crew member stood guard. "Are you Dr. Powell, sir?" he asked.

"Yes."

"The Captain's directed me to accompany you below, sir."

"Thank you."

He lifted the cable, then secured it again after they stepped through. They followed the crewman down the steps and through a narrow hallway to a hatch. He opened it and stood back for them to precede him out onto a platform looking out on the lower levels of the stern. "We're to go to the starboard side of the ship, sir. That's to your right."

Graham strode forward and stopped at the heavy metal railing that ran all the way around the deck.

Joseph signed. "The spot is coming up."

Graham unwrapped the hothouse roses he'd bought for the occasion. Just a moment or two passed before his father signaled him. This was the place his birth parents had lost their lives along with several other passengers and crewmen on a small ferry traveling back from Ireland. But not him. A Mermaid as compassionate as Katrina Larson had rescued him. It seemed kindness was a characteristic of their species. And after two such extraordinary acts of compassion, he had to believe it was so.

Graham tossed the roses, one at a time, over the railing, and watched them land and float past as the ferry moved forward. He tossed the last one, and for just a moment he thought he saw a glowing face beneath the water before the flower disappeared below in the wake of the ship. He raised his hand in farewell…and in thanks.

Katrina had never been more excited or more terrified. She'd closed her mental door for the first time in weeks, fearful of becoming confused about the input of her device.

The audiologist introduced herself as Sandy Carter. "Just have a seat right here, next to my desk."

As soon as Katrina was seated, she gripped the chair cushion to keep her hands from shaking. She had pinned too many hopes on this. She should have just held them back until after this initial activation.

But even if the device didn't work, she'd still be able to hear Drew. She had to hold on to that.

Would the actual sound of his voice be different from the sound of his thoughts? Would she be able to tell the difference?

Sandy put the processor over her ear and connected the magnet. She attached a small lead to it, and then sat down.

"We're going to program the processor for volume this time. Voices may sound squeaky at first. Your brain has to learn how to hear, since it's been deprived of sound for so long. Each week when you come in, we'll talk about how the sound has changed and make adjustments."

Katrina nodded. "Okay." Did her voice sound as breathless as she felt?

Her gaze strayed to Drew while the audiologist hit several keys.

He signed. "You okay?"

She nodded. For the past three weeks he'd kept learning sign language. It was number one on his to-do list. But okay was still his favorite sign. She smiled at him.

A high-pitched ringing sounded in her head, and her hand shot up to the device. If she could hear ringing it was working.

"Do you hear a beep?" Sandy asked.

"Ringing."

She went back to the keys and after a few seconds a distinctive beep sounded.

"It's beeping."

After Sandy hit several more keys she said, "Can you hear my voice?"

Katrina stared at her while goose bumps flooded her arms and her eyes burned. "Yes." It was the first human voice she'd ever heard. It sounded a little high-pitched, but the words were clear. Drew slid forward on the edge of his seat, his smile encouraging.

"Is it too loud?" Sandy asked.

"No. It's very high." Her heart rampaged with excitement. It was *working! Really Working!*

After a few more adjustments, Sandy turned to Drew. "Why don't you say something?"

He rose, knelt next to Katrina, and took her hand. "I love you." His voice sounded just as Cheryl had described it. Manly and deep. It fit him perfectly.

Every trick she'd used to try and get him to say it had failed. And now she'd finally heard the words. Tears glazed her eyes and an overwhelming joy burst through her.

She cupped his face. "I love you, too. I don't have to hear to know the sound of love, Drew. Every single day I hear it right here." She pointed to her heart.

Books by Teresa J. Reasor

Breaking Free (Book 1 of the SEAL Team Heartbreakers)
Breaking Through (Book 2 of the SEAL Team Heartbreakers)
Breaking Away (Book 3 of the SEAL Team Heartbreakers)
Building Ties (Book 4 of the SEAL Team Heartbreakers)
Timeless
Whisper in my Ear
Highland Moonlight
Captive Hearts

Short Stories by Teresa J. Reasor

An Automated Death
To Capture a Highlander's Heart: The Beginning
Caught In The Act

Novellas by Teresa J. Reasor

To Capture A Highlander's Heart: The Courtship
Breaking Ties (A SEAL Team Hearbreakers Novella)
To Capture A Highlander's Heart: The Wedding Night
(coming soon!)

Children's Books

Willy C. Sparks: The Dragon Who Lost His Fire
Haiku Clue (coming soon!)